Sylvia's Secret

A Family at War Book Two

Roberta Grieve

Print ISBNs
Amazon Print 978-0-2286-1530-9
LSI Print 978-0-2286-1531-6
B&N Print 978-0-2286-1532-3

BWL Publishing Inc.

Books we love to write ...
Authors around the world.

http://bwlpublishing.ca

Dedication

To my oldest friend Brenda who joined the WAAFs in the 1950s and is the inspiration for this book.

Chapter One

The noise of ringing telephones and clacking typewriters distracted Leading Aircraftwoman Sylvia Bishop every time the door opened. There were always people bustling in and out in and out of the Wing Commander's office. She pulled the sheet of paper from her machine, sighed and threw the letter down on the desk. Two typing errors. She'd have to start all over again.

Was she losing her grip? When she'd started working as the Wing Commander's personal assistant, she'd been able to type dozens of letters every day without a mistake. She was fast too. That's why she'd been promoted out of the main office.

But it was all getting too much. How many more of these 'we regret to inform you...' letters must she write? This latest batch was the last straw. Seven identical letters telling mothers, wives, families that their son had been shot down over Germany. Bomber Command was losing more planes – and people – every day.

Sylvia screwed up the spoiled letter and aimed it at the waste bin in the corner, then wound another sheet of the headed notepaper into her machine. Her fingers on the keys trembled. She couldn't do it. She covered her face with her hands, then took a breath and straightened her shoulders. She would not give way to the threatening tears. She had just managed to compose herself when the door opened but she didn't look up until Wing Commander Hugh Smythe spoke.

'Everything all right?' he asked. 'Not bad news from home I hope.'

His concerned voice was almost her undoing. He was so kind, not like some of the other officers who treated the lower ranks like skivvies, there just to do their bidding. She admired her boss for his care of the men in his charge. It must be just as hard for him, having to send out these letters every day. She knew that he also wrote a personal letter to each family as well as signing the official ones.

'No, Sir. They're all well,' she replied.

'Good. Letters done?'

'Just one more to do, Sir. I'm sorry...' She started to stammer an apology.

'I'll just sign these then.' He picked up the batch of freshly typed letters. 'Pop the other one into my office when you're done.'

'Yes, Sir.'

She bent to the typewriter once more and managed to type the familiar phrases with no errors this time. She stood up and stretched, picked up the letter and knocked on the officer's door.

At his 'come in' she handed him the letter and turned to go.

'Wait a minute,' he said, leaning back in his chair.

She noticed how tired he looked, lines etching his forehead and threads of grey appearing in his dark hair. 'What is it, Sir?' she asked as he hesitated.

'Are you happy working here?' he asked abruptly.

'Yes, Sir. Of course, Sir.'

He straightened and said. 'I just wondered if you had envisaged life in the air force to be a bit more exciting.' He gestured to the letters on his desk. 'I mean, typing, filing etc...'

'It's what I trained for,' she said, 'before I joined up.'

'But didn't it say on your application that you were interested in aeroplanes? Surely you didn't imagine you could learn to fly.'

Sylvia's face grew hot. Was he laughing at her? She managed a dignified, 'No, Sir. Of course not, Sir.'

'What is your interest then? How did it come about?'

He sounded sincere, as if he really wanted to know. Sylvia hesitated and then said. 'I live on the Isle of Sheppey where flying first started. My sister and I used to cycle up to the airfield and watch the planes.'

'Oh, yes. RAF Eastchurch. Wasn't it badly bombed a couple of years ago?'

Sylvia nodded. 'My sister was stationed there at the time. Luckily, she was all right.'

'She's in the WAAFs too?'

'No, the NAAFI. She's the supervisor at Sheerness Garrison.'

'I know the island,' Hugh said. 'I was there in 1932 when Cobham's Flying Circus did a display – National Aviation Day.'

'Really, sir? My sister Daisy and I went. We cycled over to the farm where it was held. There was such a queue for the flights.' Sylvia almost forgot she was talking to a senior officer and went on, 'We couldn't go up though – no money.'

'That's a shame. So that's what sparked your enthusiasm for aircraft?'

Sylvia nodded then felt herself beginning to blush again. 'Sorry, sir. I didn't mean to go on about it.'

'That's quite all right.' He shuffled some papers on his desk and looked up at her. 'So, it's back to the typing then.'

'Yes, sir.'

She turned to go but he stopped her, saying, 'Wait a moment. What would you say to a change of scene?'

Change of scene? What did he mean?

She looked up at her boss. 'Do you mean leave, Sir?' she asked.

She *was* due some leave, but she dreaded going home. Last time she'd visited, her sister Daisy had told her Roland Hargreaves still stationed on the island. Sylvia no longer cared about him, even less after Daisy explained how badly he had treated her best friend. It still rankled that the man she had thought herself in love with turned out to be such a rotter.

The Wing Commander smiled ruefully. 'Leave? No such luck, I'm afraid. I was thinking of a posting.'

Her heart sank. Bored and miserable as she was, she couldn't bear the thought of being sent somewhere else away from Hugh. 'Are you not satisfied with my work, Sir?'

He shook his head. 'That's not it at all. In fact...' He paused as if embarrassed. 'It's just - I've been thinking. You're far too good for this job. It must be boring for an intelligent girl like you – typing, filing.'

She felt her face flush and she stammered. 'Oh, no, Sir. I'm quite happy here.'

He smiled and spoke gently. 'You didn't look very happy when I came in. What's bothering you?'

She hesitated and then gestured to the letters on his desk. 'It's these letters, Sir. They're a bit upsetting.'

He sighed. 'Yes, they are. But it has to be done.'

'Yes, Sir, I understand.' She straightened her shoulders and stood to attention. 'Will that be all, Sir?'

He nodded but as she turned to go, he said abruptly, 'I've been posted.'

Her heart lurched. No, he couldn't go away. How could she bear not seeing him every day? She knew it was foolish to feel this way. Hadn't she vowed never to fall in love again after that disastrous affair with Roland Hargreaves? But she had – and with a married man too. And it wasn't just a silly crush as she'd tried to convince herself time and again.

'Where too, Sir?' she managed to ask.

'Top secret. I shouldn't even be telling you this much. All I can say is that it is a very important job and could help us to win the war.'

'I won't breathe a word, Sir. You can trust me.'

'I know I can, which is why...' He hesitated. 'I might be able to arrange for you to be posted to the same place – a much more interesting job. I can't tell you any more, just now. It will mean promotion, of course.'

'Promotion?'

'You'd have to go for officer training. But I think you're the sort of person we're looking for, especially given your interest in aircraft.'

Sylvia's heart raced and she wasn't sure she'd taken in what he said. 'Officer? Me?'

'Why not? I'm sure you'll pass. And then you'll be posted to RAF Medmenham – that's where I'm going.'

'Where is it? I've never heard of it.' She didn't really care. She'd do anything if it meant she could be near Hugh.

'You'll find out soon enough. Just keep it under your hat for the time being.'

'I will, Sir. And thank you.'

She came to attention again and turned to leave the room. Had he noticed the flush she knew coloured her cheeks? It was getting harder to hide her feelings, but she knew she must try. If he got the slightest inkling she would be in trouble. He was not only married but happily so, with two small children. He wasn't the kind of man to stoop to an affair and she admired him for his integrity. But she could dream, couldn't she?

Seated back at her desk she allowed her mind to wander. Fancy that – me, an officer, she thought. Mum and Dad would be so proud. She pictured herself working closely with Hugh on whatever top . secret work they would be doing. She couldn't imagine what that could be but if it involved aeroplanes and was important to the war effort, she would throw herself into it and make herself indispensable to him.

She would write to Daisy and her parents this evening, Living up to the image she'd given of her glamorous life in the WAAFs was becoming harder, especially after Daisy's heroic exposure of a black market ring and then her

Sylvia couldn't tell them anything about Hugh, and but she could boast about her promotion hint that her life was about to become more exciting.

***

Daisy threw off her coat and hung it up behind the back door, hurrying through to the kitchen. Her eyes immediately flew to the mantelpiece, her heart lurching as she saw the envelope tucked behind the clock. 'Chris,' she breathed. He'd written at last. She snatched it up, disappointment flooding over her as she saw her sister's handwriting. It was addressed to their mother, but Daisy knew Dora wouldn't mind if she opened it. Family letters were always shared.

She sat down at the kitchen table and started to read, pleased that Sylvia had written more than two pages instead of her usual single sheet saying she was well and mentioning she'd been out dancing.

She was pleased too that Sylvia seemed more cheerful, talking about a possible promotion and a more interesting job, although she didn't say what it was. Still no mention of a new boyfriend though. Daisy still felt guilty for telling her sister about that two-timing rat Roland Hargreaves. She'd felt she must warn her, after making Sylvia promise not to mention it to any of her friends, had revealed how badly he had treated Lily, her NAAFI colleague, leaving her pregnant and refusing to take responsibility. Although Sylvia protested that she was over him, Daisy worried that she was hiding her feelings, as she usually did, and was still in love with him.

Now that more than two years had passed, Daisy hoped that her sister had someone new in her life, someone who would make her as happy as Corporal Christopher Jameson made her.

Daisy sighed. If only he would write. Of course, he did write – every day. It was just that several weeks would pass with nothing in the post, leaving her consumed with worry for his safety. Then, to her relief, a whole bundle of letters would fall through the letterbox. She kept them in a pretty shell-encrusted box on her dressing table and read them every night before going to sleep.

Where was he now, she wondered. What was he doing? Was he safe? She hardly dared listen to the wireless news and watch the newsreels when she went to the pictures. Place names - Tobruk, Alamein, Sidi Barani – were as familiar to her now as London and Maidstone. Why were they fighting there? What use to either side were these endless miles of desert?

Dad had tried to explain to her but she didn't want to know. She wanted the fighting to end and for Chris to come home. And Bob too, the boy next door who'd been her childhood sweetheart until despatch rider Chris Jameson had come into her life and she had fallen in love with him. She was sorry she'd hurt Bob, but he seemed to have accepted that they'd grown apart. However, she was still fond of him and feared for his safety just as much as she did for Chris.

She shook off the gloomy thoughts and read Sylvia's letter again, glad that things were looking up for her at least.

She glanced at the clock and stood up. Better start getting a meal ready for Mum and Dad. They'd be home soon, Jimmy too.

She had put the kettle on and was looking in the larder, trying to decide what to cook when Dora Bishop came in. She pulled off her WVS hat and plonked her shopping bag down on the kitchen table. She sank into a chair, sighed and eased her shoes off.

'You look worn out, Mum,' Daisy said, setting a cup of tea in front of her mother.

'I've been sorting stuff out in the back of the shop. People have been so generous but it's getting harder. Everything's in such short supply and there's not so many donations these days.' She stood up and began to unpack the shopping. 'Not much food either. Hardly worth queuing for this.' She unwrapped the paper package to reveal a small piece of mutton. 'Thank goodness for Dad's allotment. With the vegetables he brought home earlier I can make a nice stew for tomorrow. There's a couple of sausages too. Toad-in-the-hole tonight.'

'I've already done the potatoes,' Daisy said. 'Sit down and drink your tea. I'll get the meal ready.' She reached up to the mantelpiece. 'Letter from Sylvia,' she said.

'Oh, what's she got to say for herself? About time she wrote.'

'I expect she's busy. She said she's being promoted.' Daisy busied herself with preparing the meal while her mother read the letter.

'A new job, too,' Dora said, putting the letter back in its envelope. 'She doesn't give much away though.'

Daisy put the toad-in-the-hole into the oven and sat down at the table. She poured herself a cup of tea and leaned back in her chair with a sigh.

'Busy day for you too then?' Dora asked.

'As usual. I've got a new girl, been showing her the ropes. She's a bit slow, be quicker to do it myself.'

Dora smiled. 'Not so long ago you were the new girl yourself. Give the kid a chance.'

'I s'pose you're right. I remember Muriel – Mrs Greening – was always on my back. But I was lucky. I had Lily to help.' She sighed. 'I still miss her.'

'Heard from her lately?'

'She's working on a farm, haymaking. She seems to be enjoying herself.'

'She must be recovering then. Will she come back to work in the NAAFI, do you think?'

'I don't know. She didn't say anything in her last letter.' Daisy sipped her tea, wondering how things were working out for her friend. It must be hard for her, letting people think the baby was her newest little brother. Mrs Scott had ordered Lily to say nothing, hoping that when they returned to the island everyone would accept that there was a new addition to the large Scott family. Lily could carry on as usual. Daisy wished she could tell her mother the real reason why Lily had gone down to the New Forest with her family.

When her NAAFI colleagues asked how Lily was, Daisy found it hard to keep up the pretence that her friend had been ill and was convalescing at her grandmother's down in the New Forest. Daisy hadn't even confided in June, her closest friend since Lily went away.

'Jimmy and Dad'll be home soon,' Dora said, interrupting Daisy's thoughts. 'Better get the table laid.'

Daisy stood up and together they began the well-practiced routine of getting a meal ready.

Dora took the toad-in-the-hole out of the oven, the batter crisp round the edges and the sausages, which Daisy had cut into small pieces, almost invisible. Daisy strained the vegetables just as the back door was flung open and her father and brother came in.

'Something smells good,' Stan said, rubbing his hands together.

'I'm starving,' Jimmy said.

'You're always starving, lad. Get those boots off and wash your hands.' Stan gave him an affectionate cuff round the head.

In minutes the family were seated round the table tucking into the food. 'Don't know how you do it, love,'

Stan said, wiping a piece of bread round his plate to mop up the gravy.

'I do my best but it's not easy with the rationing.' Dora sighed, then brightened up. 'Now, who's for jam roly poly and custard?'

After the meal, Daisy helped her mother to wash up in the scullery and then went into the kitchen. Stan was sitting in his favourite chair by the range listening to the wireless. She started to tell him about Sylvia's letter but he waved her to be quiet, his face grim.

They listened in silence as the newsreader spoke of losses in the desert and Daisy held her breath, her stomach churning. That's where Chris was – and Bob. So that's why she hadn't heard from either of them for so long. No chance to write letters in the heat of battle. She prayed they were both all right.

It took a few minutes for her to take in what her father was saying and she gasped, her face lighting up as the newsreader ended on an optimistic note. 'General Montgomery has now taken over command of the 8th Army,' he said.

'Did you hear that?' Stan shouted. 'The tide's turning. Monty will send them packing, soon have Rommel on the run.'

'Oh, Dad. Is it true?'

'That's what the announcer said. Well, won't be long now.' Stan leaned back in his chair and lit his pipe.

Jimmy got out his old school atlas and soon he and Stan were poring over it, tracing the progress of the two conflicting armies.

Daisy tried to join in the conversation but all she could think of was how the two men in her life were faring. Now the two of them were out there in the desert fighting the enemy side by side.

She stood up abruptly. 'I'm going to write to Sylvia,' she said and went up to her room. But when she was seated at the little table in the window, she couldn't think what to write. She sat for a long time, chewing the end of her pen and occasionally doodling on the notepad and gazing into the mirror over her dressing table. She ran her hand through her fair curls, wishing she had her sister's looks. Sylvia was also blonde, but her hair was more easily tamed into the smooth pageboy bob and she had the delicate complexion known as English rose. Daisy shook her head and concentrated on her writing. Chris loved her the way she was; what did it matter that she wasn't as beautiful as her sister?

Eventually, she sighed and scribbled a short note, congratulating Sylvia on her promotion and hoping she would be happy in her new job. She added that she hadn't heard from Chris lately but that things seemed to be looking up where he was. What else could she say? She sighed, put the letter in an envelope, sealed it and put it into her handbag to post the next day.

Another busy but, she had to admit, stressful day in the NAAFI tomorrow. Her promotion to supervisor had brought its problems and she was at a loss how to cope with them. She might as well have an early night. Perhaps a solution would come in the morning.

Chapter Two

Sylvia fed another sheet of paper into her typewriter and began to type. This would be the last condolence letter she would have to write, thank goodness. Tomorrow she would be on her way to officer training and soon after that to a new life in Buckinghamshire, she wasn't sure exactly where. She tried to suppress the excitement bubbling up. It would probably be the same boring routine, shorthand and typing. But she didn't care. In six weeks or so she would be stationed in the same place as Hugh. Never mind that nothing would come of it. Just being in the same place as him was enough. Or so she told herself.

She'd felt as if her world had come to an end when he'd told her he was being posted. How could she bear being apart from him? But then he'd offered her the opportunity of a posting to the same place. It couldn't be because he shared her feelings of course, but it was enough that he thought well of her work.

She'd had to go through a rigorous interview before being accepted and then there would be weeks of training before she'd see him again. Only when she arrived at Medmenham and was settled in would she be told exactly what work she would be doing.

When she took the letters in to be signed, another officer sat at Hugh's desk. Sylvia swallowed her disappointment. Hugh was leaving tomorrow, and she'd hoped for the chance to say goodbye as they wouldn't meet again until she'd finished her training.

Perhaps while they were apart, she would forget about him. It was wrong to feel this way. But in her heart she knew it wasn't just a silly crush. The way she felt was completely different from any previous relationship. Although she knew nothing could come of it, she smiled at the thought that in a few weeks she would be working with him again.

She tidied her desk and put the cover on her typewriter, looking around the office where she had spent so many hours – long hours made bearable by daydreaming about her handsome boss.

The other girls had already left except for Julia, her closest friend, who was waiting for her by the door. 'Come on, Syl. We'll be late for supper,' she said, taking her friend's arm. 'Don't tell me you're feeling sad about leaving. I can't wait.'

'Me too. I'm so pleased we'll be together.'

Two of the other WAAFs in the office had also been selected for special training, much to Sylvia's relief. She had been a bit worried that tongues would wag if it seemed the Wing Commander had singled her out for special treatment.

As she and Julia walked arm in arm across to the mess, they speculated excitedly about the new posting.

'Deadly secret, according to Marion. As usual, she has to pretend she knows all about it,' Julia said.

'She's always like that. Shame it's not just us two going.'

'Yes, she was quite nasty to me. Said she didn't understand why I'd been picked as I hadn't been to university and they needed clever people.'

'Don't take any notice. She's just being spiteful. I expect she's said the same about me – didn't even go to the Grammar. I passed the exam though, just...' Sylvia's voice trailed off. It was still a disappointment to her that because of her father's accident and inability to work, she'd been unable to take up her place. She shrugged the thought away. After all, if she hadn't done those evening classes in shorthand and typing, she'd never have been posted here and never met Hugh. It was those qualifications that got her in to the WAAFs.

Julia squeezed her arm in sympathy. 'I understand,' she said.

Sylvia had confided her home circumstances when they first met, pleased to find someone with a similar background. She'd been somewhat daunted when she was introduced to the other girls, all of whom seemed to have posh accents and fashionable clothes. But, as Julia said, they were all the same in uniform and all doing a worthwhile job.

'Well, I'm here now,' she said. 'And unlike some of them, it wasn't the thought of a glamorous uniform that made me join.'

Julia laughed, 'I know, you've told me often enough. Planes - you're mad about them.'

'It was growing up on the island. I'm very proud of the place. The first ever planes flew from Eastchurch – that's a village a few miles from my home. Daisy and I used to cycle out there to watch them. It's an RAF station now.'

'Don't suppose we'll see many planes where we're going,' Julia said as they entered the mess. 'Oh, no,' she whispered as she spotted Marion and Vera waving them over to their table.

Sylvia would have preferred to sit apart from them, but the mess was crowded so she and Julia reluctantly joined them. Marion was a snob and took every opportunity to belittle her. She no longer worried about it, but it had been a blow to discover that, as well as Julia and herself, she had been selected for special training.

'You all packed ready for the off?' Marion asked, 'I've packed my tennis racquet. There might be more chance to play when we get to the new posting.' She turned to Sylvia. 'You don't play, do you?'

'Actually, I do. We have a tennis club at home.'

18

'Really?' Marion's eyebrows rose. 'You've never played here.'

'Left my racquet at home,' Sylvia lied. 'I didn't think we'd have time for sports seeing as we're doing war work.'

'You must send for it. I hear the new place used to be a country estate. I'm sure there'll be courts.' She turned to Julia. 'Do you play?'

Sylvia grimaced and concentrated on her food. She couldn't admit she didn't actually own a racquet. When she could afford it, she played with Daisy at the Co-op sports ground, hiring racquets and balls for sixpence an hour. It had been fun and she missed those carefree days.

How her life had changed since the start of the war. When it was all over, would she be able to go back to that simple life? Much as she missed her family and friends on the island, she didn't think she'd be able to settle back to that humdrum existence.

Who knew what the future held though? An exciting new job, plus the bonus of working with Hugh Smythe. It couldn't lead to anything of course. But just being close to him was enough – for now, or so she told herself.

***

Six weeks later, their training complete, three WAAFs descended from the bus and gazed about them.

'Come on then,' Julia straightened her shoulders and began to march up the drive to the big house which would be their home for the foreseeable future.

Sylvia and Marion fell into step with her. 'Shame Pat isn't with us,' Marion said.

Julia agreed and Sylvia nodded. Privately, she wished it had been Marion who had failed the final test. Working closely with her over the past weeks had not made her any easier to get on with. Thank goodness for Julia, she thought.

The house was set back a long way from the road and they walked up a long drive which curved between immaculate lawns, dotted with sculpted yews. As they reached their destination, Sylvia gazed around in awe at the mansion, gleaming white in the sunshine, with its two towers, bay windows, and the ornate chimneys. It was completely outside her experience and she could hardly believe she would be living in such a posh place.

A guard at the front door inspected their papers and directed them to a side door. Apparently only senior officers and Ministry personnel used the main entrance. Inside, they were greeted by a WAAF officer who introduced herself as SO Forsyth. She led them outside again. 'Your quarters are in the huts,' she said, pointing across the grounds. 'I'll take you.'

Sylvia was a little disappointed that they would not be sleeping in the main house, but she followed the others along a path to the rear of the building.

'Just like home,' Julia joked as they came in sight of a row of Nissen huts like the ones where they'd been billeted in Norfolk.

'Hut six,' SO Forsyth said, pushing open the door. 'I'll leave you to unpack.'

Six beds, three each side with a locker alongside each, a mirror image of the place they'd left behind. So much for living in a posh mansion, Sylvia thought. She threw her kitbag down on the nearest bed and sat down, bouncing up and down to test its firmness. 'Just like home indeed,' she said, grinning at Julia.

Marion grimaced. 'I thought doing such important secret work would warrant more comfortable quarters, especially now we're officers.'

'Well, we're here now so better make the best of it,' Sylvia snapped, fed up with Marion's sniping.

As they were unpacking, the door opened and they jumped to attention at the sight of SO Forsyth.

20

'As you were,' she said. 'I just came to make sure you were settled in. Leave that and come over to the main house. I'll show you round and explain your duties.'

'Yes, ma'am,' they chorused. Forsyth nodded and left the hut.

'Don't we get to eat first? We've been travelling all day and I'm starving.' Marion grumbled.

Julia glanced at her watch. 'It's nearly suppertime. I expect we'll be shown where the mess is after our guided tour.'

She picked up the box containing her gas mask and opened the door. The others followed her.

As they walked back towards the main house, Sylvia remarked on the beautiful grounds. 'So different to Norfolk,' she said. It was a beautiful evening, the sky just tinged with pink as the sun went down. She inhaled the scent of freshly cut grass and smiled. 'I think I'm going to like it here.'

'Wait till you find out what our job is and then see if you like it,' Marion said.

'Pessimist,' Julia said, laughing.

SO Forsyth was waiting for them at the door and she ushered them into a spacious hall. Sylvia noticed the huge marble fireplace along one side, the only sign of the mansion's previous incarnation.

Maps and diagrams covered the walls and utilitarian desks and chairs replaced the original furnishings. Each work station held a lamp and various pieces of equipment which Sylvia didn't recognise.

The building seethed with activity as airmen and women, naval and army officers strode purposefully in and out of the rooms which branched off the hall.

Sylvia wondered if Hugh was among them, but she was given no time think about him as the officer opened a door and ushered them into a large room equipped as an office.

'The new girls, sir,' she said.

21

Sylvia gazed around the book-lined room, obviously the library in its former life, then snapped to attention as the officer looked up from his papers and studied the three of them.

'Welcome to RAF Medmenham. I'm Wing Commander Stewart. I hope you'll be happy in your new role. SO Forsyth will explain your duties. You will each be assigned to a different section.'

First, he explained what the different sections did. Sylvia's interest quickened when he mentioned aircraft recognition and she hoped she would be allocated to that section. She smiled as Julia gave her a surreptitious nudge. By now, everyone knew of her interest in aeroplanes. She remembered confiding it to Hugh and wondered if he had put in a word for her. She crossed her fingers behind her back and almost lost track of what the CO was saying.

Julia was allocated to L Section, located in one of the towers.

'Aircraft recognition,' the SO said.

He turned to Sylvia and she tried to hide her disappointment when he told her that she would be in a different section. It sounded interesting though.

'You will be looking for anything unusual on the ground – disguised buildings, new structures,' SO Forsyth explained. 'Don't worry. You'll soon get the hang of it.'

Later that evening, her head whirling from the introduction to her new life, Sylvia decided to write to her sister and pass on her new address. In her last letter she had only said she would be moving soon but not where to. She and her friends had signed the Official Secrets Act and had been given strict instructions not to divulge the exact whereabouts of their new home or to say anything about the nature of their work. They had to use a Post Office box number as their address.

Sylvia sat on her bed, chewing the end of her pen. She had only got as far as 'Dear Daisy...' but what could she say? She longed to describe the lovely mansion house where she would be working and the beautiful gardens surrounding it, but they had been warned that no one must know the existence of the so-called RAF station. The work didn't sound all that exciting so far. The excitement came from the secret nature of her new job, but she couldn't tell her sister any of it. In the end she wrote, 'Not much to tell really. We are in huts, just like Norfolk, and it's the same old thing, boring shorthand and typing. Luckily, Julia is still with me, so it doesn't feel too strange. I'll write more when we are settled. Love to Mum and Dad and little brother.'

***

When Daisy read the letter, she smiled. Poor Sylvia. She had been so proud of being in the WAAFs, feeling so superior to her sister's humdrum job in the NAAFI. But it was Daisy who'd had the excitement, not that she'd want to live through that again. She was quite content now with being supervisor and spending free time with her friends. The problems she dealt with at work were minor in comparison to what others were suffering. Three years at war and no one knew when it would end. She tried not to think of Chris and what he might be going through out there in the desert. No word for weeks and none from Bob either.

She'd answer Sylvia's letter, she thought. That would take her mind off her worries. And then she'd write to Lily.

She still missed her friend and was sad that she had decided not to return to her job in the NAAFI. Still, she was pleased Lily had decided to keep the baby, although it would be hard for her to manage as a single mother. She seemed happy enough though, working on a farm just outside the village where her grandmother lived, while Mrs Scott looked after the baby.

After finishing the letter to Sylvia and wishing her well in her new job, she picked up her pen again and wrote, 'Dear Lily...' She paused, wondering how she could tactfully say what was on her mind.

When Lily had been left pregnant by Roland Hargreaves, she'd told Daisy that her mother was prepared to take on the baby and bring it up as her own. Another addition to the large Scott family would not be remarked on. Mrs Scott, Lily and her younger brother and sisters had left for the country, ostensibly to escape the threatened bombing. Lily had been unwell, I and it was natural that she would go with them to convalesce. That was the story Lily had given to her NAAFI colleagues. Only Daisy knew the truth. The family would return when the baby was born, and Lily could go back to her job in the NAAFI.

It had been quite a blow to learn that Lily would not be coming back. Daisy started to write again. *'I can't tell you how much I still miss you. Things go on much the same here. The new girl Shirley has settled in nicely and sometimes comes to the pictures with us. Mavis has come out of her shell a bit, but she and Shirley are still a bit shy of letting their hair down in front of me now I am supervisor. I tell them that I'm a different person away from work although I have to be strict when on duty. They still act a bit nervous around me though. Thank goodness for June. I'm pleased you and baby Mikey are doing OK. Lucky you to have your gran and your mum to look after him while you're at work.'*

She didn't mention Christopher – it was too painful to admit that she hadn't heard from him for ages. So she finished by saying her mum and dad were well and that Jimmy was still her annoying little brother, 'although he's grown up bit lately now he's joined the Home Guard'.

She signed her name and folded the sheet of paper, putting it into an envelope. She'd post both letters in the morning on her way to work.

As she got ready for bed her thoughts turned to Christopher. Perhaps she should have written to him again. But what was the point, she thought with a sigh, when he never wrote back. She picked up the little snapshot of him which she kept on her bedside table. He smiled out at her, his eyes crinkled against the sun, his hand pushing back his mop of dark curls. It had been taken by one of his mates a few days before they left for Africa.

She pressed the picture to her lips and pushed it under her pillow, telling herself not to be so silly. How could he write out there in the desert, the battle for the valuable oil fields on the North African coast going first one way then another? Even if he had a chance to write, how would the letters get through and how did she know if he even got hers? It wasn't so much the lack of letters that upset her. It was the constant worry for his safety.

Chapter Three

After six weeks at Medmenham Sylvia had only caught a brief glimpse of Hugh. He'd been talking to her boss when she went into the office to hand him a report she had typed.

He'd glanced round and smiled, returning her salute. Her boss said a brief 'Thank you,' and turned back to his discussion and she left the office, pausing outside the door trying to control her erratic breathing. This was silly, she berated herself. She couldn't go to pieces every time she saw him. What's more, no one must ever suspect how she felt. Perhaps it was just as well she had so little contact with him since being posted here. She was beginning to think it had been a mistake accepting the posting here – so near him. Perhaps she would have forgotten him in time – or so she tried to tell herself.

A few days later she and Julia had just finished work for the day and were walking across the lawn to their hut. Deep in conversation with her friend, she started when a voice addressed her.

'Good afternoon ladies,' Hugh said catching up with them.

Sylvia felt the blush creeping up her neck to her cheeks and murmured a greeting.

'I just wondered how you were both settling in. Are you finding the work interesting?'

Julia smiled and nodded enthusiastically. 'Better than typing letters,' she said.

'And you, SO Bishop?'

'Yes, sir,' Sylvia managed.

'Enjoy your evening then,' he said and hurried away.

'Well, fancy that,' Julie said. 'A high-ranking officer deigning to speak to the likes of us.'

'He was just being polite,' Sylvia said. 'Besides, we're commissioned officers now. Why shouldn't he greet us?'

'I suppose he had to speak, seeing as you worked for him back in Norfolk.'

Sylvia didn't reply. She was trying to still the rapid beating of her heart and hoped Julia hadn't noticed her confusion. Once again, she told herself off for being silly. There was no way he could be interested in her and if he was, she wouldn't encourage him. She'd done some daft things in her time but getting involved with a married man was definitely not on the cards. It didn't stop her daydreaming though.

Julia gave her a little push and giggled. 'You've gone quiet. I do believe you've got a crush on him. I don't blame you. He is rather good looking. Very distinguished with that pipe – a bit like Leslie Howard or Leo Genn.'

Sylvia managed a laugh. She knew it wasn't just a girlish crush, but she had to pretend. 'Give over. I was just thinking about our night out. I'm broke and I was hoping we could get someone to buy us a drink,' she lied.

'Bound to be some good-looking officer willing to treat us.' Julia ran her hand through her dark curls and laughed.

Sylvia envied her friend's ability to be so carefree. Julia never had any trouble finding someone to escort her, buy her drinks and take her dancing, never seeming to take any of them seriously. Sylvia often made up a foursome with her but since her disastrous relationship with Roland Hargreaves, she was wary of becoming involved with anyone else. And now? Falling for the most unsuitable man she could imagine, sent her determination to stay fancy free out of the window. Try as she would to put Hugh Smythe out of her mind, just seeing him brought all those forbidden feelings rushing back.

As they got ready to go out for the evening, Julia chattered non-stop. When she turned from applying her lipstick in front of the mirror she noticed that Sylvia was still not ready. 'Come on Syl. We'll be late.'

'I'm sorry, Julia. I have a dreadful headache. I don't really feel like coming out. Do you mind going without me? You're sure to catch up with some of the other girls.'

'What's the matter? You were all right a minute ago.'

'It came on suddenly, just tired I expect. An early night will see me right. You go, enjoy yourself.'

Julia shrugged and grabbed her handbag. 'Night then.'

The door slammed and as soon as she'd gone, Sylvia burst into tears and threw herself down on her bed.

After a few minutes she sat up and wiped her eyes. She went over to the washbasin in the corner of the hut and splashed water on her face. Peering at her red-rimmed eyes in the mirror, she frowned. She hoped none of her hut mates would come in and see her liked this. She couldn't bear their teasing. Marion was the worst offender and she wouldn't stop until she found out what was wrong. Then it would be all over the station.

Sylvia got into her pyjamas and climbed into bed. She tried to read for a while, but she couldn't concentrate, the thoughts going round and round in her head. She put the light out and pulled the covers over her head. She would pretend to be asleep when the others came in.

Lying there, unable to sleep, she remembered the first time she had met Hugh. His courtesy and kindness to the young recruits under his command impressed her and her feelings for him had gradually

28

developed over the following months. When he informed her of his posting, she realised how she really felt and how devastated she would be not to see and speak to him every day.

When he'd recommended her for this posting, she'd been filled with joy and she wondered if he'd pulled strings to get her sent here to be near him. Perhaps he had feelings for her too. A foolish thought of course. After all, he had never said or done anything to give her hope. Besides, he was married.

Since her arrival in Medmenham, however, he had made no attempt to single her out and their brief meetings in the course of duty had soon brought her down to earth.

She turned over in bed, thumping her pillow. Put him out of your mind, you foolish girl, she told herself. He's married with a family. And even if he was by any chance attracted to her, she would not be drawn into a sleazy affair. Her brief fling with Roland had taught her there was no future in that.

She was just drifting off to sleep when the door of the hut burst open and her colleagues tumbled in with a flurry of giggles and murmurs of 'shsh' when they realised Sylvia was in bed.

She sat up, rubbing her eyes.

'Sorry, did we wake you?' Julia said, plonking herself down on the bed. 'You should have come with us. We had a super time.'

'I wouldn't have been very good company,' Sylvia said.

'Oh, sorry, I forgot. Your headache. How is it now?'

'A bit better.'

'We should let you sleep.'

'No, it's all right. Tell me about your evening.'

'Well, I met this gorgeous naval officer. Just passing through, unfortunately. We danced a lot though. It was fun.'

The other girls were getting ready for bed, still chattering about their evening when Marion spoke up. 'Come on girls. Let's get some shut eye, early start in the morning.'

They all groaned. 'Bossy boots,' Julia whispered. 'Still, she's right.'

Sylvia nodded and settled down in bed again. She pulled the pillow over her head to shut out the giggles and whispers that continued. Once upon a time she would have been doing the same, having fun, dancing and drinking with any good-looking officer who looked her way. Yet here she was mooning over a man she couldn't have.

When she woke next morning, she made a decision. Next time the girls asked her to join them, she would.

She would go out dancing and have fun. And when on duty, she would concentrate on her work and not think about Hugh. She was beginning to get a feel for what they were doing, and she felt good knowing how she was contributing to the war effort. Pity it was so secret. She would love Daisy and the rest of her family to know what she was up to. Her parents would be so proud. As for Daisy, since her promotion to supervisor in the Sheerness NAAFI, she had seemed a little dismissive of her sister's job as a shorthand typist. Little did she know, Sylvia thought.

She hugged the thought of her secret life to her – the important work she was doing and her forbidden love. It was hard to write home about her seemingly mundane life but there would be plenty of time for confidences after the war.

**

When the orderly placed the post on his desk, Hugh snatched it up eagerly and leafed through the pile of envelopes. At last. A letter from Margaret. It was weeks since he'd heard from her. He scanned the one page and sighed. More of a note than a proper letter. He had hoped for news of how the boys had settled into their new school in Oban and whether Margaret had managed to find a job that suited her. She had said she would find some war work that would fit in with the children's school hours. But, to his disappointment, the letter contained no real news.

'It is so cold here in Scotland, not like summer at all,' he read. 'I don't know why I had to move so far away. Can't we move nearer to you, now that the threat of invasion is over? Or you could come here? I'm sure your job isn't so important that you can't get some leave.'

He sighed again and screwed up the sheet of paper, throwing it into the waste-paper bin. Why didn't she understand? Of course, he couldn't tell her the exact importance of his work but she must realise, especially after him explaining, several times, that he had signed the Official Secrets Act.

'But surely you can confide in me. I'm your wife,' she had said, coming close to him and stroking his hair. When they were first married, he would have been tempted to give in, anything to make her happy. But now, he just got impatient with her. Perhaps it was just as well she was so far away.

He stood up and went to the window, grimacing at the steady downpour. Not much better than Scotland, he thought. It was the end of the morning shift and he smiled as three young WAAFs ran across the lawn laughing. They didn't seem bothered by the weather. He spotted Sylvia Bishop with them, wondering what it was about her that caught his attention. She was young, pretty and full of life – just like all the other girls in her section. It wasn't just her looks though.

She might be carefree and fun loving when off duty but at work she was serious, totally absorbed in what she was doing – and doing very well too. He had been right to recommend her for officer training and posting here. *She* not only understood the importance of their work, she showed real aptitude.

His thoughts turned to Margaret again. Of course, if he could only explain, he was sure she would understand too – or would she? Before the war, her world had revolved round the boys and entertaining. She loved holding dinner parties for their friends, mostly fellow officers. It was a world she understood. He knew that the one thing that would make her really happy was if he was a pilot, or in charge of an operational station, something she could boast about. And make the boys proud of their father - she'd said so often enough.

He went back to his desk and sorted through the rest of his mail, most of it official forms for him to sign. Then he picked up the latest batch of photographs which had come through from the print room.

Several of them had notes attached and he recognised Sylvia's neat handwriting. He smiled. How was it that with so little training she was able to pick up on things the others missed?

He snatched up one photo and studied it, gasping as he realised its significance. 'This can't wait,' he muttered, picking up the phone and asking for SO Forsyth.

When she entered the office he said, 'I know SO Bishop has just gone off duty, but could you ask her to come in if she's still on the station? I need to talk to her about this.' He waved the photo at her. 'Please apologise for interrupting her evening but this could be important.'

'Yes, sir.' SO Forsyth saluted and left the room.

While he waited for Sylvia to return, he asked himself it he was attaching too much importance to the photo and her note. Or was it just an excuse to speak to her? Of course not, he told himself.

Still, he had to admit he was spending far too much time thinking about Sylvia Bishop and it wasn't just because she was so efficient at her work. He shook his head. As if she would be interested in him. He was far too old, he told himself, running his hand through hair which had recently begun to show threads of grey. Besides, he was a married man and he still loved his wife, even if she sometimes seemed to have little love for him. Still, if it wasn't for the boys...

His thoughts were interrupted when Sylvia entered the office and he forced himself to concentrate on the matter at hand.

'You wanted to see me, sir?' Sylvia said, trying to catch her breath.

'I'm sorry. I know you're off duty but this couldn't wait.' He picked up the photo and handed it to her. 'Please tell me what you spotted that seems significant to you.'

Sylvia took it and studied it for a few moments. 'Well, sir. It's this – up in the top left-hand corner. I wasn't sure but I thought it worth taking another look.' She leaned across the desk and pointed it out to him.

He caught the scent of her hair and inhaled sharply, then shook his head. Keep your mind on your work, he told himself. 'Yes, you could be right. We've certainly never seen anything like this before.'

'What do you think it is, sir – a new type of plane?'

'Not sure. I have an idea, but I'll need to consult with my superiors.' He took the photo from her and straightened up. 'Thank you SO Bishop. Well done. You've a keen eye. If you spot anything else like this, bring it to me at once.'

'Yes, sir.'

'Off you go and enjoy the rest of your evening.'

The smile she gave him almost took his breath away and it was almost a relief when she closed the door behind her. He shook his head to clear the thoughts which insisted on intruding.

Perhaps he ought to take the leave he was due, get away. He should go up to Scotland and spend some time with Margaret and the boys. That would take his mind off these foolish thoughts. He couldn't, of course, they were far too busy, and this work was too important. It had nothing to do with Sylvia Bishop, he told himself.

Chapter Four

Sylvia caught up with Julia and the others on their way out of the gate.

'What kept you?' her friend asked. 'Hurry up, we'll miss the bus.'

They were just in time to catch it and Sylvia threw herself down on the seat next to Julia. She hoped her friend would not pursue her questioning. She could say truthfully that she had been called into the office · to discuss her work but feared her tendency to blush would give her away. And Julia was sharp enough to pick up on it. She couldn't bear the inevitable teasing about her 'crush' on the handsome senior officer that would ensue. She knew in her heart it was more than a crush - unlike any feeling she'd had before. It was too precious to share. Talking about him would spoil it.

The other girls were discussing the pub they would visit. Vera and Jane had been there the longest and knew their way around. 'Let's go to the Hare and Hounds,' Jane said.

'We might meet some chaps,' Vera said.

Sylvia forced herself to join in with the banter. 'Perhaps you'll meet your naval officer again,' she said with a smile.

'No such luck. Ships that pass in the night,' Julia said ruefully.

'There'll be others,' Vera said, giggling.

'We're just going for a quiet drink, not to meet men,' Marion snapped.

'Speak for yourself,' Vera retorted. 'I need some fun after being cooped up in that room for hours.'

'Well, don't drink too much. You know what you get like when you've had a few.'

'Marion, don't be so stuffy. We have to let our hair down now and then.'

She was right though, Sylvia thought. It wouldn't do to let anything slip about their work when they were out enjoying themselves. And Vera did get a bit silly with a few gin and tonics inside her.

The bus pulled up outside the pub and the girls tumbled out, laughing and chatting. Determined to enjoy herself and to stop thinking about Hugh, Sylvia joined in when someone started up on the piano and everyone joined in singing.

The bar was crowded with WAAFs and military personnel and it started to get very noisy and smoky. Sylvia looked across the room and noticed one of her hut mates sitting by herself. Iris was quiet and shy but always tried to join in with the rest of the Hut Six gang. Sylvia joined her at the table and fanned her face with her hand. 'Getting a bit hot in here. Need a rest,' she said.

Iris looked up with a smile and nodded. 'I'm not really one for pubs. My parents are teetotal. They'd faint if they knew I was in here.'

'I'm not much of a drinker either. I'd rather go to the pictures or go dancing.'

'Me too. I don't think my boyfriend would like me dancing with other men though.' Iris's shoulders slumped. 'I don't even know where he is though. Somewhere at sea.'

'I'm sorry. It must be hard. What's his name?'

'Freddie. He's a stoker on board a merchant ship.' She took a sip of her port. 'Do you have a boyfriend?'

'No one special.' Sylvia felt the blush creeping up her neck. If only they knew. But she couldn't confide in anyone.

She was saved from having to say more when Julia joined them with two army officers in tow. 'Come and dance,' she said, grabbing Sylvia's hand. 'This is Harry. I said I'd introduce you. And this one's Ted.' She slipped her arm through his and smiled up at him.

The other man smiled and said, 'Julia tells me you're a good dancer. Will you do me the honour?'

Reluctantly, Sylvia returned his smile and stood up. As they circled the small space in the centre of the room, she began to enjoy herself. She'd always loved dancing and it was easy to let herself imagine she was in Hugh's arms.

She was quickly brought down to earth when Harry said, 'Your friend is right. You're a good dancer.'

'Thank you. I used to go to dance classes with my sister, before the war.'

'And what do you do when you're not dancing?'

'Work, mostly. I don't get a lot of time off.'

'What work is that?'

Was it idle curiosity, was he just making small talk? She had to say something. 'Just shorthand and typing,' she said. 'Nothing important.'

'Women's work, eh? I bet you even make the tea.' He laughed and Sylvia felt her hackles rise.

She pushed him away. 'Yes, sometimes. It all helps the war effort. Tea is good for morale, I'll have you know.'

'Hey, don't get shirty. I was just joking.' Harry took her hand. 'Come on, let's dance again.'

'No thank you. I'm rather tired. All that tea making is exhausting.' She made her way back to the table leaving Harry staring after her, a puzzled frown on his face. 'What did I do?' he muttered.

Iris was still at the table. She had finished her drink and she stood up as Sylvia approached. 'I'm going back,' she said. 'I want to write to Freddie before bed.'

'I'll come too. Just wait while I say goodnight to the others.'

'You don't have to come with me,' Iris said.

'I'm tired and, anyway I want to get away from that Harry.' Sylvia picked up her bag and gas mask case and crossed the room to where her colleagues seemed to be having a good time. She tapped Julia on the shoulder and told her she was leaving with Iris.

'Oh, didn't you get on with Harry then? I thought I was doing you a good turn introducing you.'

Sylvia shook her head. 'Not my type,' she said.

Julia laughed. 'Well, I'm staying. Tell me about it when I get back.'

Outside, the two girls hurried towards the bus stop hoping they wouldn't have to wait too long. They linked arms and Iris started talking about her Freddie. She was madly in love and had eyes for no one else. Sylvia envied her. She felt the same about Hugh but there was no one she could confide in.

When they got in, Sylvia got ready for bed, leaving Iris to write her letter. She hoped she'd be asleep when the other girls came back, not feeling up to joining in their chatter as they re-hashed their evening out.

She thought about Harry and his dismissive words. Women's work! If only he knew. But that's how most men thought; she knew there was nothing she could do about it. She'd just have to put up with it. Times like this she really missed Daisy. The sisters always used to do everything together and at night, snuggled up together in bed they would whisper their secrets, hiding their heads under the covers to smother their giggles. She thought about Roland and how shocked Daisy had been on hearing she had gone up to his hotel room, something she bitterly regretted. But Daisy had kept her secret. If only she could see her again. She couldn't talk about her work of course, but she could confide her feelings for Hugh. Not the sort of thing she could mention in a letter. She was pleased her sister had found love with Christopher, but she still felt a bit sorry for Bob. Both families had fully expected the two to get together after the war until Chris Jameson had appeared on the scene. Sylvia sighed and turned over in bed.

***

At that moment Daisy was thinking about Sylvia. She was proud of her sister. Who'd have thought she'd ever be an officer. Still, she had always been the clever one, the one who would do well. Unlike her, Daisy had never been ambitious. Until the war started and her life had changed so dramatically, she had always thought she would marry Bob, perhaps move in with his widowed mother next door, start a family. A safe contented life, much like her parents. Then she'd met Chris, the tall, curly haired soldier who had stolen her heart.

She still felt bad about hurting Bob, but he seemed to have taken it well. Perhaps realising, as she had, that they had grown out of their childhood romance. The war made them grow up quickly.

She sighed. So many changes in the past three years. Would life ever return to what her mother called 'normal'? And did she really want it to?

When – if – Chris came back would they still feel the same about each other? She relived the moment when they'd said goodbye more than a year ago. That passionate kiss, so different from anything she had felt before. She had promised to wait for him and, of course, she would. He loved her and she loved him.

***

Chris took his boots off and shook the sand out. He removed his helmet and leaned back into the meagre shade of his motorcycle, wiping his hand across his forehead.

The rest of the troop sat or lay in the shade of their vehicles, some of them smoking but most too exhausted even for that.

He looked across at Bob who took a swig from his water canteen, then wiped his mouth and started to speak but Chris forestalled him.

'If you say it's bloody hot one more time...' He shook his head. 'Talk about stating the bleeding obvious.'

'Sorry mate.' Bob took another swig.

'Better save some of that water, mate. We'll be moving on soon and God knows when we'll get a chance to fill up.'

Bob didn't answer but he screwed the lid back on the canteen and struggled to his feet. 'Wish I knew where we'd be moving to. Back and forth across this bloody desert. It all looks the blooming same.'

'Well, we just have to trust that the brass know what they're doing.'

'Some hopes,' Bob grumbled.

Chris was getting a bit fed up with Bob's moaning. His view was if there was nothing you could do about it, just put up and shut up. But he didn't want to upset his mate – to his surprise they had become good friends over the last couple of years.

At first, knowing how Bob felt about Daisy, he had kept quiet about his feelings. Then one night as they lay sleepless under the starry desert sky, Bob had confessed that he had fallen in love with a French girl while he was on the run after Dunkirk.

'I know I'll never see her again, but I can't get her out of my head,' he told Chris. 'I felt bad about hurting Daisy and I would never have told her about Francoise.' He gave a little laugh. 'And then you came along.'

'Not funny, mate. I knew about you and I didn't know what to do. I thought I should step aside and was about to. But then, when she was in danger, I couldn't hide how I felt.'

'Glad you were there, mate.' Bob had turned over and they tried to sleep.

Next day they didn't mention their late-night conversation but from then on they'd been friends, looking out for each other in the heat of battle.

Now, as the order came for them to move on, Chris pulled his boots on and stood up. He held out a hand to help Bob up and they shrugged on their kit.

Bob climbed up into the gun carrier and took his seat behind the armoured shield beside the gunner. He gave a little wave as Chris mounted his motorcycle and roared off to the front of the column.

The officer at the head of the column waved him to a stop. 'Communications are out,' he said, handing Chris a pouch. 'Go back to our last position and give this to the Brigadier, then catch up with us if you can,' he said.

'Yes, sir.' Chris saluted and stowed the pouch in the pannier.

What's that all about, he wondered as he opened the throttle and concentrated on keeping the bike in the tracks left by the armoured column. There was no road, just a faint track and the deep ruts where the German tanks had gone through. It made manoeuvring the motorcycle easier than when they'd driven across pristine desert a few days ago. Each time they stopped Chris had to strip the engine down and clean the sand clogging it up.

He left the line of armoured gun carriers far behind and approached the small encampment where the brigadier and the remainder of the troop had stayed. Their job was to hold their position and give the main contingent time to catch up with the rest of their battalion.

Suddenly, Chris pulled on the brakes, throwing up a flurry of sand as he skidded to a halt. He had caught movement out of the corner of his eye off to the south.

He pulled his binoculars out and tried to focus on the movement. Had the chief moved out? But why was he going south instead of catching up with the rest of the troop?

He looked again, gasping as he brought the moving vehicles into focus. Germans!

What should he do? Torn between carrying out his orders to pass the message on to the Brigadier and turning back to warn his mates, he hesitated, his foot on the kick-starter.

He looked towards the camp, just visible on the horizon, and swallowed hard. The column of smoke must mean they had been attacked. And the fact that the enemy vehicles were moving away told him that the remainder of his troop had been defeated.

Whatever the message in his pouch might be, it was useless now. Chris sighed, pulled his goggles down and turned the bike back towards the column. He had planned to write to Daisy tonight, but it looked like they were in for another battle.

Chapter Five

After a long night shift, Sylvia should have gone back to her billet and rested. Despite her tiredness she knew she wouldn't be able to sleep. Julia was on a different shift, otherwise she would have asked her to go into town with her.

As she crossed the grass in the direction of the huts, she saw Jane, one of her hut mates, wheeling her bicycle towards her.

'Where are you off to?' Sylvia asked.

'Back to the hut. I'm too tired to go out today. What about you?'

Sylvia hesitated. It wouldn't hurt to ask. 'I was going to get the bus into town, but I wondered...' She hesitated again.

'You want to borrow the bike?'

'Yes, please. It's a dreadful cheek but...'

'That's Ok. So long as I get it back in one piece.' She laughed to show she was joking.

'Oh, thank you, Jane. It will save so much time.'

'You're surely not going shopping. There's nothing in the shops in Henley.'

Sylvia sighed. 'I know, but I must try to find something for Julia. It's her birthday soon.'

'Why don't you go to Reading? More choice there.'

'Takes too long on the bus. I prefer Henley.'

'Good luck then,' Jane said, handing the bicycle over. She gave a little wave and walked off.

Sylvia mounted the cycle and set off, wobbling a little at first. It had been a couple of years since she last rode. Passing the guard at the main gate, she

43

turned into the road, thankful there didn't seem to be much traffic about. It was a mild autumn morning and she breathed deeply, savouring the few hours of freedom ahead.

The road wound between high hedges, now showing their autumn colours. She caught occasional glimpses of the river between the trees. It was beautiful here, she thought as she freewheeled down the hill towards the town centre. So different from her island home. She found herself remembering cycle rides with Daisy, sometimes up into the more undulating countryside of the eastern end of Sheppey where the cliffs fell away to the sea, or out across the marshes. Most of the time she was so immersed in her work that she hardly thought about home and her family, although she wrote frequently to her sister and enjoyed getting letters in return.

She crossed the bridge and cycled into the market square, leaning the bicycle against a wall. It was a pretty town with quaint old buildings and little shops. She wandered along looking into shop windows, hoping to find something suitable for a birthday present.

She was about to turn back when she spotted a tiny gift shop on a corner. She crossed the road and went inside. The shop keeper had done his best to make the most of the meagre stock and it was very prettily laid out. As she was browsing an elderly man came through from a back room.

'What can I get you, miss?' he asked.

'Not sure. I'm looking for a present for a friend.' Sylvia picked up a china vase painted with a garish pattern in red and purple. She didn't think Julia would like that. She sighed and looked around. Then something else, high on a shelf, caught her eye. 'Oh, could I see that please,' she asked, pointing.

The man sighed and fetched a short step ladder. As he handed the china cat down to Sylvia, he began to cough and wheeze.

'Are you all right?' she asked.

'It's the dust,' he said. 'Not many customers these days and I haven't touched that top shelf for weeks.'

Years, more like, Sylvia thought, but she smiled and took the ornament from him.

He produced a duster from behind the counter and handed it to her. As she wiped the grime away, revealing a ginger tabby with green eyes, she smiled. 'I knew I was right,' she said. 'My friend has a cat just like this. She keeps a photo of it by her bed. She'll love this.' Holding her breath, she asked the price, sighing with relief when she realised she had just enough.

The shopkeeper wrapped a piece of newspaper around the cat and Sylvia put it in her bag.

Outside, she glanced at her watch. Just enough time to find a cafe and have a cup of tea before cycling back up the hill.

She walked on and soon found herself beside the river where she paused to take in the view. The few boats moored alongside and the trees in their vibrant autumn colours on the opposite bank were reflected in the water. No cafe though, so she turned back and almost bumped into someone. 'Sorry,' she said automatically, glancing up and gasping as she recognised her superior officer.

'Oh, sorry, sir,' she said, with a belated salute.

'No need to apologise. I didn't mean to startle you,' Wing Commander Smythe said. ''Are you enjoying your day off?'

Sylvia recovered her composure and said, 'Oh, yes, sir.'

'It's lovely here, isn't it? I find a walk along the river very relaxing after a long shift.'

'Me too. I've just come off night shift, so I ought to be getting back,' she said, starting to walk away.

'Did you come on the bus? I can give you a lift back if you like.'

Sylvia's heart started thumping at the thought of a lift in Hugh's car, sitting beside him, trying to make conversation. But she managed to reply politely. 'No, thank you, sir. I cycled. I left my bike near the town hall.'

'That's where my car's parked.' He walked alongside her, not speaking and she tried to calm herself. He was just being polite as he always was when their paths crossed at work.

As they turned a corner into the marketplace, he said, 'I was thinking of having a cup of tea before I go back. The stuff they serve in the mess is awful. Would you join me?'

'I don't know, sir. I should be getting back.' She longed to say yes but she felt a little awkward. Suppose someone saw them together? She could imagine the gossip, especially if someone like Marion heard it.

'Come on. Just a cup of tea. There's a nice little tea shop I know of near here.'

Sylvia nodded. 'All right,' she murmured.

The cafe was in an old building with low beams and small windows. Hugh led her to a table in the corner and Sylvia sat down, taking in the lace tablecloths and small posies of flowers on the table. To her relief the place was empty, and she began to relax. Why not enjoy this interlude even if it didn't mean anything to him? She could dream, pretend they were a couple, that he wasn't married with a family. It would be a memory to treasure.

She started out of her reverie when he said, 'Just tea? Or would you like something else? They do nice scones here.'

She nodded. 'Yes, please.' He must have been here before. A sudden thought struck her. Had he brought other young women here? Of course not. He wasn't another Roland.

The waitress brought a tray with a pot of tea and a plate of scones. Sylvia thanked her and looked up at Hugh. 'Shall I pour,' she asked.

'Yes, please.' He smiled. 'Now, I know this is your off duty time and we shouldn't talk about work, but I wondered – how are you finding it?'

'It's fascinating, sir. And I get so caught up in it, the time flies by.'

'You're doing very well. It's very important work, you know.'

'Oh, yes, sir. I appreciate that. It's good to be doing something worthwhile.'

He smiled again and there was a twinkle in his eye as he said, 'Better than shorthand and typing, eh?'

She felt the flush creeping up her neck. Had he heard her complaining to Julia? She took a deep breath. 'Well, sir, I know that *everything* we WAAFs do is important, but I feel this is more so.' She bent her head and concentrated on buttering her scone.

When she raised her head, he was looking at her intently. 'I knew I was right about you when I suggested this posting.'

She felt a fluttering in her stomach and her heartbeat quickened but she managed to say, 'Thank you, sir.' She hesitated. 'I sometimes wonder why I was picked for Photo Interpretation. I was just a shorthand typist, no real qualifications.'

'Well, Sylvia.' He put his cup down and leaned towards her. 'You don't mind me calling you Sylvia?'

She shook her head.

'Well, you must call me Hugh. Less of this 'Sir' business – only when we're off duty, of course.'

'Of course.' She'd almost said sir, but whispered, 'Hugh.'

'Well,' he continued. 'We knew of your interest in aircraft and your connections with Sheppey, the home of flying.'

47

'But I don't really have anything to do with planes,' Sylvia said.

'It wasn't just that of course. Remember the hobbies you listed on your application form? Jigsaw puzzles?'

'Yes, I nearly didn't put it down, It didn't seem important.'

He smiled. 'Just think about what you're doing now.'

Sylvia thought for a moment. 'I see what you mean. I hadn't thought of it before. Some of the photos we look at are part of a sort of jigsaw, aren't they?'

He nodded. 'Now, that's enough talk about work. Let's finish up these delicious scones before it's back to base.'

As they ate and drank, Hugh spoke about the town and its history. 'An interesting place, the sort of town I'd like to live in after the war.'

They were silent for while as they concentrated on eating their scones.

Sylvia was the first to speak, anxious to know more about him. 'Where do you come from?' she asked.

'A little village near Chichester in Sussex.'

'Will you stay in the air force after the war?' Sylvia asked, searching for something to talk about.

'Yes. I'm a career officer. Joined up as a cadet. I couldn't think of doing anything else.'

'What about flying?' Knowing of his interest in aircraft, Sylvia had often wondered why he wasn't a pilot.

'I've done my share.' He glanced at his watch. 'I suppose I ought to get back. Are you sure you won't have a lift? I could put the bike in the back.'

'No thank you, sir - Hugh. It's a lovely day. I'll enjoy the ride.'

Hugh paid the bill and politely opened the door for her.

'My bike's over there,' Sylvia said, pointing.

'Thank you for joining me. I've enjoyed your company, Sylvia. We must do this again.'

'I don't think so. It was nice of you to ask me and I enjoyed it too, but I don't think it would be right.'

He looked down and shuffled his feet. 'Perhaps you're right, Sylvia. Sensible girl.' He walked towards his car, a dark green Alvis, without looking back and Sylvia bit her lip. Why had she said that? A walk by the river, tea in a cafe. Where was the harm in that? No harm at all, but it was what it could lead to. It was an enticing thought, but she wasn't the sort of girl to start an affair with a married man.

She got on the bike, crossed the river and started up the hill towards Medmenham. As she freewheeled down the other side she started laughing. Tea with a senior officer. What would the other girls make of that? But she knew she must keep it to herself. She couldn't tell even her closest friend. It was a secret far too precious to share.

***

'You fool,' Hugh muttered as he started the car. When he had spotted Sylvia gazing into the river he should have just walked on. But the chance to spend time with her, to get to know her outside the work environment had been too good to pass up. If he hadn't been so angry with Margaret, he would never have done it. And after all, it had just been an innocent meeting, a cup of tea and a chat. If it had happened in the mess with others around no one would have remarked on it.

Well, it wouldn't happen again. From now on he would keep his distance and act professionally at all times.

His thoughts turned to Margaret and her latest letter. He couldn't believe what she had done without consulting him. They had agreed that the boys should not be sent away to boarding school until they were much older. But she had ignored his wishes and done it.

'It's for the best, darling,' she had written. *'I'll be able to come down and spend time with you. I'll stay at the Hare and Hounds in Sonning. It's all fixed. I know you'll say you are too busy for us to see much of each other but it's better than nothing. And it'll only be in term time. I'll go back to Scotland for the school holidays.'*

He should have been pleased. They had been apart for months and at first, he had missed her. But he had become so involved with his work and life at Medmenham that days passed without him even thinking of her. Besides, she hardly ever wrote. Today's letter had been a shock, the news about the boys a bolt from the blue. How could she do it? It's not as if she had signed up for any kind of war work and had no time for them.

'I'll be there on Friday,' her letter continued. 'Please meet me at the station. And do, please, try to get some leave.'

He had no time to write back and stop her coming. She would be on her way before a letter could reach her. Anyway, she would never understand how impossible it was to get leave - a few hours off at the most in this most critical time of the war.

He could just hear her now. 'You're a senior officer, darling. Surely you can delegate to others.'

As he ran through the probable scenarios in his head, he was forced to admit that he didn't really want to see her. She had never understood his dedication to the job and would resort to tears if she didn't get her own way. Too often it ended in rows which upset the boys. He had been glad of the excuse to send her to her aunt in Scotland to escape the bombing of the airfields near where they lived.

Hugh steered the car through the gates and parked in his usual spot. He sat for a few minutes, resting his forehead on the steering wheel. All the pleasure he'd felt during that brief interlude with Sylvia had evaporated. He sighed. Yes, he was a fool, nothing could come of it. He must make the best of things with Margaret.

Perhaps she had decided to come down because she missed him and would try to understand when he couldn't just drop everything to be with her. He would take her out to dinner, try to recapture some of his earlier feelings for her. It would be different this time, he told himself.

And he would put Sylvia Bishop out of his mind and treat her like any other WAAF under his command.

***

Sylvia sought Jane out when she got back to reassure her that the bicycle was back in one piece.

Jane laughed. 'I never doubted it. Did you have a good time?'

'Wonderful,' Sylvia said, unable to contain her happiness at the way her outing had turned out.

'I didn't think a bike ride to Henley was all that exciting. You look a bit flushed too. What have you been up to?'

Sylvia put a hand to her cheek, then brushed a hair away from her face. 'It was a bit windy coming back and that hill out of town's a bit steep.'

'Only teasing,' Jane said. 'Did you manage to get something for Julia?'

Sylvia fumbled in her bag and pulled out the newspaper wrapped package. She unwrapped it and showed it to Jane. 'Do you think she'll like it?'

'Bound to. She's mad about cats.' She linked an arm in Sylvia's and they walked across to the mess.

'You were gone a long time. I didn't think there was much to do in town.'

'After I'd bought Julia's present, I walked along the river and had tea in a little cafe.' Sylvia hoped Jane wouldn't comment on her pink cheeks. Just thinking about that chance encounter brought a curious fluttery feeling and she took a deep breath. She must try to act normally. If Marion or one of the other girls got the slightest inkling that she had spent time with a superior officer, it would be all round the station in no time. The fact that Hugh was married would cause a scandal and would certainly mean her being sent away. She couldn't bear that. Even though she had done nothing wrong she realised she must be very careful, for his sake as well as hers.

They joined their friends in the mess and the talk became more general. No one, apart from Julia, would be interested in how she had spent her free time and her friend was still on duty.

Back in the hut after supper, she unwrapped the cat ornament again and put it on her locker. I do hope Julia likes it, she thought. I must wrap it up nicely for her - but what with?

Iris strolled across and picked it up. 'Where did you get this?' she asked.

'Little curio shop in Henley. It's for Julia's birthday. I wish I had some pretty paper to wrap it in.'

'You'll be lucky,' Iris scoffed, then paused. 'Wait a minute. I've got a little box in my locker. It had sweets in it, sent from my brother. I think it'll be big enough.'

'But you were keeping it,' Sylvia protested. 'I can't take it.'

'Nonsense. I'll get it for you.'

The box was just the right size and Sylvia thanked her friend. Jane came over to have a look. 'When is Julia's birthday?' she asked.

'Tomorrow.'

'Oh, too late to get her anything then.' She thought for a moment. 'I have some red ribbon. We can tie it round the box, make it look really special.'

Sylvia was touched. 'We can say it's from all of us then.'

'What a nice thought,' Jane said.

Sylvia finished wrapping the present. 'I'll leave it on her locker. It'll be a nice surprise when she comes off duty in the morning.'

They said their goodnights and got ready for bed. Sylvia lay for a long time savouring her eventful day. She thought she would never get to sleep. But a long shift, followed by a cycle ride in the fresh country air, soon had her nodding off.

When she woke the next morning, she immediately thought of Hugh, sure that she had been dreaming. But as she came fully awake the memory flooded back. She really had sat in a tea shop with him, and he had asked her to call him 'Hugh'.

It was a memory she would hold close to her heart because she knew without doubt that it would never happen again. It mustn't.

Chapter Six

Sylvia leaned back in her chair and rubbed her eyes. Thank goodness the long shift was nearly over. Much as she loved her work, the hours spent peering through the stereoscope at hundreds of photographs took their toll.

She glanced round to see Julia just clearing her desk. She was so pleased her friend had been moved to her section to fill in for one of the girls who was on leave. It meant they could go out together this evening for a belated birthday celebration.

She began to clear her own desk, stacking the photographs with their attached notes in the tray for collection. Julia smiled across at her and lifted her hand in a drinking motion, raising her eyebrows at the same time.

Julia was always up for a drink. Sylvia smiled. She wasn't one for going to the pub, but she had promised to join Julia and the other girls for a birthday drink. Besides, tonight she needed a distraction from the turmoil of her emotions.

She joined her friend and they linked arms as they crossed the grass towards their hut.

'Everything all right?' Julia asked. 'You're a bit quiet.'

'I'm fine. Just a bit tired.' How could she confide in Julia how she felt?

'Well, I know the cure for that and it's not skulking in the hut all night. We're meeting some chaps at the Hare and Hounds.'

'What chaps? Oh no, Jules. I thought it was just us and the girls from our hut.'

'Whose birthday is it anyway? We need a few chaps to liven things up. You remember - those Army blokes we met the other night.'

'All right. I've said I'll come.' Sylvia groaned inwardly but managed a smile. She wasn't keen on seeing Harry again.

'You need to get out more. What is it? The job getting you down?' By tacit agreement, the PIs never talked about their work.

'No. I love it. I feel I'm doing something worthwhile, you know.'

'Well, what is it then?'

Sylvia shrugged. 'As I said, just tired.'

'If you say so.'

They entered the hut and began to get ready for their outing. Marion and some of her cronies were laughing together at the other end of the hut. 'We're off to Abingdon for a dance. You coming?' Marion called.

'I thought you were coming to the Hare and Hounds for a drink,' Julia said.

'Dancing's more fun.'

'Well, it's my birthday treat. I'm buying. Besides, we're meeting some chaps.'

'Anyone we know? Perhaps we will join you.' Marion turned to her friends. 'What do you think?'

Sylvia sighed with relief when they insisted they preferred to go dancing. It would just be the four of them – Julia, Iris, Jane and herself. Perhaps she'd get a chance to talk to Julia alone. If only she could be sure she could trust her friend not to tease, or worse still, blurt it out to everyone. It would be good to confide in someone.

The Hare and Hounds was packed, and it took some time for the girls to get served. They pushed their way through the crowd of service men and women, soldiers, airmen and even a couple of Navy officers, most in uniform.

They managed to find a table near the window and set their drinks down.

'Where are the boys then?' Jane asked, looking around.

'They'll be here soon.'

'We should have waited, let them buy the drinks,' Jane said.

'They can buy the next round,' Julia said. 'I'll tell them it's my birthday. We don't have to say it was yesterday.'

The door banged open and there was a burst of laughter and greetings. Three Army officers made their way over to the table where the girls sat. They pushed their chairs together and grabbed a couple from a nearby table.

Sylvia recognised the soldiers Harry and Ted from their last evening out. She smiled across at them but moved further away, ostensibly to make room. She didn't want to get into a conversation with Harry again. She had forgiven him for his 'woman's work' remark but he seemed to want more than just friendship. And, nice as he was, he did not compare with the man who constantly occupied her thoughts. She couldn't avoid him though. He moved closer and offered her a cigarette.

'No, thank you. I don't smoke,' she said.

'Really? I thought all you modern misses smoked.' Harry laughed and lit his own cigarette.

Sylvia shook her head. She didn't like to say that she had never tried it. The smoke irritated her eyes and throat and made her cough. Harry shrugged and turned to Julia.

After a couple of gin and tonics Sylvia started to relax and enjoy the banter and laughter around the table. Even shy little Iris was joining in.

As the evening wore on, the bar became smokier and noisier and Sylvia was ready to call it a day. But when she suggested to Julia it was time to go, her friend shook her head.

'The night is young and I'm having fun,' she said, downing a large swig of her gin. 'Anyway, we can't go yet. We have to wait for our lift.'

Harry moved closer and out his arm around her. 'Surely you don't want to go yet?' he asked.

'Headache,' Sylvia said and shrank back into her corner where she sat quietly sipping her drink and watching the comings and goings. She put her empty glass on the table and looked up as the door opened. She gasped as she recognised Hugh and her stomach did a little flip when she saw that he was not alone. The woman with him was beautiful, tall and slim, with a shiny blonde chignon, partially covered with a little blue hat. She was wearing a well-cut costume in dark blue, the jacket fitting close to her tiny waist and flaring out over the straight skirt. She could have been a model in a magazine, Sylvia thought.

The woman clung on to Hugh's arm possessively and Sylvia bit her lip. It must be his wife, she told herself. He wouldn't be with anyone else - would he? She watched as they walked past her table and through to the snug. She shrank back, hoping he would not spot her.

'Hey, isn't that your Wing Co,' Julia said, slightly slurring her words.

'Don't be silly, Julia. He's not *my* Wing Co. I think you've had too much drink.'

'Well, I wonder who that is with him?'

'I think it's his wife. Julia, do be quiet. We don't want to make a show of ourselves in front of him.' Sylvia hoped the heat of the room would account for her flushed face and that her friend would not remark on it. She picked up her glass and drained it. 'Will you get me another,' she asked, smiling at Harry.

'Same again?' He picked up her glass and pushed his way to the bar while Sylvia sat smiling and joining in the conversation as if her heart wasn't breaking. She had made the right decision she knew now. She would keep her distance unless it was unavoidable at work. It was easy to fool herself while Hugh's wife was far away in Scotland but now, she was here. Besides, how could she compete with the glamorous Mrs Smythe?

***

Hugh guided Margaret to a table in the corner of the snug and asked what she'd like to drink. After eating in a restaurant in Reading, he suggested they had a drink before she went up to her room.

'I don't think so,' she said. 'It's so noisy in here – not the sort of place I imagined when I booked the room.'

'We're private enough in here, darling. Don't take any notice of them in the bar. They need to let off steam when they're off duty.'

A burst of singing filtered through the closed door. 'So rowdy. It's not how I expect officers to behave. I hope you don't join in when I'm not around.'

Hugh laughed. 'Of course not. Now, let me get you a G and T.'

'If you insist.'

He left the room and fought his way towards the bar.

'Good evening, sir. Care to join us?'

He turned to greet a fellow officer. 'No, thank you. My wife's come down from Scotland and she's waiting for me in the snug.'

'She's welcome to join us too.'

'Another time maybe.'

He grinned. 'I understand. Mustn't keep the little woman waiting.'

Hugh bought the drinks and said goodnight to his friend. As he made his way back, he passed a group of WAAFs sitting at a table by the window with some army officers. They were all laughing and smoking, and the table was littered with half empty glasses. He spotted Sylvia, the only one not smoking. He wanted to go over and speak but instead, he pushed past, hoping they hadn't seen him. Taking a deep breath, he opened the door to the snug.

'You were gone a long time,' Margaret said. 'I thought you'd left me.'

He forced a laugh. 'As if I would. But darling, I must go soon. I managed to get a few hours off, but my shift starts at midnight.'

'Your shift? Sounds as if you work in a factory.'

'I suppose it is a bit like that. A sort of conveyor belt, the work comes in from one department and then I send it on to the higher ups.'

'I thought *you* were one of the higher ups.'

'I am, but some are higher than others.' Hugh spoke lightly. It was useless trying to impress upon her the importance of his work, especially as he could not tell her much about it. She probably thought he was little more than a clerk. And that was not good enough for her.

They sipped their drinks almost in silence. After the months apart he felt a little awkward. And seeing Sylvia, apparently enjoying herself, hadn't helped. He must put her out of his mind, especially now Margaret was here.

He fumbled in his pocket for his pipe and tobacco pouch and Margaret frowned. 'Oh, darling. You're not still smoking that filthy thing, are you?'

'It helps me to think,' he replied, stuffing the bowl with tobacco. But he didn't light it.

'What is there to think about?'

'Well, for one thing – your decision to send the boys to boarding school. I thought they were quite happy in the little school in Oban. And didn't we agree that we should wait till they're a little older before sending them away?' He tried to keep his voice reasonable. He didn't want a row the first time they'd met for months.

'I thought it would be good for them. Besides, it means I can spend more time with you, darling.'

'But I explained. I work long hours, sometimes all night. I wouldn't always be able to get away.' He paused, horrified as her eyes filled with tears.

'I'm so bored up there away from all my friends. I hate it.'

'I'm sorry. It's unavoidable.'

'I don't understand. It's not as if Medmenham is an operational station. What's so important?'

If only he could tell her. But even if he could, he doubted she would understand. 'I can't say. Besides, it would only bore you if I tried to explain.'

'It seems to me your work is more important than spending time with your wife,' she said, taking out a handkerchief and dabbing at her eyes.

'Oh, darling, please don't cry. You know it can't be helped.'

'I don't believe you. I've come all this way and now...' She picked up her glass and drained it.

He sighed, looked at his watch and stood up. 'I'm sorry, darling, but I must go.'

'Must you?'

'Yes.' He spoke firmly, took her arm and walked with her through the passage at the back of the pub, pausing at the bottom of the stairs.

'I'll say goodnight then,' he said.

'Aren't you coming up? I thought you would stay here during my visit.'

'I'm sorry. I did tell you I have to be on duty tonight. I'll phone in the morning and let you know when I'll be free.'

She pouted. 'This is not how I thought our reunion would be. I hope we'll be able to spend some time together. Aren't you going to apply for some leave?'

'Couldn't manage it. Sorry, darling.' He was relieved he did not have to lie.

She sighed and started up the stairs.

He sighed too and waited till he heard the door to her room close, then left the pub and made his way back to Medmenham.

The long night shift left him no time to dwell on the meeting with his wife. He knew she was annoyed that he couldn't stay but he tried not to think of it. He would make it up to her somehow.

Pale streaks of dawn lit the sky as he made his way back to his quarters and got ready for bed. He was exhausted but he couldn't sleep. He was still angry with Margaret for sending the boys away to school and then turning up here with so little warning. As usual, she expected him to drop everything and be on hand to cater to her every whim. Thank goodness he had the excuse of his work for not spending too much time with her.

When did everything change, he asked himself. He remembered their first meeting, a dance in the officers' mess. She was the most beautiful girl in the room, and he could hardly believe it when she agreed to dance with him. Not only that, she spent the whole evening with him and let him take her home.

Things moved quickly and within six months they were married. That first year was a whirlwind of social activity, moving house to his new post at Tangmere, dinners in the officers' mess, dances in Chichester. A year later Peter had arrived, and Hugh's happiness was complete. Margaret settled down to motherhood and they were both delighted when a second son, Bobby was born.

War came and he was posted to a Coastal Command station in Norfolk. Margaret rented a small cottage near the airfield and he had been able to spend time with his family. She had been happy, enjoying the social life. But as his workload increased, became more demanding, throwing tantrums when yet again he let her down over some dinner engagement or social occasion. She didn't seem to understand how the war changed things and that their

61

life just couldn't continue as before. Things became strained between them and Hugh wondered how he could carry on.

Then the airfield had been bombed and it had given him the perfect excuse to send her and the children away. Margaret had reluctantly agreed to go and stay with her aunt in Oban on the west coast of Scotland. He missed them at first, especially the boys, but as time passed, he began to realise that Margaret wasn't the woman he had married. She was spoilt and selfish, happy when things went her way, but throwing a tantrum when she was thwarted. She was still beautiful, still vivacious in company, the envy of his friends. But they only saw her good side. When they were alone, she showed a different aspect of her character – spoilt, selfish, and demanding.

Now that she was here, could they recapture their early love? He hoped so, they must and, if only for the boys' sake, he would give it a damn good try.

He sighed and turned over in bed. A fleeting image crossed his mind, of Sylvia, her golden head bent over her work, her eyes lighting with enthusiasm as they discussed a problem. But he mustn't think of her. When he'd seen her this evening, she had been enjoying herself with friends her own age, not to mention a soldier who seemed rather keen on her. He would put her out of his mind, concentrate on mending his marriage.

***

Sylvia woke with a headache, not used to drinking so much, although she blamed the smoky atmosphere of the pub. The memory of seeing Hugh with his wife swept over her and she groaned.

How foolish she had been to imagine that he was interested in her – although she had dared to dream since that walk by the river and tea in the cafe. She got out of bed and splashed her face with cold water, took two aspirins and thanked goodness she wasn't due on duty till 12 o'clock. Julia was still asleep, but the other girls were stirring, some like her wincing at the bright sunlight streaming into the hut.

'Good night, wasn't it?' Jane said. 'Pity we have to suffer for it next day.'

Sylvia smiled. 'Better take more water with it next time,' she said.

'Too right. Well, it was worth it. I've got a date with that Tom.' She went over to the washbasin in the corner of the hut and began to brush her teeth. 'How did you get on with Harry? I was surprised you were talking to him after he upset you at that dance.'

'He's all right. He's asked me to go to the pictures with him. I said I would - tomorrow.' Sylvia hadn't really made up her mind until then. But she couldn't stay here and brood while her friends were out having fun.

The other girls were awake now and getting ready for breakfast. They strolled across to the mess chatting about their evening out. 'You should have come to the dance instead of sitting in a smoky old pub all evening,' Marion said. 'So boring.'

'Not at all,' Julia said. 'You'll never guess who we saw.'

Marion gave a superior smile. 'No one interesting I'm sure.'

'Wrong. Wing Commander Smythe came in with his wife. A real glamour puss – like a film star. I think she's staying at the Hare and Hounds.'

'Fancy. He doesn't seem the type to have a glamorous wife.'

Sylvia closed her ears to their speculation. She didn't want to think about Hugh. Seeing him last night had really brought home to her how silly she was being. He had a beautiful wife and two lovely little boys – she had seen their photograph on his desk – so even in the unlikely event that he was interested in her, she was not about to become a home wrecker.

No. She would go out with Harry, enjoy his company, write to him when he was posted abroad as he'd asked her to. It wouldn't come to anything of course, but it would help to take her mind off this hopeless infatuation. Yes – infatuation she told herself. It wasn't love. How could it be when she really hardly knew him?

The thoughts churned round in her head as she picked at her breakfast while the other girls talked and laughed around her.

Julia noticed how quiet she was and asked, 'Hangover?'

'Not used to drinking,' Sylvia replied.

Marion laughed. 'You'll soon get used to it if you keep going out with these three.' She gestured with her spoon at Julia, Jane, and Iris.

'Hey, don't include me with these boozers,' Iris protested. 'I made one drink last all evening, kept topping it up with tonic water.'

The laughter and banter continued until SO Forsyth came over to their table. She pointed at her watch. 'Time you were out doing your PT. No shirking.'

They all groaned good-naturedly and stood up. Compulsory exercise was the bane of their life.

'I know it's supposed to be good for us, but I hate it,' Julia complained as they changed into their kit.

'Me too. I'd rather do a twelve hour shift,' Sylvia said.

They joined their colleagues and, after two hours of physical training exercises and a good run round the perimeter of the station, they were ready for lunch.

'Thank goodness that's over,' Jane said. 'I could do with a sleep now. Shame we're on duty this afternoon.'

Sylvia smiled. To her surprise she was feeling much better. The fresh air helped to drive her headache away and she was looking forward to her shift. And concentrating for several hours on the hundreds of photos that would have come in during the morning was the best way to distract her from her thoughts.

It was a fine day and the pilots would have been up since dawn, their cameras whirring. By the time Sylvia started her shift a massive amount of material would have been delivered and it would be heads down over their stereoscopes for the next eight hours.

She soon became lost in the work, knowing how important it was. They had been keeping a daily watch on the location and movements of the German battleship Tirpitz. The heavily armoured ship was proving a real danger to allied shipping. RAF bombers attacked several times, but failed to sink it. Now it was reported to be lurking in the Norwegian fjords, but it was proving elusive. Sylvia thought how proud she would be if she was the one to pinpoint its location.

The time passed quickly and towards the end of her shift she sorted out the photographs she thought would be of interest, attaching notes to some of them. She placed them in the basket ready for the orderly to take through to the next section. She hadn't spotted the elusive battleship today, but she would keep trying.

She and Julia walked across to the mess together, both ready for their supper. The food was terrible, but they had got used to it, although Sylvia longed for some of her mother's cooking as she forced down what passed for shepherd's pie.

'This is disgusting,' Marion said, pushing her plate away.' Sometimes I long to be home and eating one of Cook's delicious meals.'

"Well, I'm hungry so it will have to do,' Julia said.

'I expect that's why they make us do these physical jerks, so we'll be so hungry we'll eat anything,' said Sylvia.

'If you're going out with Harry tomorrow, perhaps he'll buy you some chips,' said Julia.

By the time they'd finished their meal it was almost dark outside and there was a chill in the air. Soon it would be time to change the clocks and before they knew it winter would be upon them.

Chapter Seven

Daisy was in her office cashing up after a busy afternoon, but it had quietened down now, and she set the girls to clearing up and wiping the tables down. As she added up a column of figures, her tongue protruding as she concentrated, she was interrupted by a knock on the office door. She gave a little huff of annoyance but before she could react the door opened and June burst in. 'Your brother's here,' she said breathlessly.

'Jimmy?' She put a hand to her mouth. 'What does he want?' Had something happened to Mum or Dad?

Before June could reply, Jimmy pushed past her. 'Sorry to interrupt, Daisy, but I didn't think you'd want to wait for these.' He waved a bundle of letters at her. 'See – Lofty hasn't forgotten you.'

Daisy pushed her chair back and snatched them from him. 'Don't call him that. His name's Christopher.' She examined the envelopes. 'You'd better not have opened them,' she warned.

'As if I would.' Jimmy looked hurt.

'Well then, that's all right. But what do you mean bursting into my office like that? You frightened the life out of me. I thought the house was on fire or something.'

'Sorry. I thought I was doing you a favour,' he muttered.

'All right, but you didn't have to come tearing down here with them. It could have waited till I got home.'

'Well, you've been moping around, getting all moody 'cause he hasn't written.'

Daisy muttered a thank you. Her brother so often annoyed her, but he meant well.

'Aren't you going to read them?'

'I'm busy. I must finish this.' She pointed to the papers on her desk. 'Wait for me and I'll walk home with you.' She was desperate to read the letters. It had been weeks since she'd heard from Chris and she had been imagining the worst. But she couldn't open them here. It would have to wait till she reached the privacy of her bedroom.

Later she would read out any bits of interest to the family. Dad always wanted to hear what was going on in North Africa, not that there was much. The letters would be heavily censored.

She hastily finished cashing up and filling in the ledger then took them through to Mrs. Green's office. 'I'm off now, Muriel,' she said.

'Have a nice evening,' the manager said. 'Did I hear your Jimmy out there?'

'He brought me some letters.'

Muriel smiled. 'I can guess who from,' she said.

Daisy nodded. 'Can't wait to get home and read them.'

Usually she enjoyed the walk home, taking a detour up to the seafront and walking along the prom towards the Catholic Church, trying to ignore the barbed wire and gun emplacements. It took a little longer but after being rushed off her feet in the smoky canteen it was good to get some fresh air.

Today, however, she and Jimmy took the shorter route past the station up to the High Street. When they reached the Clock Tower in the centre, Jimmy spotted one of his pals and rushed off. 'See you later,' he shouted, and was gone.

Daisy quickened her steps. She hoped her parents would still be out and she could read her letters in peace. Dad would be at the Home Guard station or on his allotment and Mum was probably at the church hall where the WVS met.

She opened the back door and called out. 'Mum, I'm home' but there was no reply. She smiled and ran up the stairs to the room she had shared with Sylvia until the start of the war. Peace and privacy, she thought as she flung her jacket on the bed and sat down at her dressing table. She withdrew the bundle of letters and carefully put them into date order. The first went back six weeks and she smiled. He had been thinking of her while she had been pining and imagining all sorts of things.

She settled down to read. There were seven letters in all, most just scribbled notes, obviously written in the intervals between the fighting. She skimmed through them quickly. One looked a bit more special and she put it aside to read more thoroughly later. The letters said little about the actual fighting, just remarking on the heat and the sand. *'Properly mucks up my engine,'* he wrote.

She smiled. Him and his precious motor bike. Still, she was glad he was doing what he loved best – riding his bike. Not like poor Bob, marching through the desert behind the gun carriers like she'd seen on the news reels.

She read on. *'Things are going better now we've got...'* The next few words were blacked out, censored. Then the word 'American' and more crossing out. *'The air force are great though. They fly ahead of us, bombing the anti-tank positions and shooting up anything resisting our advance. We'd never have got through if it wasn't for them.'*

I'll have to tell Sylvia about that, Daisy thought. She wondered briefly if her sister's work was connected with what was going on over there. Of course not, she thought. She's just a typist. It still rankled a bit that Sylvia had got into the WAAFs while she had to make do with the NAAFI. And, as she never said anything about her work, Daisy concluded that it couldn't be anything exciting.

Chris's letters as usual all ended with saying how much he loved and missed her and longed to be back in Sheerness with her.

She went to the top of the stairs and listened, but all was quiet. No one was home yet.

She retrieved the letter she had saved till last and took out the card enclosed with it. The note was brief. *'This just tells you what I want to say but can't find the words,'* he wrote.

The card had a heading in fancy letters: 'Greetings from Egypt – to someone dear at home,' followed by a short poem. She murmured the words, tears oozing down her cheeks. *'Across the sea my thoughts are ever wending, such loving thoughts of home and you. For memories' sake this card I'm sending, I love to think that you remember too.'* She kissed the place where he had signed his name followed by a row of crosses and put the card under her pillow.

She would write back after tea, she decided.

She wiped her eyes and glanced at her watch. Mum should be home soon, and she hadn't even put the kettle on. Dora always longed for a cup of tea as soon as she got home after being on her feet all day.

Daisy folded the remaining letters and put them in the little shell-encrusted box where she kept all of them since he went away, then went downstairs and started to make the tea.

The kettle had just boiled when the back door opened, and Mum and Dad came in together.

Dora glanced at the mantelpiece where letters were always placed. 'You got them then?'

'Jimmy brought them down to the NAAFI. Seven letters, Mum. He wrote them weeks ago.' The light went out of her eyes. 'I suppose I'll have to wait another six weeks now before I get any more.'

'Can't be helped, love,' Dad said. 'You're lucky they got through. Things are pretty bad out there.'

'Give over, Stan. She doesn't want to hear that,' Dora protested.

Daisy went through to the scullery and brought the tea through. She laid the table and got out the pie which had been warming in the range. Mum did wonders with the rations and even managed to make a tasty meal out of Woolton pie, a concoction dreamed up by the Minster of Food.

As they sat down, Dora said, 'Where's our Jimmy got to? I thought he'd be home by now.'

'He got off early. Didn't he walk home with you, Daisy?'

'He saw one of his mates and disappeared.'

'He'll come home when he's hungry,' Dad said.

It was an evening like any other, the family sitting round the table talking about their day, then Dad demanding silence as he switched on the wireless for the news. Much as she loved her family, Daisy sometimes envied Sylvia being away from home, meeting new people and, she was sure, having fun when she was off duty.

She stood up and said, 'I'm going up to write to Chris.' She would write to Sylvia too.

***

Sylvia and Julia had been to the pictures with Harry and Tom. She had enjoyed the film, 'The Road to Morocco', a comedy with Bing Crosby and Bob Hope. It had rather a silly plot, Sylvia thought, but it was funny and helped to take her mind off of Hugh and his wife. She had even submitted to Harry putting his arm around her. She could tell he was a bit put out that they weren't alone.

'I'm being sent away for training next week,' he told her as they left the cinema. 'I'll miss you. Can I write to you?'

71

'I'm not sure, Harry. I did tell you I've already got a boyfriend.'

'Just as friends. Please?'

'All right. But don't read anything into it, OK? Just friends.'

He grinned. 'Anyway, we won't be away long, just a few weeks and then I'll be back to pester you again.' His grin faded. 'We'll be off for good soon though. Not sure where they're sending us.'

Sylvia felt sorry for him. She touched his arm. 'I'll write, wherever you are.'

'Thanks.'

Their bus came along then, and they all waved goodbye. Julia slipped her arm through Sylvia's. 'There, you enjoyed it after all. I think you really do like Harry.'

'It was a nice evening, but I don't want him getting ideas. Besides, they're off for training next week and then shipping out soon after.'

When they got back to their billet Sylvia found two letters on her locker, one from her mother and one from Daisy.

The one from her mother was very short, just hoping that she was getting enough to eat and not working too hard. She gave a wry chuckle. When she wrote back, she would reassure her, but also say how much she was looking forward to one of Dora's tasty pies.

The letter from Daisy was much longer. Sylvia smiled. Her sister always had a lot to say for herself. She settled down to read and was delighted at Daisy's first piece of news. She had heard from Chris at last. The letter continued with a long rambling account of how long the letters had taken to reach her and how worried she had been. She then proceeded to give news of the goings-on in the NAAFI, finishing with love from the rest of the family.

Sylvia read it through again. I'll answer it in the morning, she thought, as she settled down to sleep.

And she would pass on the remarks that Chris had made to her superior officer. He would be pleased to hear how much the RAF was appreciated by the Army.

***

A few days later the girls had just finished their compulsory exercise. As the weather had stayed fine, they had done their 'physical jerks', as Julia called it, out on the lawn in front of the huts. Sylvia hated it, not so much the actual exercise but being out in full view of passers-by. She found it hard to ignore the whistles and remarks from the orderlies. Julia, of course, took it all in her stride, even smiling and waving back - that is, until she was spotted and threatened with being put on a charge.

'I can understand why we have to do it,' Sylvia said to her friend as they strolled back to their billet. 'We need the exercise and fresh air after being on duty for such long hours. But why can't we choose our own way?'

'What do you suggest?' Julia asked.

Sylvia knew her friend wasn't keen on any form of activity apart from walking to the pub or an occasional game of tennis. 'I like to swim. Wish there was a pool here.' She thought back nostalgically to her dips in the sea before the war. She hadn't even minded splodging through the mud to get to the sea when the tide was out. As a child it had been fun.

'There's the river,' Julia said. 'Why not have a swim there.'

Sylvia shuddered. 'No thanks. I walked down by the river the other day and it was full of weed – that long trailing stuff that you can get tangled up in. Don't fancy that.'

'I can't swim,' Julia confessed. 'Anyway, I've had enough exercise for one day so I'm going to have a rest until it's time to go on duty.'

'I've got some letters to write,' Sylvia said.hen she'd finished her letters, she glanced across at Julia and saw she was sleeping. Shrugging, she put her jacket and cap on and went out, closing the door quietly. Reaching the gate, she stepped to one side as she heard a vehicle behind her. It was Hugh's car and she turned away, hoping he would drive on. But he stopped and opened the window.

'Need a lift?' he asked.

'No thanks. I'm just going to the post box on the corner.' She held up the envelopes.

He smiled. 'Letters home?'

'Just answering my sister's.' Sylvia hesitated, but just as he was about to drive on, she said. 'My sister's boyfriend is out in Tunisia or Morocco or somewhere near there. Not sure where actually.' She paused, not sure how to go on.

'Yes? I hear it's pretty rough out there. I hope he's all right.'

'Well, he told Daisy – my sister – that they're all very grateful for the RAF. He said they wouldn't have got through without the air support.' She paused wishing she hadn't said anything.

'I'm glad you told me. I'll see that his comments get to the right people. Anything to boost morale. When you write back you must tell your sister to let her boyfriend know that we appreciate his kind remarks.'

'I will, sir.'

He smiled. 'Better let you post your letters.' He started the car and drove off, leaving Sylvia staring after him. Even that mundane little exchange left her breathless and confused. He was obviously going into town to meet his wife. Good job I didn't accept a lift, she thought. I can imagine what she would say.

74

***

Hugh's thoughts exactly mirrored Sylvia's. What possessed him to stop and offer her a lift? He could just picture Margaret's reaction if he pulled up at the Hare and Hounds with a pretty WAAF in the passenger seat. Thank goodness Sylvia had refused.

He wasn't looking forward to seeing Margaret. He hadn't managed to get away for a couple of days and he knew she would be sulking. He had to make it up to her somehow. After all, she had made the difficult journey down from Scotland to be with him, despite him having warned her that he would not have much time for her. She just didn't understand the importance of his work and he was tired of trying to explain.

He decided that he would drive her over to Reading and treat her to a decent meal. The food at the Hare and Hounds was passable given the shortages but it didn't satisfy Margaret's high standards.

She was waiting for him in the lounge bar of the pub, sipping a gin and tonic and tapping her foot on the floor.

She looked up, glass in hand. 'Oh, you're here at last,' she said. 'I had to buy my own drink.'

'I did say I might be late.' Hugh tried to hide his irritation. 'Well, I'm here now. Shall we go?'

'I haven't finished my drink.' She pouted and took another sip. 'Aren't you going to have one?'

'Not just now. I thought we'd get on the road.'

'Where are you taking me? Somewhere better than this dump I hope,' she said.

'If you don't like it here, you could always stay at a hotel in Reading, although I wouldn't have time to come over very often,' he said, sitting down. He stifled a sigh. 'Look, darling. I know this isn't what you had in mind when you came down. You might as well go back to Scotland.'

'I want to stay.' She touched his arm. 'I've had an idea. Why don't we rent a cottage here? The boys could come down in the school holidays. And we could spend more time together as a family.'

He liked the idea of seeing the boys, but it didn't seem fair to uproot them again. They'd only just got settled in Oban and then Margaret had packed them off to boarding school. Hugh tried to think of a way to put her off. It would be all right for a week or two, but she would probably get bored and start complaining that she never saw him. 'It's a nice idea, darling, but I don't think you'd be happy,' he said. 'You'd be alone a lot of the time in a strange place and...'

'But we'd be together some of the time.'

'I'll think about it. We can talk about it later.' He stood up. 'Finish your drink then. I don't have a lot of time and it's a bit of a drive to Reading.'

'What are we going to do there? Will there be dancing?'

'Surprise, darling.' He took her arm and they went out to the car.

On the way he tried to direct the conversation away from her wanting to rent a place. It wasn't that he didn't want to spend time with her, but his mind was almost constantly on his work and its effect on the progress of the war. It was too important for him to be distracted by a discontented and demanding wife. If only he could make her understand.

They pulled up outside the hotel. 'They do a good dinner here. Much better than the Hare and Hounds – more your sort of place,' he said, opening the car door for her.

Margaret looked up at the hotel's facade. 'Not bad,' she said. 'Let's see what the food's like.'

The maitre d' greeted them and showed them into the dining room. Hugh had phoned ahead to book a table, asking if they could have an early meal. He needn't have done as the place was deserted.

Margaret sat down and said. 'Well, aren't you going to order me a drink?'

'Of course – your usual?'

She nodded and glanced round at the empty room. 'The food can't be that good – there's no one here.'

'It gets very busy later on, but I booked an early meal as I have to be back on duty.'

'So you won't be coming back to the pub and staying then?'

He shook his head. 'Sorry, darling – no.' Before she could protest, the waiter returned with their drinks. 'Would you like to order, Madam, Sir?' he asked.

'In a moment,' Hugh said, picking up the menu. He glanced at it and handed it to his wife.

'Not much choice is there?' she said, frowning.

'They do their best – and what they do have is very good.'

'How do you know?' She narrowed her eyes and looked closely at him. 'You've been here before, I suppose. With some floozy no doubt.'

'Of course not. Where did you get that idea?'

'There must be some reason why I've seen so little of you. I refuse to believe that you're working all these hours.'

'Margaret, don't talk nonsense. I tried to explain – I'm doing very important work.'

She scoffed. 'Important! In an office? Tell me what it is then.'

He had to try and make her understand once more. 'I can't – as I've already told you - the Official Secrets Act.'

'Huh. Surely you can give me some idea. I'm your wife and I'm not going to go gossiping about it all over the place, am I?'

Hugh wasn't so sure, especially after she'd had a few drinks. He could imagine her boasting to her friends about the important job her husband was doing.

He took her hand. 'Of course not, darling. But I could get into real trouble if someone found out I'd been blabbing.' He leaned over and took the menu from her. 'I think we'd better order.'

She shrugged. 'I'll have the beef. Let's hope it's not too well done.'

'I'll have the same.' He beckoned the waiter over and gave their order.

When the food had been served, Margaret returned to their earlier conversation. 'You're not going to fob me off, you know. I intend to stay. I need to keep an eye on you with all these pretty WAAFs around.'

'You're talking nonsense, Margaret. I have always been faithful to you and I intend things to stay that way.' He really meant it too. He must put Sylvia out of his mind. A fleeting thought crossed his mind, remembering that walk by the river and the tea-room. He had enjoyed her company. Such simple pleasures. He could not imagine Margaret doing the same. She had to have bright lights, music. Even now, she was looking around, a discontented frown creasing her forehead.

'What a dismal place,' she said. 'I know it's wartime but surely they could do something to cheer it up.' She chewed another mouthful of beef. 'And this meat's overdone,' she said.

Hugh nodded. He thought it was perfectly fine but to disagree would provoke another row. He concentrated on his food, mulling over what she had said about staying. He hoped she wouldn't be able to find a place. Accommodation in the area was in short supply, much of it requisitioned by the services. If she couldn't find anywhere, perhaps she would give up and go back to Scotland.

'Are you listening, Hugh? I said we could find an estate agent in the morning. There must be somewhere to rent in the area.'

He brought his attention back to her but as he was about to reply, she said, 'Of course, if you're too busy I can go alone.'

'I'm afraid you'll have to. And while we're on the subject we ought to be getting back.'

'But we haven't had dessert,' she protested.

'Duty calls.' He called the waiter over for the bill.

Margaret followed him out to the car, protesting vehemently. Good job she'd only had one drink, Hugh thought, though goodness knows how many she'd had before he picked her up.

The drive back to Sonning was completed almost in silence, Margaret having run out of complaints. Hugh was too tired to continue trying to justify himself. It was no good anyway. She wouldn't listen.

When he pulled up outside the pub, she got out and slammed the door. He sighed and leaned back in his seat. He watched as she stalked across and threw open the pub door without glancing back at him. No use following her and trying to mend fences. When she was in this sort of mood she was best left alone. Besides, he had to get back. He really did have to be on duty this evening.

***

Sylvia finished her shift and reluctantly agreed to join her friends in the pub.

'Just a quick drink then,' she said. She didn't want to go to the Hare and Hounds now that she knew Hugh's wife was staying there. Seeing them together was too painful.

'Relax, have fun,' Julia said.

They cadged a lift into Sonning and pushed their way into the crowded bar. They managed to find seats at their favourite table in the corner and Julia went to get the drinks.

Marion looked round. 'No one we know here tonight,' she said. 'I was hoping we'd meet up with those Army friends of yours, Syl.'

'They're off training somewhere,' Sylvia replied. 'Getting ready to be sent off, goodness knows where.'

'You'll miss that Harry. He's taken a shine to you.'

'Nothing serious,' Sylvia assured her.

'Do you have someone back home then? You never talk about it but there must be a man in your life – you're always writing letters.'

'No one – and for your information I write to my family, my sister mainly.'

Julia returned with the drinks and the conversation turned to the concert that was being planned back at HQ. Sylvia didn't join in. She looked forward to the concert, especially after overhearing that Hugh had a beautiful tenor voice and was taking part. She couldn't wait to hear him. She hoped the others wouldn't mention it, concerned about the embarrassing flush she knew would stain her cheeks, and the inevitable teasing that would follow.

She sipped her drink, trying to make it last. She hadn't been used to drinking before joining the WAAFs. The smoky atmosphere, chatter and laughter reminded her of rare treats back home when her parents would allow her and Daisy to accompany them to the Ivy Leaf Club down a little alley off Sheerness High Street. They weren't allowed in the bar but sat in the ladies' lounge with Mum and her friends, drinking lemonade and eating crisps.

She had lost track of her friends' conversation, but she looked up when the door opened with a crash and someone came in.

'Isn't anyone going to buy me a drink?' The voice was loud and slightly slurred, and the girls looked round curiously.

Marion nudged Julia. 'I say, isn't that the Wing Co's wife?'

Sylvia sat up straight and looked across at the woman at the bar. Yes, it was her, but where was Hugh? How embarrassing for him.

One of the RAF officers offered Margaret a drink.

'How kind. G and T if you please,' she said.

When the drink arrived, she turned to face the room, lifted her glass in a toast and said, 'It comes to something when a girl has to beg a drink because her husband's too busy to buy her one.'

The man who had bought the drink tried to move away but she grabbed his arm and planted a kiss on his cheek. He pulled away and there was general laughter in the bar.

Undeterred, Margaret finished her gin in one gulp and, waving the glass, said, 'Isn't anyone going to keep me company?'

When no one took up her invitation, she slammed the glass down on the counter and walked unsteadily towards the stairs. 'Oh, well, nighty night everyone.'

There was an embarrassed silence for a few moments and then the laughter and chatter swelled up once more.

Marion giggled. 'Well, well. Fancy that,' she said.

Julia shushed her. 'It's none of our business.'

'Huh, just wait till everyone hears about it.'

'Marion, please. Don't spread it around,' Sylvia begged.

'All right. I wasn't going to really. Poor chap, being married to a lush.'

Sylvia agreed but she tried to be sympathetic. 'I expect she's upset. After all, she's come down from Scotland to see him and he's too busy to give her the time of day.' She tried to inject some indignation into her voice.

'She should have thought of that before coming all this way,' Julia said.

'Let's try and forget about it. I'll get another round of drinks,' Sylvia said standing up.

When she had pushed her way through the crowd at the bar, she had to wait to get served. She couldn't help overhearing the conversation between two officers who were talking about the drunken woman. 'Old Snowy missed a trick there,' one of them said, referring to the officer who had bought Margaret a drink.

'He's too decent to take advantage,' his friend said. 'Besides, she's had too much to drink already. Probably wouldn't behave like that if she was sober.'

'I wouldn't mind, drunk or not.'

'Well, she is very beautiful I must admit, but not my type, old man,' his companion answered.

'I wonder who she is,' the first man said. 'I might take a drink up to her.'

'I wouldn't, if I were you. If she's staying here, she's probably come down to visit her husband. Didn't you spot the wedding ring? Steer clear, mate, if you don't want a bloody nose.'

'You're probably right. Shame though.'

Sylvia seethed. She was about to intervene and tell them what she thought about their ungentlemanly conduct when the barman came up and asked for her order.

When she returned to her friends, Julia said, 'Who's upset you then?'

'I'm not upset, just annoyed.'

'Just because he took his time serving you?' Marion asked, referring to the barman.

'No, of course not. It's those two officers over there saying nasty things about Mrs Smythe.'

'Well, she was a bit tipsy, wasn't she?'

'Perhaps she'd had a row with her husband,' Julia said. 'He didn't come in and see her up to her room, did he?'

'As you said before, Julia – it's none of our business. Let's talk about something else,' Sylvia said. She spent the rest of the evening trying to put the horrid little scene out of her mind. But she couldn't help praying that the gossip wouldn't reach Hugh's ears. He would be terribly hurt.

Someone at the other end of the room started playing the piano and a few people started singing.

Marion picked up her drink and stood up. 'Come on, let's have a sing song.'

The others joined her, and Sylvia followed. She had never felt less like singing but as the evening progressed, she found herself joining in and even enjoying herself.

Chapter Eight

'Coming to the pub?' Julia asked.

Sylvia was lying on her bed and she shook her head. She had just come off a very busy shift which had left her with a slight headache. The last thing she needed was an evening in a noisy pub.

Before she could speak, Julia came over and pulled at her arm. 'Come on. It'll do you good. You never want to come out with us these days. There can't be that many letters to write.'

'I'm just tired.'

'Aren't we all? I know what's really wrong,' Julia said.

Sylvia sat up. 'What makes you think there's anything wrong?' Had Julia guessed about her feelings for Hugh? She had tried so hard to hide it.

'You haven't seen Harry lately.'

'Harry? Don't be daft. Anyway, he's gone away, remember.'

Julia laughed. 'Just joking. You need a drink and a night out, that's all.'

'All right, I'll come.'

The other girls were already there when Sylvia and Julia arrived.

'Looks like we'll have to buy our own drinks as the lads aren't here,' Julia said.

They got their drinks and joined Jane and the others at their usual corner table and Sylvia looked round. To her relief there was no sign of Hugh, unless he was in the snug or upstairs with his wife. The thought pained her, and she took refuge in her drink, the gin biting at the back of her throat.

'Looking forward to the concert?' Jane asked.

'That's if we can go. Depends what shift we're on.'

'I hear the Wing Co's going to sing,' Marion said. 'I'm not sure I want to spend my off-duty time listening to a bunch of amateurs.'

'It'll be a laugh, if nothing else,' Julia said. 'You'll come, won't you Syl?'

'If I can.' Sylvia's heart thumped. She knew Hugh could sing and had often heard him humming as he worked. She'd love to hear him perform and couldn't wait for the concert. She prayed she would be off duty on the night.

As the girls chatted, Sylvia's thoughts wandered until a burst of laughter from the bar made her look up.

'What's going on over there?' Jane asked.

A group of soldiers were gathered round to the sound of feet stamping and cheering and glasses being thumped down on the bar. 'Give us the money then,' a shrill voice demanded.

'Oh, look. It's Mrs Wingco,' Marian said laughing.

'Never,' Julia said, standing up for a better look.

Sylvia pulled her down in her seat. 'Take no notice,' she said.

'It's a drinking contest. She's just downed a full pint.'

Iris frowned. 'She's drunk. Disgusting.'

'Ignore them,' Sylvia said.

But it was hard to ignore the shouts and laughter and Mrs Smythe's shrill voice declaiming, 'I've won – again.'

'No money this time. I demand a kiss,' a burly sergeant major said, grabbing Margaret round the waist.

She didn't struggle but put her arms around his neck and returned the kiss, just as the door opened and Wing Commander Smythe entered.

Silence descended on the bar and the sergeant major hastily pushed Margaret away. She turned and, with no appearance of embarrassment, said, 'Oh, there you are, darling. I'd about given you up. But these kind gentlemen have been keeping me company.'

Hugh's face betrayed his fury, but he spoke quietly. 'I'm sorry I'm late.' He took her arm. 'Perhaps you'll join me in the snug.'

'She shook his hand off. 'I'm quite happy here.'

'I'm sure you are. But I need a private word if you don't mind.'

Pouting, she followed him into the small room next door. Gradually conversation resumed and the noise level rose.

'Well, what do you think of that?' Marion declared.

'The poor man must be so embarrassed,' Iris murmured.

During a lull in the conversation they could make out raised voices from the snug. 'What am I supposed to do, stuck here on my own?' they heard Margaret scream.

They could only hear a faint murmur as Hugh replied.

Sylvia couldn't bear it. 'I think we ought to go. He'll be mortified if he sees us.'

Iris agreed and they hurriedly finished their drinks.

**

There was an excited buzz in the hut as the girls got ready to go over to the main house for the concert. Unfortunately, Marion, Vera and Iris were on duty, but Sylvia, Julia and Jane were looking forward to an evening of entertainment, Sylvia was the most excited of all, although she tried to hide it. She was looking forward to being able to express her admiration of Hugh without any teasing from her friends and would be applauding hardest of any of them.

'Not sure I'm that keen,' Julia said. 'It'll be like the entertainment at the church socials I was forced to attend back home.'

'What do you mean?' Jane asked.

'The church organist would be playing the piano, some dreary sonata, Mrs Briggs would sing.' Julia laughed. 'As kids we used giggle at her bosom heaving as she tried for the high notes.'

'I'm sure it won't be anything like that. I heard that our Wingco has a splendid voice.'

'*Your* Wingco, you mean,' Julia said with a little giggle.

'Julia, I wish you'd stop saying that, especially now his wife's here. You know perfectly well I'm not interested in married men.' Sylvia turned away, knowing that her face betrayed her. She took her jacket down from its hanger and said, 'Come along, we'll be late.'

As they hurried across to the main house, Jane said, 'Take no notice, Syl. She's only teasing.'

'I know, but I'm getting fed up with it.'

Julia took her arm and squeezed. 'Sorry, Syl. Didn't mean to upset you.'

'I forgive you,' Sylvia said with a smile. 'Just don't do it again.'

They entered by the side door and went through to the main hall. Some attempt had been made to hide the room's everyday function. Chairs had been laid out in rows and a makeshift stage erected against the far wall.

As they took their seats near the front, Julie nudged Sylvia and pointed to the piano. 'What did I tell you?' she whispered.

She and Jane laughed. 'It's something different, breaks the monotony,' Jane said. 'Better than sitting in our hut darning our stockings.'

The room was filling up, a buzz of chatter swelling as people took their seats. A Flight Lieutenant who Sylvia didn't recognise stepped onto the stage and the noise died away.

He welcomed them and then introduced the first item on the programme – a comedy skit performed by two officers, one dressed in woman's clothing. The jokes were a bit risqué, but Sylvia and her two friends rocked with laughter along with the rest of the audience.

When the performers had taken their bows and skipped off stage, Sylvia said, 'Definitely not like your church socials, Julia.'

'Nothing like,' Julia replied, mopping her eyes.

The audience settled down for the next act, a banjo playing officer who did a passable impression of George Formby leaning on a lamp post. The programme continued with a girl trio singing popular songs, the inevitable piano solo, more comedy skits and a recitation of 'The Little Yellow Idol'.

Sylvia was enjoying it as much as her friends were, but she was waiting impatiently for Hugh's appearance.

After a brief interval the MC came on to the stage and announced, 'And now, the one you've all been waiting for –' a brief pause, then, 'Our very own Wing Commander Smythe, RAF Medmenham's answer to Bing Crosby.'

There was an outburst of applause, whistles and catcalls, which died down the moment Hugh stepped on to the stage.

Sylvia sat entranced as he started to sing, a lump in her throat rising as Hugh's clear tenor voice filled the room with the words of *'Danny Boy'*.

As he finished to a storm of applause, Julia leaned over and whispered, 'He's good, isn't he, better than Bing.'

Sylvia nodded, unable to speak.

Hugh's next songs were more light-hearted and he encouraged his audience to join in with a popular medley including *'Pack up your Troubles* and *'Run, Rabbit, Run'*. Sylvia sang along with the rest, clapping until her hands hurt.

'And now, to round off the evening, Wing Commander Smythe will sing *'Now is the Hour',* said the MC.

'Now is the hour, when we must say goodbye...' Hugh sang and the audience listened in silence. Sylvia's weren't the only eyes that were damp when the final words trailed away.

All too soon the evening was over and the girls wandered back to their hut in thoughtful silence.

Julia was first to speak as they began to get ready for bed. 'Not what I expected at all. That man should be a professional singer.'

Jane agreed. 'And the rest of the programme wasn't bad either.'

Sylvia didn't reply. She was still in a daze, thinking of the words of that last song. Hugh wouldn't be 'sailing far across the sea' but at the end of the war, she would be returning to her humdrum life in Sheerness and he would be back with his wife and children. Until now she had persuaded herself that just working with him and seeing him almost every day was enough. Who was she kidding? Oh, why, oh why did I have to fall in love with a married man, she asked herself.

***

Days later, Sylvia still found herself humming the tune of *'Now is the Hour'*. She couldn't stop thinking about the concert and Hugh's singing. It was as if he had been singing just for her – a foolish idea, of course.

While she was on duty, she managed to put him out of her mind – the work was so absorbing and she loved her job even though she returned to her billet exhausted after each shift. It was the off-duty hours that were hard.

She had stopped going to the Hare and Hounds with the other girls after witnessing Mrs Smythe's drunken behaviour. She dreaded witnessing a similar scene, worse still if Hugh was present.

She had turned down Julia's invitation to the cinema, saying she had letters to write.

'You're always writing. Can't you do it tomorrow?'

'I really don't feel like traipsing into town tonight. Sorry Julia, I'm just so tired. And I haven't answered Daisy's last letter.'

'Please yourself. But you're better off coming out with us instead of moping around here.'

'I'm not moping.'

Julia shrugged. 'Sez you.' She put on her jacket and said goodnight.

In the quiet of the hut, Sylvia pulled her chair closer to the pot-bellied stove in the centre of the hut. It was well into autumn now and the evenings were getting chilly. She rested her writing pad on her knee and chewed the end of her pencil. What could she write? Daisy had been so excited, telling Sylvia in her last letter about receiving the bundle of seven letters from Chris. *'I worry about him all the time. Sometimes the news from North Africa is not good but it was good to hear from him,'* she'd written. Then she asked what her sister was up to. *'Met any good-looking officers yet?'* she teased.

Sylvia desperately wanted to share her feelings. It would be a relief to confess to someone and Daisy was sure to understand. They'd always shared secrets when they were children. The problem was, letters were read by everyone in the Bishop household. Her mother would be shocked, even though Sylvia had done nothing wrong – so far, she thought. If only... But she thrust the thought away.

In the end she wrote a short note. *'I can't tell you anything about my work. I've had to sign the Official Secrets Act. Besides, it's not that exciting and would only bore you. When we are off duty we go to the pictures or the pub (don't tell Mum). We had a concert the other day. Great fun. Some of the officers sang.'*

She sighed and sat back in her chair, reading the letter through. Yes, she would mention Hugh. *'My boss, the Wing Commander, sang a couple of solos. He has a lovely voice. It reminded me of Mr Hobbs singing at the church socials. He's quite good-looking too. Unfortunately, he's married and his wife is staying in the village, so don't get any ideas,'* she wrote. There, that should satisfy Daisy's thirst for gossip without giving anything away, she thought, signing the letter and sealing it into an envelope.

***

The excitement of receiving Chris's letters had worn off a bit, but Daisy still sat up in bed each night before going to sleep and read through them. The card with its lovely poem was getting a bit creased from constant handling but it seemed to bring him closer. But now she was back to waiting for the postman every day, her eyes going to the mantelpiece the moment she got in from work. The last letter from him had been dated several weeks before. Who knew what had happened to him since then?

She wrote to him every day telling him about the little things that happened in the NAAFI and about her friends and their outings to the pictures, Mr Jacobs's fish and chips and the scatty doings of her brother. She hoped that it would remind him of the few weeks they had spent together before he had embarked for North Africa and the grim business of war in the desert.

91

Her father listened to the news every evening and had his say about the progress of the war. She didn't want to know, finding the newsreels at the cinema hard enough to endure.

Her work in the NAAFI was getting harder too. She knew some people thought she had it cushy, serving meals and cigarettes to an assortment of sailors and soldiers. But just lately she could hardly keep the shelves stocked due to the increasing shortages of food and other sundries.

They still managed to dish up nutritious meals for the hungry men who still seemed to prefer the NAAFI cook's offerings to their regular mess food. As supervisor, Daisy was responsible for ordering and making sure they didn't run out of anything. Razor blades were increasingly hard to come by. Still, it was a lot better than sitting at a desk typing letters all day like Sylvia, she thought.

It had been a long day as Daisy had stayed late to do a stock take with Muriel Green, the manager. The walk home seemed longer than usual and when she got indoors, all she could think of was taking her shoes off and sitting down with a cup of tea.

'Thank goodness you're home,' Dora greeted her as she opened the back door. 'I was getting worried. 'I don't like you walking home now it's getting dark in the evenings.'

'I told you I'd be working late, Mum.' Daisy tried not to sound irritated. Her parents had been over-protective since she had been kidnapped and held prisoner by the former canteen manager a couple of years ago. He was now in prison and Daisy felt quite safe walking the familiar streets of her hometown.

'I forgot,' Dora said. 'Anyway, here's your tea. I managed to get some sausages.' She took a covered plate off the pan of hot water on the range and put it on the table.

'Where's Dad and Jimmy – not still working?

'They've gone to some meeting up at the club,' Dora said. She poured a cup of tea and passed it to Daisy. 'You're looking tired, love. Get that down you, you'll soon feel better.'

'Thanks, Mum.' Daisy glanced up at the mantelpiece. 'No post?'

'Oh, yes – from Sylvia.' Dora felt in her apron pocket and pulled out an envelope. 'What does she mean, don't tell Mum? I hope that's a joke'

'What?' Daisy reached for the letter. Ignoring the plate of food, she read it quickly, laughing when she reached the relevant sentence. 'Mum, of course she's joking. She knows we read each other's letters. Anyway, she's old enough to go in pubs and I'm sure there's no harm in it. They work hard and need a bit of fun when they can.'

Dora frowned. 'I suppose you're right. It's just – girls didn't go in pubs in my day unless they were with someone like a husband or fiancé.'

'Things are changing and after the war, there'll be more changes, you'll see.' Daisy started to eat her meal, smoothing the letter out beside her plate and re-reading while she ate.

'She seems to be enjoying life up there,' she said.

'Yes – concerts indeed. I bet that boss of hers doesn't sing as nice as Mr Hobbs despite what she says.'

Daisy nodded. 'I always look forward to him singing at the church socials.' She finished her sausage and mash as the back door crashed open.

'That'll be Jimmy,' Dora said. He hadn't changed much from the noisy boisterous schoolboy he had been.

Stan was close behind.

'Good meeting, love?' Dora asked.

'OK. Tell you about it later.' Still with his coat on, Stan reached across to switch on the radio. 'Let's hear the news first.'

Daisy suppressed a yawn. 'I'm going up. Nice meal, Mum. Thanks. Goodnight all.'

Upstairs she read Sylvia's letter again. She smiled at the comment about her sister's boss. 'Quite good-looking,' she murmured. 'Don't say she's fallen for him.'

She decided to write back after she'd written her usual letter to Chris. She was so lucky to have met him. She prayed that he would come back safely. If only Sylvia could find someone to love and be loved by.

It suddenly occurred to her that just lately her sister's letters hadn't mentioned any of the 'gorgeous' officers which had peppered her earlier letters. Sylvia had always been a bit of a party girl, loved dancing and having fun. She seemed to have changed since moving to Medmenham. I really do hope she hasn't fallen for her boss, Daisy thought. A married man! Mum would go mad - to her it would be far more scandalous than drinking in pubs.

Chapter Nine

'Hey, Sylvia, look at this.' Julia beckoned her friend over to where she was studying the notice board on the wall of the mess.

'What?' It couldn't be anything interesting. Most of the notices were about fire drills and instructions on procedure in case of an air raid and other boring stuff. They had been here long enough not to need reminding.   ·

'Have a look,' Julia said, pointing. 'Sounds like fun.'

'Can you dance, sing, act? Would you like to take part in a Christmas extravaganza for the delectation and entertainment of your fellow officers?' Sylvia read out loud. She turned to Julia. 'Oh, no, not me. I'm hopeless at that sort of thing,' she protested.

'Come on, it'll be fun. Look, it says, *'Report to Squadron Leader James in the mess at 10 am on Wednesday or, if on duty, Thursday at 6pm.'*

'You're not thinking of going, are you?'

'Yes. Oh, do say you'll come too. We don't have to sign up for anything, just see what's what. It'll be a bit of a giggle.'

Sylvia really wasn't interested but it suddenly occurred to her that if they were holding auditions, she might get the chance to hear Hugh sing again. He was sure to take part. She nodded. 'OK, I'll come just to keep you company, but you won't get me agreeing to take part. I can't sing for toffee.'

'Something to break the monotony anyway.'

As they walked back towards the main house, Julia linked her am in Sylvia's and said, 'This Squadron Leader James – he works in your section, doesn't he?'

'Yes. I don't really know him though.'

'Wasn't he the one who arranged the concert? He's not bad looking.'

'Julia – so that's why you want to go to this meeting. Haven't you got enough young men falling at your feet?'

Her friend laughed and Sylvia gave her a friendly push. 'Time we were back and you - keep your mind on your work.'

Back at her desk, all thoughts of Christmas and entertainments went out of Sylvia's mind as she bent her head and adjusted the stereoscope. Other PIs had been logging new types of German and Italian aircraft, their numbers and dispositions. Sylvia had been tracking their movements. She sat back and rubbed her eyes, then looked again. Yesterday, this had been an operational airfield. Now there was only one building standing. But it definitely hadn't been bombed. Squadron Leader James had just come into the room and she beckoned him over. 'Have a look at this,' she said, pointing to what looked like a smudge in the corner of the photo. 'Only one building. Where have all the others gone, and the planes? What do you think?'

'Are you sure it's the same area?' he asked.

'Positive.' She picked up a photo taken a few days ago from the tray on her desk and showed it to him.

While he compared the two photos Sylvia studied him. She hadn't really taken much notice of him before but now she smiled. His bushy moustache did nothing to compensate for the thinning hair. Not Julia's type at all, she thought.

'You're right. I think they've moved,' he said. 'We'll have to find out where. I'll show these to the

Wing Commander. Better keep an eye on this area over the next few days Section Officer.'

'Yes, sir.' As he turned to go, Sylvia said. 'You're the officer who's organising the Christmas show, aren't you?'

'That's right. Are you coming to the meeting tomorrow? We need all the volunteers we can get.'

'I'm not sure. I don't sing or anything. My friend Julia is keen though.'

'See you both there then.' He turned away and Sylvia went back to studying the hundreds of photos that still awaited her scrutiny.

That night, she found it hard to get to sleep. Although mentally exhausted from the long shift, it was impossible to relax. She hadn't seen Hugh for several days and tormented herself with thoughts of him with his wife. It was near dawn before she fell asleep.

It seemed only minutes later that she was woken by a shake of her shoulder. 'Come on, lazybones. We don't want to be late for the meeting,' Julia said.

Sylvia rubbed her eyes and sat up. 'What meeting?'

'The Christmas show. Come on, get dressed.'

'I told you, I'm not really interested.' She had been so wrapped up in her work she had quite forgotten the poster calling for volunteers and Julia's eagerness to take part.

Julia turned to their hut mates. 'We're all keen, aren't we girls?'

There was a chorus of agreement except for Iris, who was still in bed. She never said much but she was more reserved than ever since she had heard recently that her fiancé's ship had gone down with all hands. Sylvia tried to persuade her to join them.

'You need something to take your mind off it,' she said, although she knew it was a daft thing to say. But it wasn't good for her to stay in the hut moping.

97

'All right, but it's not really my kind of thing,' she said, reluctantly starting to dress.

'I'm looking forward to it. I used to belong to my local dramatic society back home,' Jane said.

'But it's not Christmas for ages,' Marion protested.

'We'll need time to rehearse.'

'OK. I suppose it will fill our off-duty time now we can't play tennis,' Marion said.

'You're right. Not much we can do in this weather.'

It had turned very cold with unremitting rain for the past week. Autumn was quickly turning to winter. Sylvia sighed and began to dress. 'Just don't expect me to volunteer for anything.'

When they entered the mess, Squadron Leader James approached them, a clipboard in his hand. 'Can I ask each of you what your skills are – singing, dancing, painting scenery?' he asked.

Sylvia hung back but Jane spoke up. 'I can act, sing a bit too,' she said.

He made a note. 'Any experience?'

'Am dram, back home,' she said.

'Great. What about you?' he asked Julia.

'Not done anything since school, but I'll have a go at anything.'

'Good – and you?' He turned to Sylvia.

'Oh, no. I'm hopeless at performing.'

'Why are you here then?'

'I thought I might be able to help in some way.'

'Good. I'm sure we can find something for you to do – backstage, costumes, scenery. Plenty of choice.' He scribbled something on his list and turned to Iris.

'What about you?'

'I'm not sure. I suppose I could help with the costumes.'

'Just the job,' he said enthusiastically. 'Now that's everyone.'

He asked them all to find a seat and proceeded to outline his plans. 'I thought we'd have a pantomime for a change instead of our usual variety concert – Cinderella.'

There was a chorus of groans from the back of the room. James waved them to silence. 'It's not compulsory, you know. But you have volunteered. Come on, chaps it'll be fun.'

'Who's going to be Cinderella?' someone called.

'You, Jock,' his companion answered to a chorus of laughter.

'Now then, no messing around,' Squadron Leader James protested. He scanned the room, waiting for the laughter to die down. 'Look around you, chaps. There's plenty of pretty young WAAFs to choose from.'

More laughter and some whistles from the back.

Julia nudged Sylvia and whispered. 'I'm going to put my name down. I might get to meet Prince Charming.'

'Some hopes. Don't you know he's always played by a girl in panto?'

'There'll be other blokes though.'

'Yes, the ugly sisters – played by men.'

Julia started giggling and Squadron Leader James called, 'Quiet please.'

He produced another sheet of paper and waved it in the air. 'This is the cast list. I'll pin it on the notice board. Please put your name down for any part you fancy. There'll be another meeting this evening and I'm hoping for more volunteers. I'll be holding auditions later in the week. That's all.'

Thank goodness that's over, Sylvia thought, glancing at her watch. Just time for a cup of tea and a sandwich before going on duty. Julia and Jane were laughing and joking about who would be chosen for the part of Cinderella. Sylvia didn't really listen. She was trying to hide her disappointment at not seeing Hugh. She had been sure he'd be there, given his lovely singing voice and his obvious enjoyment when taking part in the recent concert. It had been her main reason for attending the meeting.

'So, what have you put your name down for?' Jane asked.

Sylvia shook her head. 'I can't since or dance, but he said he can find me a job,' she said.

'Like the Squadron Leader said, they don't just need performers,' said Jane.

'General dogsbody, I expect,' Julia said with a smile. 'You shouldn't have volunteered.'

***

To Julia and Jane's chagrin, the role of Cinderella went to Marion who, it turned out, had a lovely soprano voice. They soon got over their disappointment though and took to their parts in the chorus with gusto. These days the hut rang with song and laughter even at the end of the long shifts when they were all so tired.

Sylvia had been quite surprised when she was appointed assistant stage manager and for the next few weeks nearly all her free time was taken up with rehearsals and meetings with Squadron Leader James who had asked her to call him Bill when they were off duty. It was turning out to be more enjoyable than she had anticipated although Bill took his duties as combined producer, director and stage manager very seriously and sometimes got quite irate when things didn't go well.

Of course, the main reason for her enjoyment was that Hugh had been chosen to play Baron Hardup and, except when his duties took him away, he attended almost every rehearsal. Sometimes, listening to him sing, Sylvia became so entranced that she almost forgot why she was supposed to be there. To her disappointment he missed the last rehearsal, the job obviously taking precedence when there was work to be done.

She, too, had to concentrate on her work as things were hotting up, especially in North Africa. One day, peering though her stereoscope at a long line of tanks, she thought about Bob, the boy next door, and Daisy's boyfriend, Chris. She had not had the chance to meet him, but her sister had sent a snap of the two of them taken just before he went abroad. They looked so happy together and Sylvia was pleased for her, although she felt sorry for Bob, Daisy's childhood sweetheart. Were they down there in that line of tanks she was looking at? She prayed they were both safe.

At the end of her shift, Sylvia went over to the mess to meet Bill. He wanted to make some changes to the script and had sought her advice. They sat at one of the tables with cups of tea and Bill showed her his pencilled amendments. Sylvia thought for a moment, wondering how she could tactfully tell him that no changes were necessary.

He put his cup down and said, 'Well?'

'I see what you mean,' she said, hesitantly.

'But? I sense a but coming.'

'It's only two weeks to performance day. It's a bit late to ask people to unlearn their lines and learn new ones. Most of us are so busy, there's not really much time...'

Bill shuffled his papers together and sighed. 'You're right of course. It's just - I want it to be perfect.'

'You worry too much. It's coming along well. They'll love it.'

'Are you sure?'

Sylvia reassured him and finished her tea. 'Was there anything else?' she asked.

'Could you check on the costumes in case they need any alterations?'

'OK. I'll speak to Iris.' She made to stand up but changed her mind when she saw Hugh enter the room. Her heart started thumping and she found it hard to move. It had been weeks since their encounter in Henley and, since then, she had only spoken to him in the course of her work or in general conversation with others about the show.

She allowed herself to daydream when she listened to him singing but apart from that she was steadfast in her determination to put any romantic notions out of her head. His wife was still staying at the Hare and Hounds and she had stopped going there with her friends. She dreaded seeing Hugh with her, worse still witnessing another scene.

Julia had come into the hut one evening after a night out and threw her bag down on the bed next to Sylvia's. 'You should have come with us, it was fun,' she said.

'Too tired,' Sylvia replied, her standard excuse.

'You'll never guess who we saw in the cinema?'

'No, I expect you'll tell me.'

'Wingco's wife - and she wasn't with him.'

'So what? He's always working, and she can't be expected to stay in every evening.'

'She was with a soldier – a major I think. Couldn't see much of him as she was all over him. What a cow! The poor chap's working all hours and she's...'

'Julia. It's none of our business,' Sylvia interrupted. I just hope H... er he doesn't find out, that's all.' She had almost said Hugh.

'Someone should tell him.'

Sylvia had ended the conversation and got into bed.

Now she remembered what Julia had told her and felt embarrassed for Hugh. She wondered if he knew about his wife's behaviour. Of course, he had seen her the worse for drink but being unfaithful was something else.

***

Hugh almost turned round and left when he spotted Sylvia sitting with Bill James. It was hard enough seeing her at work. She seemed to be spending a lot of time with Bill and he supposed he should be pleased she had found someone. But a little spurt of jealousy stabbed his heart and he had to steel himself to join them when Bill called him over.

'Did you want to see me?' Bill asked.

'I just wanted to apologise for missing the last rehearsal. Couldn't be helped.'

'No need. We're all under pressure at the moment.'

Sylvia stood up. 'If there's nothing else, Bill, I should get back.'

Bill nodded.

'Goodbye then.' She looked at Hugh. 'Goodbye, sir.'

As she walked away, Hugh gave a short laugh. 'So, you're Bill but I'm sir.'

Bill grinned. 'You're a senior officer, sir. We're more informal away from the office.'

'SO Bishop doing a good job, is she?' Hugh asked for something to say.

'Very efficient,' Bill replied. 'Lots of good ideas too.'

Hugh nodded. He couldn't trust himself to continue talking about Sylvia. 'I'm afraid I'll have to miss another rehearsal if you can manage without me.'

'Extra duties?'

'Not this time. As you know, my wife has been staying nearby but the boys will soon be home for the school holidays, so she needs to go back to Oban. I must spend some time with her before she goes. She's seen little enough of me while she's been here.'

'I'm sure she understands.'

Hugh nodded. He wasn't so sure. He hadn't even told her about the show. Bad enough being busy at work. He'd never hear the last of it if he told her he was at rehearsals.

Bill shrugged. 'Pity she'll miss the show though.'

'Yes. So - you can manage without me for now?'

'Sure. Your scenes are almost perfect. We can get a stand-in if necessary. So long as you're here for the dress rehearsal.'

'Of course. I won't let you down.' Hugh walked away deep in thought. He was dreading saying goodbye to Margaret. There was sure to be a scene. She'd been badgering him to ask for leave and seemed incapable of understanding why it was impossible.

'Just a couple of days, darling,' she pleaded, winding her arms around his neck and pouting. And then when he'd pushed her away, she'd stamped her foot. 'Anyone would think you don't want to spend time with your family. And what about the boys? This will be the second Christmas without you.'

The argument had gone on and on and he'd had difficulty controlling his temper. Now he had to go through it all again.

***

It had turned bitterly cold with a biting wind and Hugh turned his collar up as he got out of the car. Inside, he went straight upstairs to the room where Margaret was staying. He entered without knocking and she turned abruptly.

'You're early for a change,' she snapped.

'You should be pleased. After all, you always complain when I'm late.'

'But I'm nowhere near ready – as you can see.' It was nearly noon and she was still in her nightgown and negligee, an open suitcase on the bed.

He smiled grimly. 'We need to get a move on if you're to catch that train,' he said.

'No need to rush, darling. There'll be other trains.' She smiled and came towards him. 'As you're here, we've time for a proper farewell.' She loosened the belt on her negligee. 'After all, it's the last time we'll be together for a while.'

He had always found it hard to say no to her but now he stood firm. 'Darling, I'm sorry. There's no time. You must get that train. I've booked you on the sleeper. If you miss that one, you'll have difficulty getting a seat on another.'

'I don't care.' She pouted and ran her hand down his arm. 'Come on, darling, there's plenty of time.'

He gently pushed her away and said, 'Go and get dressed. I'll finish packing for you.'

She went into the bathroom, slamming the door, and Hugh grabbed the rest of her belongings and put them in the case. If only she wouldn't do that, he thought, although he should be used to it by now. She had always used sex as a way to get what she wanted. And it usually worked. Not now though. He was tired of it – the constant quarrels and making up.

She came back in, dressed in a flimsy cotton frock, hardly suitable for the weather. She threw the nightclothes and her wash bag into the case and picked up her coat from the back of a chair. 'Come on, then, if you're in such a hurry.'

He put everything in the case, getting a whiff of her perfume as he folded the nightgown. It brought a brief flash of nostalgia which he quickly suppressed. Snapping the case shut he opened the door for her, and she brushed past him.

Downstairs, Hugh stopped to pay the bill. To his relief there were no customers, but as he turned to go, Margaret leaned over and grabbed the landlord by his lapels. Pulling him across the bar towards her, she gave him a smacking kiss and said, 'Thanks for having me. I *have* enjoyed my stay.'

Hugh stood by the door and waited for her to join him. If she's waiting for a reaction, she'll be disappointed, he thought, as she pushed past him and walked across to the car. She stood tapping her foot until he opened the door for her.

The drive to the station was completed in silence and when the car stopped, Margaret got out without waiting for him. She leaned over and picked up her case.

'No need to see me off, darling. Just give me my ticket.'

'I'll wait with you,' he said.

'The ticket, please.' She sighed as he fumbled in his pocket. He handed it to her, and she snatched it from him, leaning down for a brief kiss on his cheek.

'Goodbye, darling,' she said.

'I really should...' he began.

But she was walking briskly away. At the station entrance, she raised a hand in farewell without turning round and then she was gone.

Hugh sat in the car for a long time, his emotions in turmoil, a mixture of relief and regret. He waited till he heard the train pull in and then start up again. Then with a sigh, he started back to Medmenham.

Chapter Ten

Sylvia was really enjoying being involved in the pantomime. Although she was tired all the time, she seemed to take on a new lease of life when she attended rehearsals. Bill was a perfectionist, so she did her best to make sure all the props were in place, the costumes ready, and all the other little things required to make the show a success.

Bill was going through the script one more time before the dress rehearsal when Sylvia joined him, carrying a list.

'Ah, there you are,' he said. 'Everything all right?'

'Fine. Stop worrying,' Sylvia chided him.

'I know - it'll be all right on the night as they say.'

'Well, it will – it must after all your hard work.'

'I'll be glad when it's all over.' Bill ran his hands through his hair.

'No, you won't. You've loved it. You won't know what to do with yourself after this.'

'It's true. I love the theatre.'

'So, will you stay on in the air force after the war?'

'Oh, no. It's civvy street for me as soon as poss. I'll try for some theatrical work, but it won't be easy.'

'Good luck then.' Sylvia shoved her list at him. 'Now then, let's get this checked one last time. The cast will be here soon for the rehearsal.'

'Yes, full cast and costume, for a change.' He sighed. 'I know it's difficult – the job comes first, of course. But Baron Hardup hasn't been here for the last few rehearsals.'

'He doesn't need to rehearse really though, does he? I've listened in and he's word perfect.' Perfect in every way, Sylvia added under her breath.

Bill nodded. 'Here they are,' he said as the door banged open.

The rehearsal went well. Everyone knew their parts and the music was good. Sylvia, watching from the wings, script in hand, held her breath as Hugh came on for his big scene. Even in costume and with makeup, he still looked tired. She knew Margaret had returned to Scotland and she wondered if he was missing her. He should be relieved, she thought. One more scene like the one she and her friends had witnessed could cause a real scandal. She hated thinking of him being the subject of malicious gossip.

She thrust the thought away and listened entranced as he began to sing. His voice thrilled her as usual, but it wasn't just that. She had discovered that he had a gift for comedy, and she found herself laughing out loud.

There were no mishaps, no one forgot their lines, the makeshift scenery only wobbled a little and the Fairy Godmother's wings stayed in place. If it went like this tomorrow it would be a resounding success and poor Bill would be able to relax, Sylvia thought.

'Well done, everyone. Drinks all round,' Bill called.

They gathered in the bar and the room was soon filled with chatter and laughter. Sylvia found herself standing near Hugh. She had been listening to one of the lads telling a joke and hadn't noticed his approach. She took refuge in her drink, but he touched her arm and said, 'Well done. Bill's just been telling me what a good job you've done. A woman of many talents.' He smiled.

Sylvia's cheeks flushed and she said. 'Everyone has done well. Team work.'

'Of course. But I was thinking about your PI work as well. You're very good.' He paused and Sylvia took another sip of her drink. She didn't know what to say.

He continued, 'It's been a bit frantic, what with the show as well. You must be exhausted. I wonder...' he hesitated.

'What?' Sylvia's stomach was churning. She was torn between pleasure that he'd stopped to talk to her and concern lest anyone noticed.

'I did enjoy our chat down by the river all those weeks ago. I know I shouldn't ask, but I wondered if we could do it again...'

'No, no.' She shook her head vehemently.

'I'm sorry. Please. You misunderstand. After the show tomorrow – I'd like to take you for a Christmas drink to celebrate.'

'But, sir, there'll be an after-show party, won't there? We can have a drink together then.'

Hugh's face fell. 'Of course. But these occasions are so noisy. I thought - a quiet drink so we could talk properly.'

Sylvia longed to say yes but it was too dangerous. She could imagine the gossip if they were seen together. It would mean a disciplinary action for him as well as for her. Even an innocent drink and chat could be misconstrued. Something like that could harm her career – and his. She knew that Hugh's career was very important to him – for her too, especially now that she could see no other future after the war but to stay on in the WAAFs. She couldn't imagine returning to her humdrum life back home.

As she hesitated, he said, 'Please Sylvia. I need someone to talk to and I do enjoy your company.'

She sighed and gave in. 'All right, sir. Just a drink.'

'Of course. And I've asked you before - please call me 'Hugh' when we're off duty.'

She smiled and was about to reply when Julia approached. 'Well done, sir,' she said. 'You were brilliant. Well everyone was. It was fun, wasn't it? Let's hope it goes as well tomorrow.'

Hugh smiled. 'I'm sure it will.'

109

Julia chattered on, seemingly oblivious to the tension between the two. To Sylvia's relief Hugh moved away to talk to Bill and she watched him go, until Julia nudged her. 'You're not listening, Syl. Don't tell me you're still going all moony-eyed over the Wingco. There's no future in it, my dear.' She took a sip of her drink. 'Mind you, I wouldn't blame him for going astray considering the way that wife of his behaves. Good job she's gone back to bonny Scotland.'

'Hush, Julia. Someone will hear. I keep telling you, you've got it all wrong. He's my boss and we get on well together – at work, that is.'

'If you say so. But if you don't mind me pointing out, you're blushing again.'

Sylvia shook her head in despair as she felt the tide of colour flood her cheeks. How she hated this tendency to blush so easily. But there was no stopping Julia, who always had to tease, especially when she'd had a couple of drinks.

'It's a bit hot in here, that's all. I need some air,' Sylvia said.

'You're not going? The party's only just started.'

'I'm on early shift tomorrow and then there's the setting up for the show. I must get some sleep.' She put her glass down on a convenient shelf and pushed her way through the crowd towards the door, relieved that Julia didn't try to detain her.

As usual, sleep did not come easily, the brief conversation with Hugh re-playing over and over again in her head.

***

Sylvia was exhausted after her busy shift, more so than usual due to her sleepless night. She had found it hard to concentrate on the pile of photographs that littered her desk. She pushed her chair back, stood and stretched. Just time for a quick nap before going back to the main house to get ready for the show. There was a lot to do before the curtain went up.

As she left the building, Hugh came up behind her and held the door open for her. 'My big night or rather, afternoon,' he said with a grin.

'Good luck, sir.' She started to hurry away.

'You still all right for later?' he called after her.

She nodded, hoping no one had heard. She shouldn't have agreed to meet him after the show, but she kept telling herself it didn't mean anything - just a chat, that's all.

Back at the hut there was no chance of a nap. The other girls were fussing around, checking their costumes and makeup. Marion was gargling and singing scales, practising for her big moment onstage. Sylvia gave up and decided to go for a walk to clear her head.

It was a cold day with clear blue skies, and she enjoyed wandering through the grounds, breathing in the sharp air. Since she had arrived at Medmenham the place had changed. Much of the once pristine gardens had disappeared, smothered by more rows of huts. So many people now worked here that Sylvia hardly knew anyone. There were personnel from all the forces and a recent influx of Americans, much to the other girls' delight.

Sylvia wasn't interested. Her life revolved round her work, trying to get enough sleep – and day-dreaming about Hugh. Her heart beat a little faster and there was a fluttering in her tummy as she anticipated their coming meeting after the show.

She looked at her watch. Time to go back.

She was checking the list of props in the main hall, which had been miraculously transformed into a theatre, when Julia and her friends came in.

'There you are. We wondered where you'd got to.'

'Busy little bee, aren't you,' Marion said. 'You've made yourself quite indispensable to Bill James, I see.'

Sylvia had become immune to Marion's sniping. 'I'm just doing a job. Besides, it's Iris he likes but they're both so shy,' she said.

'I thought she was still grieving over sailor boy. She got over it pretty quick,' Marion said.

Julia rounded on her. 'Why do you have to be such a cow? Doesn't she deserve to be happy?'

There was a shocked silence and they dispersed to don their costumes and get made up. Sylvia was shaking as she continued checking that everything was in place. So, it's not just me she has to have a dig at, she thought, deciding to ignore Marion in future.

She calmed down and finished setting up for the first scene, looking round with pride. The scenery might be a bit makeshift, but they had done their best. Everyone had mucked in and all were determined to make the show a success. Bill had worked hard on the production and they did not want to let him down.

Sylvia could hear the audience arriving and she took a deep breath. Bill had gone backstage to wish them all luck. When he returned, he gave Sylvia a thumbs up. 'Places please,' he said and the Ugly Sisters, together with Cinderella, came on to the stage. When they were settled, he whispered to Sylvia, 'Curtain up.'

She held her breath and pulled back the makeshift curtain to reveal Marion as Cinderella, face dirty and dressed in rags, sweeping the floor. Her sisters – a flight lieutenant and a squadron leader in drag – sat by the fire toasting their toes.

Sylvia was kept busy backstage, only stopping to listen for a moment when Hugh came on and did his big song.

It seemed only moments before it was all over, and the cast took their bows and clustered backstage to receive a well-deserved pat on the back from Bill.

'Right, folks. Well done. But no time to rest on your laurels. You've to do it all again later on.'

There were a few groans from the cast and some good-natured banter.

'Why do it twice in one day, why not over two days?' Marion asked, the only one to have a moan.

'I explained,' Bill said patiently. 'It was to give those on duty this afternoon a chance to see it.'

Jane touched Marion's arm. 'It's a big part, tiring for you I know, but at least we have a day off tomorrow.'

'Yes, Christmas day.' Julia said. 'Come on, Marion. Cheer up. You were great. The lads in the audience have all fallen in love with you.'

'You looked beautiful in that frock in the last scene with Prince Charming,' Jane said.

Marion smiled and did a mock curtsey. 'Some Prince Charming,' she said with a laugh. 'But I've got a date with one of the 'sisters' next week.'

'And there's the party after the next performance,' Julia said. 'Perhaps I'll find my own Prince Charming.'

They looked across to where Iris and Bill had their heads together. 'Looks like Iris has found hers, doesn't it,' Sylvia said.

They all joined in the laughter.

The second performance was even better than the first and there was a heady mixture of laughter and banter at the party afterwards. The drink flowed freely but soon, the number of people dwindled as those on the night shift left.

Sylvia took the opportunity to slip away and walked down to the main gate where Hugh had arranged to pick her up. He wasn't there and she was tempted to turn round and go back to her hut. She really shouldn't be doing this.

She was about to walk away when she heard the car. It glided to a stop beside her and Hugh leaned over and opened the door.

'I'm so pleased you waited,' he said. 'I had a job getting away.'

'Basking in the admiration of your fans, I expect,' she said.

Hugh laughed. 'Something like that. It was a good show though, wasn't it?'

'I enjoyed it.' Sylvia wasn't about to start congratulating him on his singing. She might say too much. It was enough to be sitting beside him as he negotiated the country lanes.

They drove in silence for a few miles and Sylvia peered out into the darkness as they came to a crossroads. 'Where are we going?' she asked.

'I know of a nice little pub in a small village near here.'

She wondered how he had come across it, out here in the countryside. Perhaps he had brought Margaret here. The thought unsettled her, and she almost asked him to take her back. What was she doing miles from Medmenham with a married man? If they were seen, no one would believe it was an innocent meeting. The thoughts churned round in her head, but she thrust them away and concentrated on the pleasure of being with him. She might not get another chance.

They pulled up in front of a whitewashed building with a thatched roof, the very picture of an English country inn. So different to the pubs on the Isle of Sheppey with its Victorian pubs on every street corner, Sylvia thought.

Hugh came round and opened the door for her. He held her arm as she stumbled on the gravel forecourt.

The bar was quiet, only a couple of elderly men sitting in the corner with their pint pots in front of them. An attempt had been made to decorate for Christmas with a string of dusty paperchains and some sprigs of holly along the mantelpiece. A log fire blazed in a huge open fireplace and Sylvia's nose wrinkled at the smell of burning wood. It reminded her of helping her father on the allotment when he would light a bonfire and she and Daisy and Jimmy would roast potatoes in the embers. Such happy, innocent pleasures.

The whiff of nostalgia made her once again question the wisdom of being here with Hugh, but her thoughts were interrupted when he asked what she would like to drink. She opted for a shandy instead of her usual gin and tonic. 'Just a half,' she said.

'Go and sit down and I'll bring it over,' Hugh said.

She would like to have sat near the fire but instead took a seat in the far corner away from the two old men. They were probably not at all interested in her, but she couldn't face anyone listening to her conversation.

When Hugh joined her, sitting opposite at the table, they sipped their drinks in silence for a few moments. While she was wondering what to say he said, 'So you enjoyed the panto?'

'Very much. It was great fun and Bill did a marvellous job.'

'You seem very friendly.'

'We were working closely together, that's all. I think he rather fancies his chances with my friend Iris. But he's so shy and so is she. I told him he had nothing to lose by asking her out.' She picked up her glass and drank a little, trying to make it last.

'Let's hope he takes your advice,' Hugh said.

Sylvia nodded, then putting her glass down she took the plunge. 'You said you needed someone talk to. Is there a problem – at work I mean?' She wondered if someone had made a mistake in their reports and he wasn't sure how to deal with it.

Hugh didn't answer immediately. He reached into his pocket for his pipe and tobacco. 'Do you mind?' he asked.

Sylvia shook her head.

He took his time filling the pipe and lighting it and Sylvia waited impatiently. This wasn't how she'd imagined the evening would go.

'Well, er – I expect you heard that my wife has gone back to Scotland.'

'To spend the Christmas holidays with your sons?'

'That's right. That wasn't the only reason though. She was unhappy.' He drew on his pipe and then said, hastily, 'My fault, I suppose. I was too busy to spend time with her. She said it was a waste of time coming all this way and she was lonely.'

Not that lonely, Sylvia thought, remembering the scenes in the Hare and Hounds and the rumours she'd heard. She hoped that Hugh had no idea of her goings on. He would be so hurt.

Hugh continued, 'I'm sure she thought that working in an office meant I would be doing office hours and would be free to take her out – dining and dancing and such.'

'But surely she understands how important your work is.'

'I don't think so.' He sighed. 'It's so hard when you're not allowed to talk about what you're doing - the secrecy, you know. I tried to explain but...'

'I understand.' She smiled. 'My sister is very dismissive of my work – thinks I'm just a shorthand typist. Her job is much more important of course – supervisor in the local NAAFI.'

'The thing is, Sylvia, everyone's job is important in this war. From the lowliest clerk or cook to the Air Marshal in charge of the RAF and the Prime Minister himself. We're all cogs in a wheel; we must all play our part.'

Sylvia nodded. 'I agree.'

Suddenly, Hugh put down his pipe and leaned across the table, seizing hold of her hand. 'Why doesn't she understand? You understand, don't you?'

She gently pulled her hand away and picked up her glass. Where was this leading? Was he going to trot out that old cliché about his wife not understanding him? He did seem genuinely upset.

116

'The reason I understand, sir, is that we are doing the same work. Everyone in the unit is working together. We know that we can't always have time off when we want it, that sometimes we're called upon to do extra hours.' She didn't know how she managed to keep her voice so steady.

'You're right of course.' He sighed. 'Let's talk about something else.'

'Tell me about your boys. Do you have a photograph?'

He reached into his pocket and pulled out his wallet, extracting a snap of two little boys. One had fair floppy hair falling over his eyes, the other darker like his father. 'That's Bobby,' he said, pointing, 'and that's Peter.'

'How old are they?' Sylvia forced an interest. She couldn't help thinking that things might be different if Hugh didn't have children.

'Seven and nine, growing up fast.'

'You must miss them.'

He nodded. 'They're home for the holidays at the moment, but they'll be back at school by the time I'm granted some leave – if ever. It's ages since I last saw them. They probably won't recognise me when we finally get together.'

Sylvia sympathised. She felt the same about her brother Jimmy. Last time she had leave he had been evacuated to Wales, just a schoolboy. Now he was old enough to join the Home Guard. 'I miss my brother and sister too.' She sighed. 'How much longer will this wretched war go on?'

Hugh took her hand again. 'To be honest Sylvia I really don't care. The longer it lasts the longer I can keep seeing you. I don't want to go home.'

Sylvia's heart beat faster. 'You don't mean that, Hugh.'

'I do, really.' He ran his hand through his hair. 'I know I shouldn't be saying this, but I can't stop thinking about you. Sometimes the work and the responsibility weigh heavily but when I'm feeling down, the thought of you in the next room brightens my day.'

She should stop this before it went any further, she told herself. But she could not bring herself to pull her hand away. Instead she put her hand over his and said, 'I feel the same way.'

'You do? I hardly dared hope. But that day by the river...' He paused, then said, 'I've felt this way for a long time.'

For a few moments they stared at each other in silence. Then Sylvia came to her senses and withdrew her hand. She took a deep breath. 'Hugh, we shouldn't be talking like this.'

'You're right. I never meant...' He sighed. 'I promised myself we would just have a quiet drink as friends, talk about the show or our work. I just wanted to enjoy your company. But it's been so hard, trying to hide my feelings.'

'Me too,' Sylvia whispered.

'I'm not asking you to have an affair with me. I respect you too much for that. I'll have to request a posting, abroad somewhere...'

'No, please, I couldn't bear it if you went away. I know it's the sensible thing to do, but I don't feel sensible right now.' Sylvia's voice choked and she was on the verge of tears.

'I really should go, Sylvia my love. It would be torture to see you every day and not...'

She looked up at him, her eyes shining through her tears. 'For me as well,' she said.

'We can't carry on like this, meeting in out of the way places, yet trying to act normally at work.'

'We can try.'

Hugh nodded. 'All right. But it's going to be hard.' He got up and came round to her side of the table, sitting down close to her on the bench. He put his arm around her and drew her close. He wiped away the tears with his thumb then bent and kissed her.

Her head told her she should pull away, but her heart won and she gave herself up to the kiss - at first sweet and tender, then becoming more passionate. When he released her, it took her a moment to catch her breath. She glanced across to the two old men by the fire, but they were deep in conversation. Thank goodness no one else had come in.

But then she forgot everything as Hugh pulled her towards him again. Between his kisses he murmured, 'I love you, sweet Sylvia. I think I really knew the moment you first walked into my office.'

'I love you too, Hugh.' She leaned into him, breathing in his scent of lemon cologne and pipe tobacco. She wanted to stay here forever but it was getting late.

The barman began clearing up, making a lot of noise, to let them know it was nearly closing time and they reluctantly drew apart.

Hugh helped her on with her coat and they went out into the cold wind. He kept his arm around her as they walked across the car park, settled her into her seat and got in himself.

Sylvia didn't want the evening to end but she was relieved when Hugh started the car and began the drive back to Medmenham. She knew that if they started kissing again things might go further than she was prepared for. He was still a married man and she wasn't about to get herself in the same situation that she had with Roland. Thinking herself in love with him, she had gone to his hotel room willingly, but she hadn't enjoyed what happened. It hadn't taken her long to realise what sort of man he was. Hugh wasn't like that – of course he wasn't, but she couldn't take the chance.

She was quiet on the drive back and Hugh concentrated on his driving. When they reached the gates of the big house, she asked him to stop. 'I'll get out here and walk over to my billet.'

'If you insist.' He opened the car door, then leaned over and kissed her cheek. 'No regrets?' he asked.

She shook her head.

'Will you let me take you out again?'

She didn't answer and, without waiting for him to open the door for her she got out and walked quickly away down the path leading to the hut.

***

Sylvia awoke on Christmas Day and for a second thought she had been dreaming. But it was true. Hugh had kissed her and said 'I love you.' The whispered words as they embraced in the dimness of that smoky pub convinced her he really meant it.

She sat up and looked round the hut, where her friends were all still asleep. She wanted to sing and shout, to tell the world, but it must remain a secret, one she could not share even with her closest friend. She could tell Daisy though, so long as their mother never got to know that she was in love with a married man. Her sister would understand. I'll write to her now, she thought, reaching over to her locker for pen and writing pad. She sat up in bed and started to write. First, she must wish her sister a happy Christmas. Although she had sent a homemade card to her family a few days ago, she wasn't sure if they'd received it. You never knew with the post these days.

She chewed the end of her pen, wondering how to tell Daisy about Hugh. She had always kept her letters light-hearted, giving the impression that, although she was doing a very mundane job, she was having a wonderful time, dancing and flirting. Would her sister believe how much she had changed since meeting Hugh and starting work as a PI?

'I know you think I'm flighty and irresponsible, but I've changed. I've fallen in love. Hugh is a little older than me, an officer, very handsome. I don't go out

120

dancing and drinking any more. We like walks by the river and quiet country pubs.' That was stretching the truth a little – one walk and one pub visit. But she hoped there would be more.

Daisy would guess that she was talking about her married boss, who she'd mentioned in earlier letters but up to then she hadn't written anything that her parents couldn't hear about.

She was just finishing when the other girls started to wake up, yawning and stretching, some looking the worse for wear after their night of partying.

'You're an early bird,' Julia called across. 'What happened to you last night? You missed a good party. It got even better after you'd left.'

'I was so tired and when it got so noisy and smoky, I just wanted to have a quiet night.'

'But you weren't here when we got back.'

'I went for a walk in the grounds to get some fresh air and then I remembered I'd left something in the office. Had to hunt around for someone with a key.' The lies came easily, and Sylvia was ashamed.

Julia looked sceptical but didn't reply. She got out of bed and started to dress.

Marion had been listening and she said with a sarcastic laugh, 'A likely story. I bet you went off with that Bill for a bit of canoodling.'

'If you mean Squadron Leader James, you couldn't be more wrong,' Julia said. 'He danced most of the evening with Iris.'

The other girls were getting up and dressed by now and the hut was filled with laughter and Christmas wishes, and reminiscing about the show and the party afterwards. Sylvia finished her letter and sealed the envelope.

'Come on, lazybones, breakfast time.' Julia said. 'I wonder if we'll get a decent breakfast as its Christmas,' she said.

Chapter Eleven

'Cinderella' and the Christmas festivities had been a welcome break from the unremitting work but now, in this very wet January of 1943, the fun they'd had was a distant memory. Mist and rain did not stop the planes from taking off and taking hundreds of photos and Sylvia and her colleagues worked frantically to keep up. The three-shift system meant that the work went on round the clock.

Sylvia was on the night shift this week and, as usual, she found it hard to sleep during the day. Several of the other girls were working different shifts and, although they tried to be careful not to disturb their sleeping hut mates, it was never completely quiet with their constant coming and going.

Hugh worked the early morning shift and Sylvia had hardly seen him since that wonderful Christmas Eve. Sometimes she almost thought she'd dreamt it - those intoxicating kisses, his murmured endearments. Had it really happened? Had he just been playing with her, missing his wife and trying to fill the void left by her absence?

Just as well they were no longer working in the same section, she told herself. She still felt the same about him, but what was the point? Nothing would come of it. When the war ended, the PI unit would be disbanded and, even if she stayed in the air force, it was unlikely they'd be posted to the same station.

I must stop thinking about him she told herself over and over. But, back in her billet trying to sleep after an exhausting night's work, she couldn't stop herself re-living those few hours she had spent with him in that smoky little pub, a Christmas Eve she would never forget. Then, she had dared to hope that their relationship might develop into something more. Not that she would let it go too far, she told herself.

Winter had come with a vengeance and it was so cold that the girls rarely ventured out to the pub or into town in their off-duty hours. Instead they huddled round the stove in the middle of their hut reading, writing letters and teasing each other. Poor Iris bore the brunt of their leg pulling, especially when she started knitting baby clothes.

'It's for my sister,' she protested. 'She's having a baby in the spring.'

'A likely tale,' Julia teased.

'Leave her alone,' Sylvia said, turning to Iris. 'Take no notice, they don't mean anything by it.'

Iris blushed. 'I know.' She smiled. 'I've always liked needlework and making things.'

'You made a lovely job of those costumes, especially with so little material to work with,' Sylvia said, leaning across to see what Iris was working on. She admired the lacy pattern. 'Wish I could knit. I'd make a scarf and some gloves – to wear indoors if this blasted stove doesn't start to warm us up.'

They all laughed.

'I could teach you,' Iris said tentatively.

'Thanks, but no. My mum tried and I just couldn't get the hang of it. My sister Daisy is the knitter in the family.'

Their talk turned to reminiscences and stories of their home life. They rarely talked about their work – each of them worked in different sections and the habit of secrecy was never broken even among their closest friends.

Sylvia's job had changed lately. Instead of monitoring the airfields and nearby installations, she had now been told to concentrate on changes in the landscape. She wasn't the only one doing this and at the end of each session all the photos with their notes attached were sent to a central office where more senior officers examined them again, comparing the notes made by each of the PIs.

Despite the bad weather the pilots were not deterred and went up whenever possible so each day hundreds of reels of film poured into Medmenham. It took time to get effective photos and with the mist and rain some of them were blurred and hard to interpret. But they still had to be developed and examined.

Sylvia pored over a batch like that one day in late February, half a dozen taken from different angles. The thing on the ground was an odd shape, like no aircraft she had seen before. She was so intrigued that she didn't make any notes to go in the out tray. Instead, she took the photos across to Flight Officer Babington-Smith who was working on the other side of the room.

'Excuse me ma'am, I wonder what you think of this?' she asked tentatively, handing her the photo. She hadn't had a lot to do with the flight officer before and was a bit in awe of her, although the other girls had told her she was quite informal and liked to be called Babs.

The senior officer picked up a jeweller's magnifying glass and peered at the blurred shape. After a few moments she sat back and said, 'I saw something similar the other day. A real puzzle. We've been asked to look out for anything strange. I wonder...' She pulled the stereoscope towards her and held it over two of the photos, turning to Sylvia with a satisfied nod. 'Yes, worth a bit more investigation. Well done. If you see anything else like this, bring them to me.'

'What do you think it is?'

'It's hard to tell. I'll pass it on,' Babs said. 'Besides, it's not our job to speculate.'

Chastened, Sylvia said, 'Yes, ma'am,' and went back to her desk.

Despite the reprimand, she felt pleased with herself. After all, the senior officer had said 'well done.' She realised there was no need to be nervous of approaching Babington Smith, although she felt sure she would never dare address her as Babs.

From then on, she kept a close watch for more of the peculiar shaped objects, but she didn't see anything else similar. She did notice, however, that there was a lot more activity in the region where she first spotted them. The heavily forested area near the coast had been cleared and something was definitely happening.

It was near the end of March and Sylvia still wasn't sure exactly what she was looking for as she scanned hundreds more photos every day. But they had been told to keep a close watch on the area. Of course, she had no idea what her colleagues had found, if anything. It just wasn't done to discuss their work outside of hours, so sometimes it was hard to tell how the things she reported fitted into the whole picture.

At the end of one long shift, she went across to the mess for a late lunch. She had been on duty since six that morning and had stayed past her time to finish the latest batch of photographs. She was dying for a cup of tea and something to eat.

The mess was deserted except for one person sitting alone, his back to the door. Her heart leapt when she recognised him. She had hardly spoken to Hugh for weeks, except on rare occasions in the course of their work.

He looked up as she passed his table to go to the counter and the smile on his face made her heart beat even faster. That look told her that his feelings had not changed either.

She collected her food and took the tray across to his table, knowing that she really shouldn't – but, she told herself, it would be silly to go and sit at another table by herself. Why shouldn't she join him for a friendly chat?

'Do you mind?' she asked, putting her tray down.

'Of course not. Don't be silly. Besides, I need to talk to you.'

She sat down and picked up her cup. 'Hugh, please don't...'

'But, Sylvia, I've hardly seen you since Christmas. I know we've been extra busy but...' He paused. 'I've missed you, my sweet. It's so hard. I'd got used to seeing you every day at work and I told myself that was enough. But then, I was moved to another section and...'

'Please, Hugh. It's hard for me too.' Her eyes shone with unshed tears.

They sat in silence for a moment or two, then Hugh reached out and took Sylvia's hand. 'I'll ask Margaret for a divorce,' he said abruptly.

She was shocked. 'You can't do that. What about your children?' She pulled her hand away.

'We'll sort something out. Don't worry, I'll make sure you're not involved.'

Sylvia sighed. She hadn't thought about that. She was more concerned about how it would affect him. 'I'm not worried about that. Besides, I'm tired and not thinking straight.'

'Then, please, will you come out with me this evening? We can go to the same place as last time. It's quiet there. We won't be seen.'

Sylvia hesitated. 'I don't like all this secrecy.'

'It's *your* reputation I'm thinking about,' he said.

'I understand, really I do.' She sighed. 'Now, let's talk about something else in case anyone comes in.'

'Very well. We'll change the subject. How are things in your section?'

'Busy as usual.' She hesitated. 'We're finding some strange stuff. I'm not sure i should be talking about it.'

'You can talk to me. After all, we're working on the same things. Have you heard anything about rockets?'

'I've seen some strange things shaped like torpedoes.'

He nodded 'It seems the Germans are working on some new secret weapon. Pilotless aircraft that can reach London.'

'I've heard rumours,' Sylvia said.

'Not just rumours, I'm afraid.'

Sylvia gasped, although it was true she thought along those lines herself. She hadn't really wanted to believe it, and having it put into words terrified her. The part of North Kent where her family lived had already been dubbed 'Bomb Alley'. Now, they could be in more danger. 'Can we stop them?' she asked.

Hugh smiled grimly. 'Let's hope so.' He took her hand again. 'That's where our work comes in. Bomber Command needs all the help we can give them.'

The door behind them opened and Sylvia let go of his hand. 'I must go,' she said, standing up hastily. She'd hardly touched her food, but she couldn't stay for fear of giving herself away. She dreaded being the cause of gossip and it didn't take much for rumours to start flying around.

'Don't go, please,' Hugh whispered as she bent to pick up her bag.

A voice behind them said loudly, 'Skiving off, Hugh old chap?'

Hugh turned. 'You too, Roddy.' He laughed. 'Anyway, it's back to the grind for me.' He turned to Sylvia. 'Keep up the good work SO Bishop.'

'Yes, sir.'

And then he was gone. How did he do it? Change his manner so quickly to the formality of a senior officer. Of course, he was a good actor. He'd shown that in the recent pantomime. The thought startled her. Had his declaration of his feelings for her just been an act? Was he just after a casual affair? She didn't want to believe it and, after all, he *had* mentioned a divorce.

After a brief greeting to the other officer she slowly followed Hugh out of the mess. He was waiting on the path. 'Sorry about that. I hope you weren't too embarrassed.' He paused. 'You will meet me though – by the gates, 6.30?'

'I don't know – I shouldn't really...'

'Please,' he pleaded. 'I'll be waiting.'

She nodded and he strode away.

She hurried back to the hut, her shoulders hunched against the driving rain. Inside, she went over to the stove and held her hands out to its warmth. Iris sat nearby, knitting as usual. She looked up and smiled, pointing her knitting needle to the two beds at the end of the hut where two of their friends were sleeping.

Sylvia nodded and quietly hung her hat and coat up before joining Iris by the stove. She gestured to Iris's knitting. 'It's coming along nicely,' she whispered.

'Yes, nearly finished. But I want to knit a shawl for the baby, so I'll need some more wool. It'll have to wait till I have time to go into town.'

Sylvia had an idea. She had been wondering how she could leave to meet Hugh without arousing curiosity. Nobody would walk or cycle into the village in this weather.

'I'll get it for you,' she offered. 'I need to go to the post office. I can get the bus into town – if I hurry, the shops will still be open.'

'You'll miss supper,' Iris said.

'I can get something to eat in town.'

'That's kind of you. I must give you the money.' She stood up to get her purse, telling Sylvia in great detail what wool she wanted and where best to get it. 'You know the shop – near the butchers in Market Street.'

Sylvia went and got her coat, still damp from her rush across the grounds. 'I'd better hurry to catch that bus. See you later.'

The rain had let up a bit, but the wind was cold and she was pleased she didn't have to wait long for the bus. She had calculated that she could do her shopping, have a quick bite to eat and get the return bus which would drop her by the gates around 6.30. Her meeting with Hugh would have to be brief. She couldn't stay out too long for fear of comments from her friends about her absence. She hoped he would understand.

***

Hugh told himself over and over that his relationship with Sylvia must go no further than the friendship of colleagues. He hoped that by moving to a new section he could put her out of his mind. But it was no use, he longed for just a glimpse of her and when she walked into the mess this afternoon all his common sense fled. No, he'd told himself firmly, as his heart beat faster at the sight of her, he would not ask her to join him.

And then she walked across to his table and sat down with him.

Now, as he waited in the Alvis just outside the gates, he half hoped she wouldn't turn up. He knew how risky it was meeting like this, especially parking here in this distinctive car. Everyone knew the Alvis.

He would never forgive himself if she got into trouble over him. And it was always the girl who got blamed, especially getting involved with a married man.

He glanced through the gates and up the dark driveway but there was no sign of her. His watch said 6.35. She wasn't coming. He'd go to the pub and drown his sorrows. He was about to drive away when a bus pulled up at the stop a few yards away to let someone off. It was Sylvia. She waited until the bus turned a corner and then hurried over to the car.

Hugh leaned over and opened the passenger door and she got in. 'Sorry I'm late. I had to go into town.'

'I could have taken you,' he said.

'Shopping for knitting wool?' she said with a little laugh. 'I don't think so. Besides, it was just an excuse to go out.'

'Did you manage to get what you wanted?' he asked. Such mundane conversation, he thought, when all he wanted to do was take her in his arms and tell her he loved her.

'I had to go to several shops and I'm still not sure if I've got the right stuff. It's for my friend Iris,' she explained.

They both relapsed into silence, Hugh concentrating on his driving. It was dark with no moon and he only had a faint glimmer of hooded headlights to see by.

'Where are we going?' Sylvia asked.

'I thought that little pub where we went before.'

'It's a long way. I mustn't be out too late. Apart from an early start tomorrow, the girls will wonder where I've been.'

Hugh thumped the steering wheel. 'Oh, God, how stupid am I? I should have thought of that. Can't you say you met a friend in town?'

'Not really, my only friends here are the girls in my hut.'

Hugh pulled into a lay-by and stopped the car. 'I'll take you back. You can say you missed the bus.'

'I hate all this secrecy and lying.' Sylvia's voice broke on a sob and Hugh groaned.

'I'm so sorry, my darling. I hate it too.' He hit the steering wheel again. 'What are we to do?'

Sylvia shook her head and fumbled in her bag for a handkerchief. Hugh took it from her, gently wiping her eyes. 'Please don't cry. I love you. I'd never do anything to hurt you – you must know that.' He pulled her towards him and kissed her.

When he finally released her, he told himself this was the last time he would taste the sweetness of her. He must stop this now before it went any further.

'We must stop seeing each other,' he said firmly, although the words cut like a knife in his heart.

'No, please Hugh. I won't ask anything of you – just to be with you now and then.'

'It won't work, Sylvia. Seeing you at work is hard enough.'

'I know - it's the same for me. But Hugh...'

He silenced her with another kiss. 'You know I'm right. Look, I promise I *will* divorce Margaret. She doesn't love me, probably be glad to get rid of me. But it will take time and I don't want you involved. So, until I'm a free man, we must remain colleagues only. No one must ever guess what we mean to each other.'

Sylvia nodded. 'I understand.' She wiped her eyes again and sat up straight. 'Now take me back, but before you do, just one more kiss – please?'

How could he resist? Sweet, tender, becoming ever more passionate – would it be enough to sustain him in the coming difficult weeks and months? He doubted it, but he must be strong for both of them.

Chapter Twelve

In the weeks that followed, Sylvia threw herself into her work so that there was little time to dwell on her love life – or lack of it. It helped that there was now greater urgency since the discovery of something unusual happening at Peenemunde on the Baltic coast. The photos she had shown to Flight Officer Babington Smith a few weeks ago proved of more than passing interest. Now it seemed pretty certain that a new weapon was being developed. Since their first encounter, Sylvia had got to know the flight officer, who insisted she be called Babs. 'That's what everybody calls me. I can't be doing with all this formality,' she'd said.

Sylvia still found it hard to address the officer by her nickname but one day, as they'd sat together in the mess, Babs asked her why she'd joined the WAAFs.

'I've always loved aeroplanes,' she said. 'Living on the Isle of Sheppey watching the aircraft was my childhood pastime. My sister and I used to cycle up to Eastchurch to watch them taking off and landing. So exciting.'

Babs smiled. 'I agree. I used to write for the Airplane magazine and travelled to all the air shows. When the war started, joining the WAAFs seemed the natural thing to do.'

They'd carried on chatting, enthusing about their interests and, since then, a sort of friendship developed.

The PIs were now working longer hours and Sylvia was glad to go to bed worn out at the end of each shift. She tried to put on a brave face during their rare leisure hours, laughing and chatting with her hut mates. But it was hard. Perhaps it would be better to try and forget Hugh altogether. She didn't believe he would be able to divorce Margaret without an almighty scandal. Despite her bad behaviour, she was still the boys' mother and Sylvia hated the thought of causing those two little boys any unhappiness.

Her concentration on her work was more intense these days, and it was almost possible to dismiss Hugh from her mind during duty hours. But just as she was beginning to think she was 'over it', convincing herself it had just been a fleeting infatuation, she would catch a glimpse of him across the mess or passing through the office and all the old feelings would well up again. She longed to speak to him, to feel the touch of his hand, but apart from a brief greeting, he kept to his resolve to treat her just as a colleague.

One day in April, she looked up from her stereoscope and flexed her shoulders, stiff from bending over the instrument for so long. As she turned back to her work, two people entered the room. Her heart leapt when she saw that it was Hugh with a man in civvies who she had never seen before.

They crossed the room and stopped at the next desk to hers and she heard Hugh introducing the man as someone from the Ministry of Supply, here to look at the work they were doing. They spoke in low tones and Sylvia bent her head to her work. It wouldn't do to be caught eavesdropping, but she had to admit she was curious.

She hoped they would speak to her, but they didn't stop long and she tried to put it out of her mind. She picked up a handful of photos and left her desk to show them to Flight Officer Babington Smith.

The older woman looked up and smiled. 'More photos? What is it this time?

'Not much different, except there seems to be more activity.'

'Let me see.'

Sylvia handed her the batch of prints and they examined the photos together, Sylvia pointing out the long shadows on the ground that piqued her interest. Babs peered through her jeweller's magnifying glass and said, 'I'm right. They *are* developing rockets. Everything we've looked at recently confirms it. I told the man from the Ministry and he seemed to agree,' Babs said.

'He came into my office with Wing Commander Smythe,' Sylvia said, pleased she could keep her voice level when saying his name. 'They didn't stay long.'

'Hugh was showing him round the place,' Babs said.

Sylvia went back to her desk feeling a little resentful. It's all right for *her* to call him Hugh, she thought. I have to say 'sir'.

***

While Sylvia and her colleagues were concentrating on discovering the sites and finding out more about the pilotless aircraft - rockets as they were now calling them – rumours were flying round about another big operation being planned. Sylvia knew that Hugh was working on it through something overheard in the mess, but she couldn't discuss it with anyone. Besides, her own work was far too absorbing to give her time to wonder what was going on in the other sections.

The long hours bent over a stereoscope were taking their toll. Sylvia started to get bad headaches and wondered if her sight was failing. She ought to see the MO but she kept putting it off, fearing to be taken off her present task, worse still to be posted away to less demanding work.

Despite taking aspirin and trying to get enough sleep, her health grew worse. She tried to hide it, but Julia noticed. 'You're not your usual self, Syl. What's wrong?'

Sylvia shrugged. 'Just tired, like the rest of us.'

'It's not just tiredness. I've seen you taking tablets. Tell me what's wrong,' Julia insisted.

They were alone in the hut so, after pleading with her friend not to make a fuss, she said, 'I'm so tired all the time and I've been getting these headaches. I think it's just eye strain. Sometimes, towards the end of a shift, everything gets a bit blurred.'

'You should get your eyes tested. Perhaps you need specs.'

'I can't. They'll take me off PI. I couldn't bear leaving here.'

Julia nodded. 'I know why too. It's that Wing Co isn't it? You've fallen for him. All that talk about Harry was just a blind.'

A sob caught in Sylvia's throat. 'Oh, Julia, I can't help the way I feel.' She grabbed her friend's hand. 'Please, promise me. You won't tell anyone.'

'You can rely on me. I did wonder if it was something serious when we were teasing you. At first, I thought it was just a silly crush but it isn't, is it?'

Sylvia shook her head.

'What about him?'

'He loves me but...'

'I know - he's married. Mind you, with that awful wife of his, I don't blame him.'

'It's not like that. It's not just a fling. Besides, we've agreed not to see each other again.' Sylvia thought it best not to shock her friend by mentioning divorce.

'Oh, well, that's that then.' Julia stood up. 'Stop thinking about him and get your eyes tested. Make sure there's nothing wrong.'

Sylvia was about to protest but Julia said, 'You must. Our work is important – it wouldn't do to miss something because you can't see properly.'

'You're right, of course. I'll do it. I promise.'

Next day Sylvia sought out Section Officer Forsyth, who was responsible for the welfare of the girls in her hut. An appointment was made with an optician in town and SO Forsyth went with her.

She was diagnosed with acute eye strain. 'Too many late nights reading with a torch after lights out,' the optician said with a laugh. He prescribed spectacles which Sylvia would only need for close work. 'They'll be ready in a day or two,' he said.

On the way back to Medmenham Sylvia was very quiet. Glasses, she thought. No one in her family had ever needed glasses, not that it mattered. What did worry her was the thought of having to change jobs and possibly being moved away

'Will I still be able to carry on as a PI?' she asked tentatively.

'I don't know. You'll have to see the MO. Meantime, no work until you get your specs.'

The medical officer gave her a thorough examination, asking about the headaches, her sleeping, appetite, and other more intimate questions. Sylvia answered as honestly as she could and was relieved when he told her to get dressed and beckoned her to sit opposite him at his desk.

'It's not just your eyes,' he said.' Although that's what is causing the headaches. The spectacles should fix that.' He paused. 'I think you've just been working too hard.'

'So have all my colleagues,' Sylvia said. 'But they don't get ill.'

He smiled. 'You'd be surprised. The jobs you are all doing can be quite a strain. Have you had any leave recently?'

Sylvia shook her head. 'Not since I was posted here.'

'Well, I prescribe a week's leave. Plenty of sleep, good food and fresh air – that's what you need.'

'But I can't take a whole week,' she protested.

'I insist – a week's sick leave. Don't worry. I'll clear it with your commanding officer.'

Sylvia left the office in a daze. It would be wonderful to go home, to see her family again. But she dreaded the reaction of her friends in Hut Six. None of them had been given leave for months. Why should she be singled out?

***

At the start of her leave, SO Forsyth drove her to Reading station. She handed her rail pass to her and saw her onto the train. 'Have a good rest and come back good as new,' she said.

'I will still have the same job, won't I?' Sylvia asked anxiously.

'Of course. You've got your new specs and after a bit of rest you'll be fine. Don't worry.'

The guard blew the whistle and the train began to move. Sylvia leaned out of the window and gave a little wave, then she settled back into her seat with a sigh. A whole week with her family. It would be wonderful to see them after so long. She couldn't wait to have a long sisterly chat with Daisy. A whole week without seeing Hugh, though. Perhaps that wasn't such a bad thing, she thought. Maybe she'd get him out of her system. Despite what she kept telling herself, she knew she wouldn't; she just knew he was the only man she could love. She'd had brief flings in the past but never thought seriously about any of them. She blushed at the thought of her infatuation with Roland Hargreaves. How could she have been taken in by him? But this was different.

The train pulled in and there was a mad scramble for the Underground. It was very crowded and, nervously, Sylvia hesitated at the top of the escalator as someone pushed roughly past her. That settles it, a taxi for me, she thought. Hang the expense.

At Victoria she found her platform and was pleased she only had a few minutes to wait. The train was packed, mainly with servicemen and women. She managed to find a seat squeezed between a sailor and a soldier. They didn't waste any time before engaging her in conversation and she learned that the sailor was rejoining his ship at Chatham. He started flirting with her and she couldn't help smiling at his cheeky remarks.

The soldier didn't join in with the banter and, after a few moments, folded his arms and appeared to be asleep. When the sailor left the train, Sylvia shifted in her seat, glad of the extra room after being squashed between the two men.

The soldier opened his eyes and sat up straight. 'Going to Sheerness?' he asked.

'Yes, I'm on leave. Going to visit my family.'

'Lucky you. No leave for me. I've just been posted to the garrison there.'

'My sister works in the NAAFI there.'

'I'll have to look her up,' he said. 'Does she have a boyfriend?'

'He's serving overseas.'

'Shame. Oh, well. What about you? Care to come to the pictures with me?'

Sylvia shook her head. 'Didn't you hear me tell that other chap? I'm spoken for.'

'Just my luck. All the pretty ones are.'

Sylvia turned away and looked out of the window, catching the eye of an older woman sitting opposite. The woman smiled and Sylvia felt embarrassed at being flirted with in public. The other people in the crowded carriage were engrossed in newspapers and she hoped they hadn't heard.

This was a through train to the island and as it went round the loop taking it away from the main line, Sylvia began to recognise landmarks. Very soon they were rattling over the old bridge that spanned the narrow stretch of water separating the island from the mainland. Home, Sylvia thought, with a lift of her heart. She couldn't believe how ardently she had wanted to get away from the place when she was younger. Now she thought affectionately of childhood adventures with Daisy, cycling all over the island, helping Dad on the allotment, singing with the Co-op choir. After a brief stop at Queenborough, within minutes they were steaming into Sheerness station.

'Perhaps we'll bump into each other while you're here,' the soldier said, lifting Sylvia's case from the rack.

'Perhaps,' she said, smiling and thanking him. They handed in their tickets and the soldier hefted his kitbag onto his shoulder and strode off towards the Garrison.

Sylvia stood for a moment outside the station breathing in the sea air before turning right and making her way along the crowded High Street. She hoped she wouldn't see anyone she knew, anxious to get home to her family, although she hadn't let them know she was coming and, as it was mid-afternoon they might all still be at work. She'd go in the back way – they never locked the back door.

She walked up the alley leading to the long, narrow back garden and opened the gate. The chickens scratched in their run, lettuces grew alongside the path and tomato plants climbed up a row of canes. Dad's been busy, Sylvia thought with a smile.

To her surprise, she saw Daisy through the kitchen window, sitting at the table and writing. She looked up when she heard the back door open, leaping up with a squeal of surprise. 'Sylvia. What are you doing here? I was just writing to you. Why didn't you tell us...?' The words tumbled out, not giving Sylvia a chance to speak.

'I only knew myself yesterday, didn't have time to write.' Sylvia put her case down and took off her cap and overcoat, hanging them on a hook behind the door. She looked round the cosy kitchen, pleased that nothing had changed.

'Where is everybody?' she asked, sinking into her father's old armchair in front of the range.

'Dad's over the allotment – where else? And Mum's at the WVS.'

'What about Jimmy? Off getting into mischief as usual?'

Daisy laughed. 'You wouldn't know him – he's so grown up. I told you he'd joined the Home Guard with Dad. But he wants to join the merchant navy when he's seventeen. Not long to go now.'

'I bet Mum's not happy about that,' Sylvia said.

'She's hoping the war will be over before he goes.' Daisy gathered up her writing things and put them on the dresser. 'I haven't even made you a cup of tea. Take your things up and then we can sit down, and you can tell me all your news.'

'Not much to tell really,' Sylvia said, picking up her case and walking slowly upstairs to their old bedroom. They had shared it all their lives until she'd joined the WAAFs. It was very neat and tidy – just like Daisy, she thought. Sylvia had always been scatterbrained, and she recalled their squabbles over her leaving her things strewn all over the room. Life in the WAAFs had taught her to be a bit more organised. No more squabbles, she thought with a smile.

She went downstairs to be greeted by an enveloping hug and something between a laugh and sob. Mum was home. 'Sylvia, love,' she said. 'You should have let us know.' Dora Bishop turned to her other daughter. 'Haven't you even made her a cup of tea?'

'Just doing it, Mum,' Daisy said.

'What are you doing home? Is everything all right? You look a bit peaky, love.' Without giving

Sylvia a chance to answer, Dora pushed her towards the only armchair in the room – Dad's chair. 'Sit down, love, and tell us your news. You wouldn't believe what's been happening here.' She rattled on, bustling around, taking the tray from Daisy and pouring the tea.

Sylvia grinned and pulled a face at her sister behind their mother's back. She sat back and smiled contentedly. Home – just like old times.

When they were all seated, Daisy said, 'Now then, we need to hear all your news.'

'Not much to tell really. Same old boring stuff at work. They've given me a week's leave and I couldn't wait to see you all.' How could she tell them it was sick leave? They'd only worry.

'I thought you might bring that young man home with you,' Dora said.

'What young man?'

'You said you'd met someone in your last letter.'

Sylvia tried to sound nonchalant. 'Oh, him. No, he's no one special. Just a work colleague.'

'That's not the impression I got,' Dora said.

Sylvia shook her head and picked up her handbag to distract her mother. 'I've got something to show you.' She pulled out the spectacle case and opened it. 'I've got to wear specs – just for reading and paperwork.' She put them on and grinned at Daisy. 'What do you think?'

'You look a proper Miss Prim,' her sister said.

'Don't tease her, Daisy. I think they suit her – like that film star, what's her name?' Dora thought for a minute. 'Oh, you know, can't think at the minute.'

The two girls shook their heads, grinning. Dora was a keen picturegoer but could seldom remember the names of the stars or the titles of the films.

'Oh, well. Doesn't matter. Anyway, Dad'll be home in a minute. Best get the tea ready.'

'I'll help,' Sylvia said. 'Better change out of my uniform first.'

'Oh, no. Keep it on. Dad'll want to see how smart you are.'

Stan came in carrying a bag of potatoes and carrots with Jimmy close behind. By the time the hugs and emotional greetings were dealt with, Dora had the meal on the table – sausages and mash with thick onion gravy.

'Lovely – home cooking,' Sylvia said.

'Don't they feed you at that place then?' Stan asked.

'They do, but it's not the same. It must be hard cooking for so many. There's hundreds of us on station.'

'I thought you'd get better grub being an officer,' Stan said.

'You'd think so but we daren't complain. We'd only be reminded there's a war on,' Sylvia said with a laugh.

Jimmy devoured his meal in record time, talking all the time, asking questions about Sylvia's work. 'What planes have you got - bombers? Do you see them loading the bombs?'

'I'm not in Bomber Command anymore. Where I am now isn't an operational station. No aircraft.'

'No planes?' His face fell. 'How can it be an RAF station with no planes?'

'It's admin,' Sylvia said, 'where they plan the raids and such. I don't have anything to do with that – it's the job of the higher ups.'

'But you're an officer,' he protested. 'You must be doing something exciting.'

'Just shorthand and typing – like I did in the solicitor's office before I joined up.'

'Boring,' Jimmy said, turning to his mother. 'Can I leave the table?'

Dora nodded and he scrambled down and rushed out of the room.

Sylvia laughed. 'I thought you said he's grown up. He hasn't really changed, has he?'

'Never still for a minute,' Stan said. 'But he's a good lad, a credit to the Home Guard. I expect you two girls will be off out too, dancing or pictures.'

'Not me. I'm tired with all that travelling. I think I'll have an early night.' Sylvia was feeling a bit overwhelmed surrounded by her family and needed some time to think. It was hard too, keeping up the pretence that her work was mundane office work.

'Me too,' Daisy said. 'I'm on earlies tomorrow.'

They helped their mother clear away and wash up and Sylvia realised how much she had missed her family, even the ordinary domestic chores which she so hated before she went away. She couldn't picture Hugh in this setting. Perhaps she should try to forget him, hard as it would be.

They said goodnight to their parents and went upstairs, Sylvia impatient to talk to her sister in private. There was so much to say, stuff that couldn't be shared in letters. She was surprised that their mother hadn't pursued the question of her 'young man'.

Once they were in bed, propped up on pillows, Daisy looked across at her and said, 'Well?'

'All right.' She sighed. 'I don't know where to begin.'

'You told Mum he was no one special but you do talk about him in your letters. And didn't you actually use the word 'love'?'

Sylvia took a deep breath. 'His name's Hugh and he's a wing commander. He was my boss at the last place. I really liked him then, but I didn't think it would come to anything especially when he told me he was being posted away. I couldn't believe it when he put in a word for me to have officer training and work with him at the new place.'

'He must like you too, then?' She paused and gave Sylvia a hard look. 'Hey, it's not that married officer you mentioned in your letter?'

Sylvia nodded. Better not mention the children, she thought.

'What?' Daisy's voice rose. 'You mean to tell me you're having an affair with a married man?'

'Shush. They'll hear. Anyway, it's not an affair. We haven't...'

'I should hope not.' Daisy said sharply. She leaned across and took her sister's hand. 'I thought you learnt your lesson with that Roland chap.'

'Don't judge me, Dais. Besides, Roland's in the past. It didn't take long for me to realise what a rat he was. But this is different.' She covered her face with her hands. 'I know it's wrong, but Daisy – I love him, really love him. He's so different from the lads I've been out with before. It's all right going dancing and having a drink and a laugh. But they're just boys wanting a good time before they go off to fight.'

'What's so special about this Hugh then – apart from being married I mean.'

'It's hard to say. I started off just liking him, admiring him I suppose. But then, as I go to know him my feelings changed.'

Daisy nodded. 'I do understand. That's what it was like for me and Chris. I couldn't help myself and I felt bad about poor Bob.' She leaned back against her pillow. 'So, what are you going to do about it?'

'He says he'll get a divorce.'

'That's what they all say,' Daisy scoffed.

'He's not like that. He means it.'

'Mum'll go mad. You won't be able to come home if you get mixed up in a scandal.'

'It doesn't have to be a scandal. He's got grounds for divorce.'

'As far as Mum's concerned it *will* be a scandal. How will she hold her head up at the Women's Guild or the WVS?'

'Do you think I haven't thought of that? Anyway, I've decided. When I get back, I'm going to ask for a posting. Hopefully, I'll be able to forget him if I don't see him every day.'

'It's probably the right thing to do, Syl.'

'It's all right for you. You've got Chris, and lucky for you, Mum and Dad approve. Even Bob has forgiven you for throwing him over.'

Daisy sighed. 'I still feel bad about Bob, but I couldn't help how I felt about Chris.'

'And I can't help how I feel about Hugh. Don't you understand?' A sob caught in Sylvia's throat.

'I do – I really do. And I'm sorry you're in such a pickle. I just don't want you to get hurt.'

'I'm hurting already. I kept telling myself just seeing him and working with him was enough, but it's not.' Sylvia threw herself back on her pillow. 'Oh, Dais, what am I to do?'

'I think you know the answer to that.' Daisy leaned over and switched off the bedside lamp.

***

Sylvia awoke next morning blurry-eyed and headachy from too little sleep. Daisy was already up, and she remembered her sister was on early shift. She could hear voices downstairs and she pulled on her dressing gown and went to join her family. Her father and Jimmy were in their Home Guard uniforms, Jimmy cramming a slice of toast into his mouth.

Dora bustled round clearing the table and glanced up as Sylvia entered the room. 'I thought you deserved a lie in,' she said. 'Do you want some breakfast?'

'It's all right, Mum. I'll get it.'

'There's some porridge on the stove and you can have some toast if you like.'

'I don't want to eat all your rations,' Sylvia said.

'Don't talk daft, girl.'

'Well, I've brought my ration book – and I've got some points to spare.'

'I'm going shopping after I've cleared up. Come with me if you've got no plans.'

'We're off,' Stan said. 'Come on, Jimmy – finish that toast. We don't want to be late.'

'See you later Mum, Sis.' Jimmy crammed the last morsel of toast into his mouth, grabbed his haversack and followed Stan out of the door.

Sylvia ladled some porridge into a bowl and added a little milk. 'What time will Daisy be home?' she asked.

'Just after two.'

'I might go to meet her then.'

After breakfast Sylvia and her mother walked into town, meeting several neighbours on the way. Everyone who greeted them admired Sylvia's uniform and she was forced to smile and say how well she was doing in the WAAFs while her mother nodded and smiled proudly.

The shopping took most of the morning and Sylvia thought how hard it was for her mother having to queue for everything. It also made her realise how spoilt she had become since joining the WAAFs. She never had to worry about where her meals came from – not to mention no cooking or washing up.

Back home after a sandwich lunch Dora went off to her Women's Guild meeting. She asked Sylvia to come with her, but she declined, saying she wanted to take a walk along the seafront and then to meet Daisy from work.

'You won't get far,' Dora warned. 'Most of the front's closed off with barbed wire. There's gun emplacements on the jetty and along by the old fairground.'

'Never mind. I just want some fresh air. I spend so long sitting in crowded offices, pounding my typewriter.' How easily the lies came – and how she wished she could boast about the important work she was doing.

She put on her great coat and cap for, as usual on the island, a chilly wind blew off the sea.

She went out the back way and was walking down the garden path when Mrs Gardner, the next door neighbour popped her head over the wall. 'Oh, Sylvia, so good to see you home,' she said.

Sylvia asked after Bob.

'Last I heard he was all right. He's out in Egypt or somewhere – never quite sure. They're not allowed to say much.'

'I was so sorry to hear that he and Daisy had broken up. How did he take it?'

'Well, as you know, they'd been together ever since they were just children really. We all expected...' She paused. 'Well, never mind. They were too young really. A shame. I'm so fond of Daisy. Still, these things happen...'

Sylvia nodded. 'Perhaps he'll meet someone else.'

'He hinted that there was someone – a girl he met over in France. But I can't see anything coming of that.'

'A French girl?'

'He was nearly captured by the Germans and she helped him get away. He says he's going back to find her after the war.'

'Let's hope he gets lucky,' Sylvia said.

Mrs Gardner nodded thoughtfully, then she smiled at Sylvia. 'And what about you? Will you be bringing a young man home to meet Mum and Dad?'

'No fear. I'm far too busy for romance.' She forced a laugh, then glanced at her watch. 'Oh, dear, better get on. I'm meeting Daisy from work.'

The week seemed to go slowly, and Sylvia longed to be back at Medmenham doing the job she was so good at. Nice as it was to spend time with her family, after a while they had little to talk about. She went to the pictures with Daisy and a couple of her friends, but she couldn't concentrate on the film.

At the end of the week, as she got ready to catch her train, Dora paused in helping her to pack. Daisy had left for work early and Sylvia had already said her farewells to her and the rest of the family.

'You're looking much better than when you arrived. All that sea air must be good for you,' Dora said.

'I'm feeling better, Mum. I was just tired, needed a break.'

'We'll miss you, love.' She gave her daughter a hug. 'Oh, when will this bloody war be over and we can go back to normal?'

'Mum, it's not like you to swear.' Sylvia was a bit shocked.

'It's enough to make anyone swear. Rationing, families split up, you miles away and Jimmy going away soon.'

'He can't go yet, surely he's not old enough.'

'Merchant navy – he's already applied.'

'Daisy said he was keen but...'

'I can't stop him. He'll have to go for training first so maybe it'll all be over before he goes to sea.'

'Let's hope so,' Sylvia said. But in her heart, she knew the war would not end any time soon. There was the fear of these new rockets hanging over them – although the general public did not know about them – yet. If they couldn't find the factories and bomb them, who knew what would happen. The thought made Sylvia even more impatient to get back to work.

She hugged her mother back, then looked at her watch. 'I must go if I want to get that train.'

'I'll come and see you off.'

They were quiet on the walk to the station, each engrossed in their own thoughts. The train was in, steam gently hissing, the driver standing alongside the engine. Sylvia got in the first carriage and put her case and coat on the rack. This time she had the carriage to herself, no flirty servicemen to fend off.

She leaned out of the window and kissed her mother's cheek, held onto her hand until the whistle blew and the train began to move. She waved until the railway line curved and the station became a small dot in the distance.

She leaned back in her seat and sighed. She was going to miss them all of course, but inside she felt a little thrill of excitement. It wasn't just the thought of seeing Hugh again, but eagerness to get back to her work. The two emotions warred within her and she began to question whether she could stick to her resolve and ask for a posting away from Hugh and the temptation she would face if she saw too much of him. On the other hand, her job was so important to her that she couldn't bear the thought of being sent elsewhere and not being involved in any exciting developments.

***

Daisy sat at her office desk, going through the NAAFI store inventory. She wished she had been able to see Sylvia off at the station, but she had to admit, she felt a bit relieved that her sister's leave was over. It had been a strain trying to keep quiet about Sylvia's relationship with Hugh Smythe. And she was getting fed up with her going on about him. She hadn't seemed interested in what was happening in Daisy's life, her constant anxiety about Chris. It was all, 'what shall I do? I can't give him up,' and Daisy just didn't know how to answer her.

One evening they listened to the wireless while their parents were out and they had started dancing round the kitchen like they used to. The tune had changed and Bing Crosby began to sing, *'If I didn't care, why would I feel this way'*, and Daisy saw to her consternation that tears slid down Sylvia's cheeks. She'd brushed them away and tried to laugh it off, but Daisy knew she had been thinking about Hugh and the impossible situation they were in. She'd tried to comfort her sister but what could she say?

It wasn't that she disapproved, she told herself now. No one could help falling in love, as she learned when she was struggling over her feelings for Chris, despite being promised to Bob. But a married man! Mum would go mad if she ever got an inkling of what was going on. Sylvia swore that nothing had happened and Daisy believed her. But if they carried on seeing each other, who knew where it would lead?

She tried to concentrate on her work and put it out of her mind. It wasn't her problem. Sylvia, being Sylvia, would go her own way as she always had. But Daisy sensed a change in her sister on this visit. What had happened to the carefree girl who only thought of dancing and having fun? It wasn't just her feelings for Hugh. She seemed more serious now, keen to get back to her work, much to Daisy's surprise.

For the first time it occurred to her that perhaps her sister wasn't just an ordinary typist. She'd hated working in the solicitor's office before the war and couldn't wait to join up and do something more exciting. A thought struck her. Perhaps she was doing something secret. Daisy couldn't imagine what and was a bit peeved that her sister hadn't confided in her. Hadn't they always told each other everything?

Chapter Thirteen

Hugh had just finished his shift and was on the way to his quarters when he bumped into Squadron Leader Bill James.

'Coming for a drink?' he asked.

Hugh hesitated. He wasn't in the mood for company, the letter from Margaret still ran round in his head. While he'd been at work, he'd been able to put it out of his mind.

Before he could make an excuse, Bill said, 'Come on. You need to relax a bit more.'

'All right, just a quick one.'

When they were settled in the mess, beer tankards in front of them, Bill said, 'You look as if something's on your mind. Care to tell me about it?'

Hugh took a sip of his drink. 'It's just the work, you know. There's a lot going on over there and we need to get to the bottom of it.'

'I thought you were working on that big bombing raid last week. A success, I heard. The info you gave must have helped.'

Hugh sighed. 'Yes, but so many men were lost. Anyway, I'm back working with Babs and her team.'

Bill grinned. 'Ah, and that little blonde WAAF – Sylvia. I knew you were sweet on her. Better take care, old man.'

'Don't talk soft. There's nothing going on. Besides, she's not here. I think she might have been posted elsewhere.' Hugh tried to sound offhand, but he didn't think Bill was deceived.

He was worried about Sylvia and hoped that Bill might know what had happened to her, but he daren't ask. He hadn't seen her for over a week and she said she might ask for a posting. But surely she would have spoken to him before she left.

They drank their beer, chatting about the raid on the German dams which was now common knowledge since it had been reported on the wireless. Of course, the part their station played was still a secret from the rest of the population.

The door opened and Jane came in with Julia and Iris. Bill waved to them and beckoned them over. He ordered more drinks and when they were settled at the table he asked, 'What's happened to your friend – you know, my stage assistant ASO Bishop? Haven't seen her around lately.'

'Why do you want to know?' Iris asked.

'Jealous are you?' Bill teased.

'Certainly not! I thought you might be planning another entertainment.'

Bill laughed. 'No. Too busy at the moment.'

'Well, if you are, she won't be able to help. She's on sick leave,' Julia said.

Hugh smothered a gasp, pretending to cough and Bill glanced sharply at him. He turned to Iris. 'Nothing serious I hope.'

'She'll be back soon. Julia had a letter yesterday.' She drained her glass. 'Enough talking about other women. I need another drink.'

Bill gathered up the glasses. 'What about you, old boy?'

'No thanks. I'm off. Letters to write.'

Outside, Hugh took a deep breath. She was all right – and she was coming back. He had to see her. But first he must answer Margaret's letter.

***

152

Sylvia walked out of the station, into the spring sunshine, her coat over her arm. It was early evening and still quite warm. After that cold wind off the North Sea which always seemed present in her home-town, it was good to feel the sun on her face. She walked to the bus stop, hoping she wouldn't have to wait too long. Now that her leave was over, she couldn't wait to get back on duty and immerse herself in the fascinating world of photo intelligence.

She hoped she would still be in Babs's section, although it was possible that in her absence her place had been filled by someone else. They enjoyed working together and bouncing ideas off each other. Babs always gave credit where it was due, although Sylvia knew that she was no match for the older woman when it came to deciphering the often-blurred images.

It was supper time when she reached her billet and the hut was empty, her colleagues either on shift or eating. She unpacked before going to join them, taking a deep breath before opening the door to the mess. She wasn't ready to see Hugh yet, especially in a crowded mess hall. She still hadn't made up her mind what she was going to say to him.

To her relief there was no sign of him, and she smiled and waved to her friends, who were sitting with Bill James. There was a chorus of welcome and it was good to know she had been missed.

'Have you eaten?' Jane asked.

'I had something on the train, Mum packed me some sandwiches. I'll just have a drink.'

'Had a good leave?' Iris asked.

Sylvia nodded. 'Good to see my family.'

She joined them at the table and Julia leaned over and whispered, 'You've just missed him.'

Sylvia ignored her and turned to Jane. 'My brother's talking about joining the merchant navy. Needless to say, my mother's not keen on the idea.'

Bill came back with the drinks and after greeting Sylvia, asked what she wanted.

'It's OK. I'll get it,' she said.

Going up to the bar gave her time to compose herself. She was furious with Julia and hoped none of the others had overheard. Was she just teasing, or had she seen them together and drawn her own conclusions? Sylvia dreaded being found out. It wasn't just her reputation that would suffer but her career. And that was important to her. And what about Hugh? An extra-marital affair could ruin his career too and, although things hadn't gone that far, the suspicion would be enough.

By the time she returned to the table she had calmed down. Julia was her friend and Sylvia was sure she could be trusted not to gossip.

The girls resumed their conversation and Sylvia retreated into her own thoughts. It was hard to join in the light-hearted chatter with so much on her mind. She finished her drink and stood up. 'Better go and report for duty,' she said.

As she walked across to the main building, she heard her name called and turned round with her heart racing. Hugh caught up with her and said, 'I'm so glad you're back. They said you were on sick leave but you're looking better.'

'I'm all right now,' she said, starting to walk away.

He caught her arm. 'I must talk to you - alone.'

'Hugh. We agreed we can't be seen together. It's no good...' A sob choked in her throat. 'I must report that I'm back. I don't even know what section I'm in now.'

'I think you're still with Babs.' He stepped away from her as two officers came into view engrossed in conversation. They saluted and walked past.

When they were out of sight, Hugh reached for her hand and said, 'Sylvia, please, just for a few minutes. It's important.'

Her resolve almost left her. There was nothing she wanted more than to be with him, to feel his arms around her, his lips on hers. But she must be strong – for both of them.

'I'm sorry, Hugh. Please, let me go.' She pulled away and walked off, her head high.

***

Hugh stood and watched until she entered the main building, his chest tight, hands clenched at his sides. She was right, of course. He wanted her so badly, but he couldn't be responsible for ruining her career, her reputation, her life. Perhaps in the future, after the war was over, it would be different. But for now, he must stay away from her, hard as that would be. It would be disastrous for both of them if their love for each other ever became public.

He put his hand in his pocket and pulled out an envelope – the reply to Margaret's letter. He had been on his way to the post box at the end of the drive when he'd spotted Sylvia and given in to the impulse to speak to her.

Margaret's words were seared into his brain and he longed to share them with Sylvia. Just a brief note with the last news he had expected.

'I want a divorce. You must give me grounds. You must agree that things are not right between us. I don't want a scandal. I'm sure we can be civilised about this.'

No mention of the boys or custody. No real reasons. On first reading he had been ecstatic. But given time to digest the stark message he had second thoughts.

She wanted him to divorce her, not the other way round. He would have to give proof of adultery. She must know that he had never given her grounds. In fact, he could probably divorce her because of her drinking and behaviour when she stayed here back in

155

the autumn. He was pretty sure she hadn't stopped at flirting with the men she'd met while staying at the pub. And back in Oban with the boys away at school, who knew what she'd been up to?

He'd sat down and dashed off a letter, telling her in no uncertain terms that she had no grounds for divorcing him and that if it came to it, he would cite her behaviour. He'd mentioned his sons. Did she not care how it would affect them?

He reached the post box but hesitated before posting. He shouldn't have been so hasty, should have thought things through. Yes, he wanted to be free of her, free to court Sylvia openly. But knowing Margaret, she would become angry and abusive. And if she got the slightest inkling of his deep feelings for another woman, well – the old saying was true, 'hell hath no fury...'

Instead of posting the letter, he tore it in two, then again. He stuffed the pieces in his pocket and walked back to his quarters. This couldn't be done in a letter. He'd have to talk to her face to face. But there was no chance of getting leave at the moment. His superiors would never allow it at this critical stage of the war.

**

Sylvia knew she'd done the right thing by walking away but now she regretted her hasty action and wished she'd agreed to meet Hugh to tell him her decision. She was determined there would be no more meetings in quiet pubs or walks along the riverbank. She would talk to him as a colleague when they were at work and, if they happened to meet in the mess, she would sit with him. It would be hard to act just as colleagues and friends, but she knew she could do it.

She was worried about him. He hadn't seemed his usual self during their brief exchange and she wondered if there was something on his mind. It must be something to do with their work, she told herself. Perhaps he would tell her when they were next on duty together.

She was pleased when she reported for duty to hear that, as Hugh had told her, she was still in the same section as Babs. They got on so well together and, when they were engrossed in their work, Sylvia found she could put her personal worries to one side. It was only when she was trying to sleep that she couldn't stop thinking about Hugh, going over their brief meetings in her mind, savouring each touch of his hand, the feel of his lips on hers.

She had just finished a long shift and a particularly intense session staring into her stereoscope and was deep in thought as she entered Hut Six. She had wanted to stay on until she had solved the problem, but Babs had insisted she go off duty.

'You've just come back from sick leave. We don't want you getting ill again,' she said.

'I'm fine,' Sylvia protested. 'Please let me stay.'

'Go – now,' Babs insisted.

Sylvia sighed and took her glasses off, putting them in their case.

The hut was filled with chatter as the girls got ready to go out. Sylvia went over to her bed and sat down, rubbing her eyes. The glasses helped but she still got headaches after a long shift. All she wanted was a long soak and an early night.

'You coming with us, Syl?' Julia's voice snapped her to attention.

She shook her head.

'Come on. We're going to a dance in Reading. The lads are back from training and picking us up so no need to get the bus.'

'I don't feel like dancing.'

'Harry will be pleased to see you.'

'I don't care.'

Julia sat beside her and lowered her voice. 'Look, Syl, I know there's something on your mind and I know what it is but staying in and brooding won't help. Besides, you don't want Marion or her cronies getting suspicious. Come with us. You might even enjoy yourself.'

Sylvia sighed and stood up. 'All right, you win. Just let me get ready.'

'No time. They'll be here soon. Just powder your nose and put on a bit of lipstick.'

Sylvia hastily complied. So much for the hot bath, she thought. She turned to Julia. 'Well?'

'You'll do.' Julia took her arm and they followed Jane and Iris outside.

'Thank goodness Marion's working tonight,' Julia said. 'I don't want her cramping my style.'

The others laughed.

Outside the gates, a lorry waited with its engine idling and an army officer standing nearby.

'Come on girls,' he called. 'We're wasting dancing time.'

'Evening, Harry. Guess who's with us.' Julia pulled Sylvia forward.

'Sylvia – nice to see you. Where have you been hiding yourself?'

Before she could reply, Jane said, 'She's been on sick leave.'

'You're OK now, I hope. Anyway, it's good to see you.' He turned to the group of girls. 'Now, who's going to sit beside me?'

'Go on, Syl. We'll go in the back.' Julia grabbed the tailgate of the lorry and eager hands reached out to pull her inside. Jane and Iris followed.

Harry grinned and opened the passenger door. 'Up you go,' he said.

Sylvia climbed in beside him, wondering if Julia had engineered this. No doubt she hoped it would take her mind off Hugh. But although she enjoyed Harry's company, that was all. She had made it plain that she was spoken for and didn't want him getting any ideas.

Still, she tried to be sociable. 'How did the training go?' she asked.

'Cold, muddy and uncomfortable,' Harry said. 'Still, it'll probably be worse where we're going.'

Sylvia didn't know what to say but she was saved from having to reply when the lorry pulled up outside the dance hall. They all climbed out and rushed inside, chatting and laughing. Music spilled out and the place was full of couples swinging and jiving.

Harry didn't give Sylvia time to protest but pulled her into his arms and swung her round. 'I've been waiting for this for ages,' he said.

'Dancing?'

'Yes – with you,' he replied.

'Harry, please. I told you I have a boyfriend.'

'But he's not here and I am. No harm in having a bit of fun.'

'As long as you understand...'

'Yes, of course. Stop worrying and enjoy the dance.'

After a while, the music and the atmosphere enveloped her, and she began to enjoy herself in spite of her earlier reluctance.

She found herself laughing at silly jokes and drinking too much and when it was time to leave, she agreed that it had been a good evening. Harry hadn't made a nuisance of himself and she unbent sufficiently to kiss him on the cheek when she said goodnight.

'We're off in a few days,' he said. 'You will write, won't you?'

'I promise – but friends only.'

'I suppose so.'

The lorry deposited them at the gate to RAF Medmenham and the giggling group of WAAFs sobered up sufficiently to show their passes and

159

salute the guard before making their way unsteadily up the drive.

'There, I told you it would do you good to get out,' Julia said as they got ready for bed.

'All right, bossyboots. You're right. It was fun.' Sylvia was forced to agree.

'You like Harry, don't you?'

'Yes, but...' Sylvia shrugged.

'I know. You've only got eyes for you know who.'

'Hush, Julia.' Sylvia looked round the hut but the other two were already in bed. 'Please, don't say anything. Besides, there's nothing going on.'

'I believe you, thousands wouldn't.' Julia said. 'But I'm worried about you.'

'You needn't be.'

'Good. I'm pleased you're being sensible. You must come out with us more often. It was good to get a glimpse of the old Sylvia tonight.'

'What do you mean?'

'When we first met, back in training in Norfolk, you were so carefree and full of fun, always up for a night on the tiles. But you changed, got more serious.'

'It's the work we're doing, that's all.'

'If you say so.' Julia climbed into bed.

'Goodnight.'

Soon they were all asleep, all except Sylvia who stared into the dark, her eyes wet. During that last slow dance when Harry pulled her close she almost pushed him away. Instead she gave herself up to the music, imagining herself in Hugh's arms. Julia had called her sensible but if she was, she'd agree to be Harry's girl. But, nice as he was, he could never capture her heart in the way Hugh had.

***

It was a few days later and Hugh had still not answered Margaret's letter. He knew he couldn't put it off for much longer. Margaret was quite capable of

160

jumping on a train and turning up here, making a scene. He couldn't allow that to happen. He sat at a table in the mess, nursing a glass of beer, the thoughts churning around in his head. He looked at his watch. Have to be back on duty soon and still no letter written.

The door opened and Bill came in, ordered his drink and came to sit at Hugh's table.

'Cheer up, mate.'

Hugh took a drink and said, 'Nothing to be cheerful about.'

'You're not still mooning after SO Bishop, I hope. I told, you. There's no future in it and you'll land yourself in trouble.'

'You're right. And, no I am not mooning after her as you put it. There's something else on my mind.'

'To do with the job?' Bill asked. 'I know we're not supposed to talk about it but...'

'Of course not.' Hugh finished his pint and set the glass down. Taking a deep breath, he said, 'It's my wife.'

'What's she been up to then?'

Hugh looked at him sharply. Everyone on the camp must know about Margaret's behaviour when she stayed here a few months ago. But Bill wasn't grinning or giving one of those knowing looks like his colleagues had recently.

'She wants a divorce,' he said bluntly.

'Look, you don't have to tell me anything. It's none of my business.'

'Well, you're my friend and I need to talk to someone. I don't know what to do.' Hugh looked down at the table, fiddling with his empty glass.

'I can't tell you what to do but if I was in your situation, I'd give her what she wants.'

'What do you mean – my situation?'

'You know very well what I mean.' Bill looked round and lowered his voice. 'Sylvia Bishop.'

Hugh raised his hand to protest but Bill carried on. 'I know you've fallen for her. And, knowing you, it's not just a fling you're after. And from what I know of her she isn't the type either.'

Hugh nodded miserably. 'When I got Margaret's letter, I was so relieved. She wanted a divorce and I would be free to court Sylvia. But then I thought about it.'

'It seems straightforward to me. What's the problem?'

'Knowing Margaret, I'm sure she won't give me grounds even if she has been playing around, which I strongly suspect she has. She will expect me to supply the evidence.'

'Simple enough. Everyone's doing it. Hotel bill, photos, all done.'

'I can't do that to Sylvia.' Hugh was horrified.

'No, of course you can't. That's not what I meant. Find a willing floozy and make sure you're seen." Bill paused for a moment to let it sink in.

Shocked, Hugh shook his head. 'I can't do that. No. There must be another way.'

'Yes, there is. You divorce Margaret. Get evidence against her.'

'I would but she's not the only one I have to think of – there's the boys. I can't let them be hurt.'

'You're right of course.' Bill picked up their glasses. 'Want a refill?

'No thanks. I should be going. Can't sit here drinking all day. Duty calls.' He stood up. 'Thanks for listening.'

'Thanks for confiding in me, mate. Don't do anything hasty.'

'I won't.' Hugh strode out of the mess and hurried across to the main house.

A few days later, he still hadn't written to Margaret, and he was going out of his mind, the thoughts churning around in his head. Only at work could he push it all to one side. There was so much going on and excitement was building as the significance of the weird aircraft and the surrounding installations became clearer.

It was with a feeling of satisfaction that he finished his shift and strode across to the mess. His work was the balm which kept unwelcome thoughts at bay.

He collected his food and joined Bill at his table, hoping his friend would not mention Sylvia and his troubled love life.

But after a few idle comments, Bill said, 'I've been thinking.'

'What about?'

'Divorce.'

'No Bill, I don't want to talk about it.' He sighed. 'I'll have to let Margaret have her way somehow or other.'

'That's what I've been thinking about. Listen, Hugh, I've remembered someone from home. His wife left him, went off with the gardener, can you believe. Anyway, after she'd been gone a couple of years, he divorced her, no fuss, no scandal.'

'What's that got to do with me and...?' Hugh couldn't bring himself to mention Sylvia's name.

'Matrimonial Causes Act 1937.' Bill leaned across. 'It means couples can divorce after two years' separation – desertion.'

'But Margaret hasn't left me.'

'She's not here, though is she?' Bill said. 'All you have to do is tell her to stay away until the two years is up, then you'll both be free.'

'I don't think she'll agree to that. And what about the boys?'

'It won't affect them much, will it? They're away at boarding school, so you don't see them much anyway.'

'I doubt they'd recognise me now – it's been so long.' Hugh pushed his plate away. He couldn't eat.

'Well, it was just a thought, mate. Only trying to help.'

'I know – and thanks. I'll think about it.' He stood up. 'I'll see you later.'

He got the car out and drove to Henley, parking in the market-place. A long walk would do him good and give him time to think. He walked down towards the river, remembering those magic hours with Sylvia back in the autumn. He strode along the path, head down, deep in thought, hardly noticing the fresh green of spring, the swans and their goslings gliding through the water. A shout from the across the river made him look up and he smiled at the sight of a group of boys fishing. One of them had caught something and they were crowding round exclaiming over the size of the fish. The lads were a little older than his sons, but he thought with a pang of Peter and Bobby. Would he ever get the chance to take them fishing? He wrote regularly to them and they wrote back but it wasn't the same.

If he took Bill's advice and didn't see Margaret for two years, would he be able to have contact with the boys? He couldn't bear the thought of not seeing them. It was hard enough now but he could at least blame the war. If he went ahead with the separation, he would only have himself to blame if he became estranged from his sons.

He turned and went back to the car, no decision made. He must talk to Sylvia. Whatever action he took, he must discuss it with her and make sure she wasn't hurt in any way.

Chapter Fourteen

Sylvia looked at dozens of photos this morning, finding nothing of any great interest. She reached for another batch of prints, flexed her shoulders and bent her head over the stereoscope once more. Ah, this looks different, she thought. It was definitely a crater and there were other signs of bomb damage. So, the raid had been successful. She put the photo to one side and selected the next one from the pile. Disappointment flooded her. Despite the evidence of the first photo, she could see that the damage hadn't been as extensive as she'd first thought.

She picked up the prints and pushed her chair back. Babs must see these. She hurried across to Babs's work-station and waited while she finished a phone call.

'Something interesting?' Babs asked as she put the phone down.

'Worrying, more like,' Sylvia said, handing the prints over.

After studying both the pictures for a minute or two, Babs nodded. 'That crater looks like a direct hit. But going by the other photos, it's in the wrong place. They were a bit too far over.' She stood up. 'I'll take these through to the boss. Well spotted, Sylvia.'

Sylvia went back to her desk feeling pleased. So much of her work gained little recognition. Often, she didn't know if the notes she attached to the photos were helpful. Babs, however, was always ready to give credit where was due. Sylvia was thankful that she hadn't been moved to a different section on her return from leave.

She pulled another basket of prints towards her. As fast as she finished one batch another landed on her desk. More and more sorties were being flown every day, each aircraft bringing back rolls of film with sometimes up to five hundred exposures. It was demanding work.

Sylvia had been here for nearly a year and in that time the workload had increased so much that more and more personnel were joining the PI service. Hundreds of men and women from all the services, as well as civilians were crammed into the main house and scattered outbuildings. Newcomers had to be billeted in the village when the on-site accommodation ran out.

Sometimes the sheer scale of things could become overwhelming and, although Sylvia was oblivious of her surroundings while she was working, she found the constant stream of new faces difficult to cope with.

Today, she reached the end of her shift, hot and tired and longing for a bath. She hurried back to her hut, thankful that she did not encounter anyone. The pleasure she'd felt at Babs's praise evaporated and the ever present problem of her relationship with Hugh intruded, as it always did apart from when she was engrossed in her work. She had managed to avoid him in the weeks since her return from leave and only spoken briefly to him when she saw him in the mess. He had tried several times to waylay her, saying he must talk to her. But she brushed him off, saying it was no good. There was no future for them. It was easy to be strong when she didn't see him, but she knew that if she gave in to his pleas to see her alone, she would not be able to resist.

To her relief there was no one in the hut and she sank down on her bed, slipping her shoes off and wriggling her toes. The weather had turned hot and she longed to exchange her regulation shoes for sandals. She sighed, remembering paddling in the sea at home and walking barefoot along the sea wall. Would those carefree days ever come again?

No good brooding, she told herself, better have that bath and then get over to the mess for some food, unappetising as it usually was. As her mother always said when she'd picked at her food, 'if you're really hungry, you'll eat it.'

The bath did little to raise her spirits, the water tepid and coming out of the taps in a frustrating dribble. She dried herself and dressed, returning to the hut to find Julia just back from the mess.

'If you're thinking of going for food, don't bother. They said it was stew, but it was nothing like any stew I've ever eaten.' Julia sat down on the bed with a thump. 'Stew! How could they serve stuff like that on such a hot day?'

'I'll force myself to eat it. I'm starving.'

'No need. I've got some goodies in my locker. I was saving them but I'm happy to share.' She rummaged in the locker and brought out a packet of crackers and a small square of cheese. 'Good old Mum. Here, have some.'

'I can't take your stuff,' Sylvia protested.

'There's plenty here. Not much cheese but I've got biscuits too.' She rummaged again and produced a packet of digestive biscuits.

'How does she manage to send you food? This looks like a whole week's cheese ration.'

Julia tapped her finger alongside her nose. 'Don't ask. Mum won't tell me. But I have an uncle in the grocery trade. Draw your own conclusions. Don't tell anyone, will you?''

Sylvia was shocked. Must be the Black Market, she thought, remembering how Daisy helped to bring a black marketeer to justice a couple of years ago. She felt a bit guilty but said nothing and took a bite of cracker and a small morsel of cheese. Like Mum said, 'if you're hungry you'll eat anything'.

Putting her qualms aside, she helped Julia polish off the cheese and crackers, followed by a couple of digestive biscuits. Just in time, she thought, as the door banged open and the other occupants of the hut entered.

Julia hastily swept the crumbs and packaging into the wastepaper basket. 'Busy day, girls?' she asked.

'As usual,' Marion replied. 'Thank goodness we've got the rest of the day off. We're going to play tennis – care to join us?'

'Much too hot,' Julia said. 'We're going over to the mess for a cup of tea.'

They strolled across the grass, Julia enthusing about a new conquest, a Naval Lieutenant.

'Is this one serious then?' Sylvia asked.

'Of course not. You know me.' Julia laughed, then turned to her friend, her face serious. 'What about you? Don't tell me – you're still stuck on the wingco.'

'Can't help it. I know it's silly and I should stick with Harry. But it's not fair, leading him on.' She sighed. 'If only Hugh wasn't married.'

'But he is, and I know you're not the type for an affair with a married man.'

'Let's not talk about it. Come on, I'm dying for that cup of tea.' She strode on ahead.

After tea they went across to the tennis courts and sat on the grass watching their friends who were playing doubles.

'How can they run around like that in this heat?' Julia asked, leaning back and chewing a piece of grass.

'They take it so seriously, especially Marion,' Sylvia replied.

'That's why I don't play with her. She hates being beaten. I just play for fun.'

'She got very cross with Jane the other day when she kept giggling and missing the ball.'

'I can never keep score,' Julia confessed. She stood up. 'Let's leave them to it. It's wearing me out just watching them.'

When they got back to Hut Six, Julia said, 'Coming out this evening?'

Sylvia shook her head.

'Do come. We don't have to be late back. I know it's early start in the morning.'

'I've got letters to write.'

'You're always writing letters. Oh, well, perhaps Jane will join me.'

Sylvia hadn't planned to answer Daisy's latest, but it was a good excuse. She took her writing case out from the locker and was surprised to see a piece of paper tucked inside. With a start she recognised the handwriting and hastily slipped it back in. Who had put it there? Not Hugh himself surely? Men, even high-ranking ones, were strictly forbidden to enter the female WAAFs' quarters. Then she remembered that she had taken her writing case in to lunch with her the other day, leaving it on the table while she went to fetch her food. He must have put the note inside then.

She looked round to make sure no one noticed her agitation. The other girls came in laughing and teasing each other after their game but they ignored her, agreeing to go to the pub with Julia.

'You not coming, Sylvia?' asked Iris.

'Too busy. Letters,' Sylvia said, holding up her fountain pen.

She waited until they'd gone out and gathered up her writing things. The heat had died down and it was pleasantly warm now. Sylvia found a quiet spot away from the huts and sat down on a bench under a tree. Only then did she withdraw the single sheet of paper from her writing case.

The note was brief. *'Dearest Sylvia – you know how I feel about you and I know you feel the same. Please don't keep avoiding me. There is a way we can be together. Please meet me to discuss it with you. I promise I will abide by any decision you make. I'll be by the main gate at 7 o'clock. I will be waiting. H'*

She read it twice, unsure how to reply. But she must hear him out. She couldn't think what he meant by them being together. Surely, he did not expect her to become his mistress. Well, she wouldn't know unless she talked to him.

She looked at her watch. Six thirty. No time for letter writing. She hurried across the grass and into her hut, pleased that the other girls had gone out. Her flushed cheeks would tell them something was up. She quickly tidied her hair and straightened the seams in her stockings. Smoothing down her skirt and uniform jacket, she put on her cap and marched down to the front gate.

There was no sign of the Alvis and she smiled at the guard by the gate, crossing the road to stand by the bus stop. She would wait five minutes and then go back to her billet. The guard had gone back into his little hut and she hoped he would not notice her getting into Hugh's car. She had been lucky so far. Julia had kept her promise not to gossip about Hugh and, apart from a bit of teasing about her 'crush' on the senior officer, her colleagues seemed unaware of her real feelings. Spending time with Harry had helped to allay any possible suspicion and Sylvia felt guilty for using him in this way. She salved her conscience by telling herself that Harry was quite aware that she wasn't serious about him. He fully believed that she was committed to someone else who was away fighting.

She looked at her watch and sighed. Hugh had obviously been delayed with some work problem or perhaps had changed his mind. She was about to cross the road when his car came out of the gate and stopped beside her. The top was down on this fine summer evening and Sylvia was nervous of getting in and being seen.

'Come on. I'll give you a lift,' Hugh said quite loudly, not that the guard could hear from this distance.

Sylvia hesitated and then, without a word, got in beside him. How she hated the necessity for this subterfuge. She felt unclean somehow as if everyone who saw them would get the wrong idea. But she hadn't done anything wrong and had nothing to be ashamed of – so far, she told herself.

'You're very quiet,' Hugh said as they drove through the village and out on to the main road to Oxford. 'I'm sorry for leaving the note. Did anyone see or ask you about it?'

'No. I was very discreet.' Sylvia's voice held a note of bitterness and Hugh pulled into a layby and turned to face her.

'I don't like this any more than you do. But you've been avoiding me at work, and I must talk to you.'

'Go on then. Talk.'

'Not here. We'll go to that pub where we went before.' He started the car and put his foot down. Speeding along with the top down and the wind in her face, it was impossible to speak. She kept glancing at him, his lips tight as if he was angry. Had she done something to upset him? But he had said in his note they could be together. She had no idea how. He had mentioned divorce but to her that was wrong, especially because of his children. Stop worrying and just enjoy being with him right now, she told herself. It might be the last time.

It had been dark when they came here last time but tonight the sun was only just setting. As they pulled into the car park Sylvia noticed several tables set under trees in the garden at the side of the pub. She looked around nervously, hoping there were no air force personnel among the customers.

Hugh came round and opened the door for her. 'Would you like to sit outside? There's a table over there in the corner.'

Sylvia nodded.

'I'll get the drinks. Usual?'

She nodded again and walked across the grass to a table set a little apart from the others. There were only two other couples sitting outside, both too engrossed in each other to take any notice of them.

Hugh brought the drinks and sat down. He took a sip of his beer and put the glass down. He leaned across and took Sylvia's hand. 'I know this is difficult for you. I don't want to you to be hurt – and you will be if I go ahead with my wife's wishes. I told you she wants a divorce and she expects me to give her the evidence. You know what that means, don't you?'

'I'll be named, won't I? But I don't care, Hugh, if it means we can...'

'But *I* care, Sylvia, my love. I won't have you involved in a scandal. We'd both be drummed out of the air force or at least demoted and sent to some awful posting far away from each other. It's different in wartime. We have responsibilities, don't we?'

'What do you suggest then? We carry on as we are, embark on a full-scale affair and try to keep it secret? I don't think I can do that, Hugh, much as I love you and want to.'

'There is another way. I didn't know this before, but I've learned that adultery isn't the only grounds for divorce. It's called desertion which means Margaret and I must not have any contact with each other for two years but after that we'll both be free. I've written to her and she's agreed to those terms.' He leaned towards her. 'I'm afraid it also means we mustn't see each other either, Sylvia.'

'Two years. That's a long time, Hugh.' Sylvia pulled her hand away.

'I haven't seen Margaret for seven months. Only one year and five months to go – that's not so long.'

'It seems like it to me.'

'I know it will be hard, darling, but we must stay apart. If Margaret gets the slightest inkling that I am in love with someone else, she'll make things difficult for us.'

'But we see each other at work. It's going to be impossible, pretending you're just another colleague.'

'We'll just have to be strong, won't we?'

Sylvia nodded and thought for a moment. 'So Margaret mustn't see anyone either?' she said. 'How will you know if she's keeping to her side of the bargain?' Sylvia was remembering those incidents in the pub last autumn. She wouldn't be surprised if Margaret was carrying on like that up in Scotland with no one to see what she was up to.

Hugh smiled grimly. 'She will. I think she's so keen to get rid of me, she'll stick to it. To tell the truth, I've a feeling she's found someone else - but she'll be discreet. And she's staying with her aunt who is very old-fashioned and would soon let me know if anything was really going on.'

'It all sounds so...' Sylvia shook her head 'Oh, I don't know. I never thought I'd ever get involved with something like this.'

'I'm sorry, darling. I never thought it either. But I couldn't help falling in love with you.'

'Neither could I, with you.' Sylvia reached for his hand again and smiled.

They sat holding hands in silence for a few moments. Then Hugh said, 'You mustn't give anyone cause for suspicion about us. Gossip is rife at Medmenham. You must go out with your friends - let them think you're having a good time.'

'I go dancing with Julia and the other girls in my hut. We meet up with a group of army chaps. I've been out with one of them and he wants to get serious. I told him I have a boyfriend serving overseas.'

'I won't be jealous if you do go out with him. Besides, what right do I have to ask you not to?'

'He's been posted abroad now. Besides, you're the only one for me. I've known that for as long as we've worked together.'

'Me too.' Hugh drained his drink and said, 'Let's get out of here. Too many people around now.'

The garden had filled up while they talked, and Sylvia agreed.

In the car, Hugh said, 'Where to, my lady?'

Sylvia laughed. 'Anywhere. I don't care.'

'Better put the hood up first. It's not so warm now.' He finished fixing it and got in beside her. Before starting the car, he took her in his arms and kissed her.

It was hard to resist, but as he became more passionate she pulled away. 'Not here, Hugh.'

He sighed. 'You're right. We must be careful.' He pressed the starter and manoeuvred the Alvis out of the car park and into the country lane. 'I take it you don't want to go back to your billet,' he said with a grin.

'I should really but – no. I want to stay with you forever.'

'For a couple more hours anyway,' he said.

Dusk was falling when they stopped beside the river. Without a word, they got out of the car and strolled along the tow path hand in hand in contented silence. There were a few people about, like them enjoying the balmy summer evening.

'Hard to imagine there's a war on. It's so peaceful here,' Sylvia said.

'We must enjoy it while we can,' Hugh said. He looked around and saw that they were alone, sheltered from prying eyes by the willows which swept down to the water. 'Let's sit,' he said.

Hugh took his jacket off and laid it down for her to sit on. They sat on the grassy bank watching the ducks and swans settling down for the night, contented in each other's company.

Finally, Hugh broke the silence. 'You realise this is the last time we can be together like this – at least until my divorce is final. We can't risk anyone seeing us.'

Sylvia turned to him, lifting her face up to his. 'Then we'd better make the most of it, hadn't we?'

Their kisses grew more passionate and Sylvia pulled him down so that they were lying in the long grass. 'Are you sure this is what you want?' Hugh asked breathlessly.

'Yes, Hugh,' Sylvia whispered.

**

As they wandered back to the car hand in hand, Hugh asked, 'No regrets?'

'None at all.'

He squeezed her hand. 'Me neither.'

They drove back each lost in thought. Sylvia had spoken the truth. She had often regretted her involvement with Roland Hargreaves, wishing she had never allowed herself to be persuaded to go up to his hotel room. She had laughed it off when Daisy questioned her, pretending it was no big deal. But she had been deeply ashamed, more so when she learned what a cad Roland was.

This was different, she told herself. She loved and was loved in return. Despite the difficulties that lay ahead she knew that Hugh would never do anything to hurt her.

The car stopped some distance from the main gate and Hugh took her in his arms. 'One last kiss, my darling. This has to last us for the coming months. Here's to November 1944 when I'll be free.'

The tender kiss lasted some minutes until Sylvia finally pulled away. 'It's going to be so hard, seeing you at work but not...'

'Hard for me too, darling. But it will be worth it in the end.'

'I know.' Sylvia opened the car door and stepped out.

'I'll wait till you've gone in. Goodnight, sweet Sylvia.'

She walked quickly away, fighting to hold back tears. How would she manage over the coming months? How could she bear it, seeing Hugh at work and not being able to even speak to him? I'll have to ask for a posting, she thought. But where could they send her? Where would she be able to do the same sort of valuable work? She really didn't want to leave Medmenham, but it might be the only solution.

Chapter Fifteen

Back in his quarters, Hugh couldn't settle. He paced the small room berating himself for giving in to temptation. He had promised himself that he would be strong. But now that he had tasted the joy of being with Sylvia in the way he knew they were meant to be, it would be even harder to stay away from her. Eighteen months - such a long time. Eighteen months during which anything could happen. Margaret might change her mind. Sylvia might meet someone else or at least decide she couldn't wait for him.

Worst of all, someone might have seen them together and it would become common knowledge that he was having an affair. He was popular enough and had no enemies as far as he knew, but there was always someone willing to spread malicious gossip and cause a scandal. And liaisons with WAAFs were strictly forbidden. More than one of his colleagues had been disciplined for just that over the past couple of years. Usually one or other would be posted abroad to keep them out of trouble and avoid scandal. He couldn't let that happen to Sylvia.

He got into bed, the thoughts still whirling round in his head. That wasn't the only problem. Margaret must never know. He was surprised that she'd so readily agreed to his terms. She wasn't one for waiting for what she wanted. He must be very careful that no inkling of his involvement with Sylvia reached her ears. She could be very spiteful when thwarted.

As he drifted off to sleep he pushed his worries away and re-lived those wonderful moments on the riverbank, memories that must sustain him in the months to come.

***

He woke early after a restless night and almost decided to skip breakfast. Work was the antidote to brooding. But as he crossed the grounds, he spotted Sylvia and a group of WAAFs going into the mess. What harm to join them and wish them good morning? Just a glimpse of her smile would see him through the long shift. On impulse he followed them in.

There were two empty seats at her table, and he put his tray down saying, 'Mind if I join you, ladies?'

Sylvia looked up and smiled, a smile that tore at his heart especially when she turned and greeted Bill James, who had just come in, indicating the other empty seat.

He swallowed his hurt and also greeted his fellow officer while the girls chattered brightly about a film they'd seen.

'You should have come with us, Sylvia,' Jane said. 'Ronald Colman - my hero.' She laughed and rolled her eyes.

Marion said, 'I prefer musicals. Bing Crosby – he has such a lovely voice.' She turned to Hugh. 'That reminds me. When are we going to hear you again, Wing Commander? It's time we had another concert.'

'You don't want to listen to me singing and anyway, I'm too busy. Besides, we have had visits from professionals. Didn't you hear Moiseiwitsch the other evening? Came up from London. Marvellous pianist.'

'He was amazing,' Jane said.

'But we could organise something ourselves, surely?' Marion persisted.

'It's not up to me. Ask Bill. He's entertainments officer.'

Bill shook his head. 'As Hugh says, we're far too busy at the moment. We're inundated with work. In fact, I hear they're going to introduce twelve-hour shifts, alternate weeks of days and nights.'

Julia groaned. 'We're already doing long hours. How can they expect us to do more?'

'We'll just have to put up with it, I suppose,' Jane said.

'We do want to win this war, don't we?' Marion asked sharply. 'We must bite the bullet.'

'She's right,' said Hugh. 'We're all in the same boat, must pull together.'

There was a more subdued grumbling, but they all knew it was no good and they finished their breakfast and departed to their various work-stations.

As Hugh walked across the grass with Bill, he said, 'You always hear everything first. Is it true about the shifts?'

Bill nodded. 'Won't be much time for concerts or any other leisure time.' He paused. 'So, did you take things any further?'

Hugh was startled for a moment, thinking of what happened yesterday evening. 'What?'

'The divorce, old chap,' Bill said with a laugh. 'What did you think I meant?'

Hugh sighed with relief. 'I wrote and suggested it to Margaret, and she's agreed - a two-year separation – got a letter today.'

'Thank goodness. No scandal then.' They entered the main building and Bill lowered his voice. 'You'll have to careful, old man. You know – you and...'

'That's all over. We won't be seeing each other – except at work of course.'

Bill nodded. 'Good. Makes sense. So divorce..?'

'It's Margaret who wants it,' Hugh said sharply. 'Nothing to do with...'

'Of course.' Bill walked away quickly, leaving Hugh staring after him. He wished he hadn't confided in him and tried to reassure himself that his friend wasn't prone to gossip. Nevertheless, he just hoped that he wouldn't let anything slip to Sylvia's friend Iris, now that they were going out together.

***

Sylvia was very subdued this morning. During a restless night, doubts had crept in about her relationship with Hugh as they so often did. She had no regrets about letting him make love to her – it was what she had dreamed of. But now, the thought of not being able to see him outside work hours set her thinking. Was he like Roland, losing interest after getting what he wanted? Were the terms of separation from his wife just an excuse to end their relationship? She couldn't believe it and pushed the unwelcome thoughts away before starting work, determined to concentrate on that and put everything else out of her mind.

She was concentrating so hard on the set of prints before her that she startled when Babs spoke to her. She hadn't heard her approach.

'Have you heard about the new shift system?' she asked.

'They were talking about it in the mess. I haven't been told officially,' Sylvia replied.

'It starts after the weekend. The rosters are up on the notice board. I'm not sure how it will work. We'll have to wait and see.'

'Nights and days, alternate weeks, I heard.'

'I think so.' Babs gathered up the prints that Sylvia had put in her out tray and went back to her desk.

The prospect of working longer hours did not worry Sylvia. She often stayed on after the end of her shift if she was working on something important. It occurred to her that if she was put on a different shift to Hugh it would be easier to keep her distance, much as she hated the idea.

She bent to her stereoscope and before long was immersed in the fascination of deciphering the images in front of her. Nothing exciting today, she thought as she typed up her report. But it had been a satisfying day's work all the same.

At the end of her shift she walked across to the mess with Julia to have a look at the rosters.

'It says the work will go on round the clock. Day shift workers will have one day on, one day off,' Julia said. 'That's not so bad. There'll still be time for a drink after work.'

'Yes, but look Julia.' Sylvia ran her finger down the list of names. 'We're going to be on nights the first week. Eight till eight in the morning. No time for the pub then. We'll be trying to sleep during the day.'

'At least we're together.' Julia laughed. 'Don't fancy nights but it might work out OK. It'll be alternate weeks of day and nights, with days off in between. We'll be able to go into Oxford or Reading for the day.'

'I don't think so. We'll be trying to catch up on our sleep.'

'Not me. I only need six hours. That leaves six hours to enjoy myself.'

Sylvia shrugged. Nothing could deter Julia if she was determined to have some fun. Still, she worked hard and was good at her job and so long as she kept up her standards, what did it matter? For her part, Sylvia was grateful she would have time to rest properly and certainly wouldn't miss going dancing or drinking.

'Well, I'm off to get a good night's sleep and then just relax tomorrow ready to start our night shift on Monday.'

'I'm going to round up the other girls and have a good evening at the pub. Might not get another chance.' Julia laughed and walked away, turning to see if Sylvia followed her. 'Come on, slow coach.'

Sylvia took a last look at the list, looking for Hugh's name. He would be doing days, she saw, with a mixture of relief and disappointment. Less chance of bumping into each other.

***

Night shifts suited Sylvia. She had no problem concentrating on her work and, once she got into the rhythm of working for twelve hours it began to seem as if she had had no other life before this. In addition, she was so exhausted at the end of the shift that most days she just tumbled into bed without even thinking of breakfast.

It was hard to sleep during the day with the comings and goings of her colleagues who were working different hours. But she usually managed to get some rest.

At midday she would wander across to the mess for some food and then go back for another sleep or, if she had the energy, write letters home. She sometimes wrote to Harry - just friendly chatty notes about her colleagues and the funny things some of them said. She hoped he would accept now that they were just friends. It was harder to write to her parents and Daisy. What could she tell them? She couldn't even say she was on night duties. They would wonder why a shorthand typist needed to work at night.

She hadn't even had a glimpse of Hugh since starting night shifts and the memory of those magical hours by the river began to seem like a dream. But she lived for the day when they would be able to meet openly.

Doubts often crept in. Did he really feel the same? How much longer could she carry on like this – without a smile, even a glimpse to sustain her through the long months? Lots of others in the same boat, she told herself. Some worse off. What about Daisy and her Chris? Her sister didn't even know if the man she

182

loved was still alive. At least she knew Hugh was safe. She must be like everyone else, just carry on and live with hope.

One morning she stumbled out of the main house, barely able to keep her eyes open. It had been a gruelling shift with hundreds of prints arriving on her desk every minute – or so it seemed. As fast as she dealt with one lot, another would appear. There was a sense of urgency in the room and everyone was more focused than ever. Something was in the wind, but Sylvia's contribution was only a small part of it.

As she made her way to Hut Six, Julia joined her and took her arm. 'Lovely morning – I don't think,' she said, looking at up at the sky.

Sylvia was so tired she hadn't even noticed the weather. Now she looked around, noticing almost as if for the first time, that the trees were almost bare and there was a gusty wind chasing dark clouds across the sky. Autumn had come without her realising. She couldn't believe how quickly time had passed. Only a little over a year to go before Hugh was free. A year was still a lifetime to Sylvia though.

'Let's hope they've lit the stove in the hut,' Julia said, intruding on her thoughts.

'It still won't be very warm yet,' Sylvia said. The big stove in the centre of the hut took a while to heat up.

'Well, I'm not hanging around in there all day,' Julia said. 'I'm off to town after breakfast. Coming?'

Sylvia shook her head. 'I need sleep.'

'Better have some food first. You're not eating properly. You'll be ill again if you're not careful.'

'All right. Don't nag,' Sylvia said with a little laugh.

'I'm not nagging. I worry about you.'

'We're all tired working such long hours. I don't know how you manage to stay so chirpy.'

Julia laughed and started to run across the grass, pulling Sylvia along with her. With a laugh, Sylvia gave in and ran with her.

They reached the mess, panting and giggling. 'That's enough exercise for one day,' Sylvia said.

When they got back to the hut after breakfast, Jane was sitting on her bed. She looked up and called Sylvia over. 'A letter for you,' she said, handing her an envelope.

'From Daisy?'

Jane shook her head. 'It must be from Harry,' she said, 'although it doesn't look like his writing.'

Sylvia took it slowly, her heart thumping. Had he been injured – or killed? Was this from one of his comrades?

'Thank you, Jane.' She went over to her bed and sat down slowly. Only then did she look more closely at the envelope, her heart leaping as she recognised the writing. Why was Hugh writing to her? Was he telling her their affair was over? That he had decided to stay with his wife?

She tore the envelope open and slowly withdrew the sheet of paper. The words blurred and she reached for her glasses. Her heart slowed as she took in the words.

'My darling Sylvia, I know we agreed not to have any contact, but I had to write. This seemed the safest way, an ordinary letter by post, rather than a note left on your desk. These past months have been torture for me, not even seeing you across the room or passing you as we go to and from our offices. How can I bear a whole year without you? There must be some way we can get together, but it would be foolish to risk being found out. I just need to know that you still feel the same way. I love you, my dearest. Your ever-loving Hugh.'

Sylvia read the letter again, then looked around the hut. Julia had already gone out and Jane was settling down to sleep. The others were on day shift.

Jane sat up. 'I hope it wasn't bad news,' she said.

Sylvia shook her head, smiling. 'Just a note from a friend,' she said. And one that could get them into a lot of trouble if anyone saw it, she thought.

'Good.' Jane lay down again.

Sylvia got ready to sleep too, first tucking Hugh's letter under her pillow. She was too excited to sleep. Her tiredness had vanished, and she felt light-headed. She wanted to dance, to sing. Hugh loved her. That was all that mattered. The knowledge would sustain her until they could be together.

As she gradually drifted off to sleep, she thought of Hugh's words. No, they couldn't risk being found out, but she couldn't bear being apart for such a long time. There must be a way for them to spend time together. They could meet in London - perhaps on one of their days off. She fell asleep dreaming of walking along the embankment, feeding the pigeons in Trafalgar Square. There were thousands of service personnel in London, uniforms everywhere. No one would notice them.

Chapter Sixteen

Hugh almost regretted writing the letter as soon as he posted it. Suppose someone in Sylvia's hut saw it and recognised his handwriting? But as he calmed down, he told himself the risk was worth it. It had been so long since they'd exchanged even a word or a glance. He just had to let her know that he was serious about her. This just wasn't a casual affair.

He was more worried about Margaret. It wasn't like her to agree so readily with anything he suggested. She always had to be in control. That was why he had to be extra careful to keep his feelings for Sylvia secret. Bill knew, of course, but he didn't think anyone else suspected. And it must stay that way. Margaret would do anything to discredit him and if she found out that she could divorce him for adultery, she would jump at the chance of getting what she wanted without having to wait, never mind who got hurt in the process.

He knew that she had been friendly with the regulars while she was staying at the Hare and Hounds. He wouldn't put it past her to keep in touch with one of them so that she would hear if there was any gossip about her husband.

As he sat in the mess brooding over a pint of beer, Bill came and sat beside him. 'Any news?' his friend asked.

'About my problem? Not really,' Hugh replied. 'It's all in hand. The solicitors have exchanged letters and they've both accepted the two-year separation as grounds for us to divorce. Now, we just have to wait.'

'What about Sylvia? Has she agreed not to see you?'

Hugh nodded. 'She knows it's the only solution.'

'Obviously you'll see each other at work, as colleagues. That can't be helped. But I hope you won't be tempted to meet privately.'

'Good advice, Bill. But I can't deny I'm tempted.' He put his hand up as Bill started to speak. 'Don't worry. I'm not going to spoil everything just for a few minutes alone with her.' He sighed. 'It's hard though.'

'I do understand, old boy. Trust me – I'll be discreet. After all, I'm in the same boat. Iris and I...'

'At least you're single,' Hugh interrupted.

Bill laughed. 'That won't make any difference to the powers that be. You know the rules. Senior officers must not fraternise with WAAFs.'

They drank their beer in silence for a few moments, each busy with their own thoughts.

'What about your children?' Bill asked.

Hugh sighed. 'I miss them terribly. They're at boarding school, you know, so they don't see much of their mother either. I expect she'll be given custody, although I'll be able to visit them and take them out at weekends. Obviously not at the moment – no chance of getting leave.'

'What about after the war?' Bill asked.

'I'll still be in the air force, so it won't be much different, unless I'm posted nearer their school.' He finished his beer and stood up. 'I'm not the only one to miss my boys. Lots of families have been apart for much longer. Some children may never see their father again.'

On that sombre note he strode out of the mess, slamming the door behind him.

***

187

Winter came with a vengeance and it was freezing in the hut. Sylvia came off duty, desperately tired as usual, but she only dozed for a couple of hours. She was so cold that she couldn't get back to sleep and at last she gave up. She got out of bed, pulling a chair close to the stove and wrapping a blanket round her. She looked across at the others. Jane and Iris were sleeping, and Julia had gone out. The other two were on duty.

Sylvia didn't know where Julia went in her off-duty hours but she usually only came back to get a couple of hours sleep before going on duty again. She would be so deeply asleep that it was a job to rouse her when it was time to go to work.

Satisfied that she would not be disturbed, Sylvia felt in her pocket for Hugh's letter.

She had read it so often that it was becoming quite crumpled and frayed. Should she have written back, just to let him know she'd received it and to say she was thinking of him? It was tempting. Should she risk it? She could slip it into his in tray among the other papers.

She pushed the blanket aside and went to her locker for pen and paper. Shivering, she went back to her fireside chair and warmed her hands at the stove before starting to write. She screwed up the first attempt and thrust it into the stove, watching it burn. She shouldn't write anything that would give them away. It must be quite impersonal, just in case anyone else got hold of it.

She started to write and had got as far as 'Dear H...' when the door opened, and Marion entered.

'Bloody cold out there,' she said, rubbing her hands together and coming to stand in front of the stove. She glanced down at Sylvia's notepad. 'Thought you'd be asleep like the others,' she said.

'Too cold,' Sylvia said, trying to cover up the letter. 'I thought you were on duty.'

'My twelve hours off. I've been into the village. Spending my sweet coupons.'

'Lucky you. I used mine up ages ago.'

Marion glanced down at the notepad on Sylvia's lap. 'More letters? Who is it this time?' She snatched the notepad and laughed. 'Dear H? Is that Harry? I thought you weren't serious about him.'

'I'm not. I promised to write when he was sent overseas. We're just friends.'

'Pull the other one. I know he's mad about you. I hope you're not leading him up the garden path.'

'Don't talk rot.' Sylvia snatched the notepad back. 'Why don't you leave me to write my letter in peace?'

'All right. No need to get shirty.' Marion flounced off, leaving Sylvia trembling. She could hardly hold the pen, but she must finish before anyone else came in and interrupted her. In the end it was just a brief note. 'I must see you. It is torture for me too,' she wrote, signing it with just her initial. Hardly impersonal but it would have to do. She folded the sheet of paper and put it in her jacket pocket.

When she went on duty that evening, she still hadn't decided whether she would leave the note for Hugh. Suppose someone else read it?

She sat at her desk, forcing herself to concentrate. As usual, once she got started it was easy to lose herself in contemplation of the stream of prints that landed on her desk. The work never lost its fascination, especially when something particularly interesting came her way. Tonight, there was nothing worth reporting but she attached notes to each one and put them in the tray for collection.

Near the end of her shift, she typed up her report and stood up to put her jacket on, putting her hand in her pocket to feel the folded note. She walked across the room to hand in her report and went out, hesitating as she approached the room where Hugh worked.

189

The door was open, and she peeped in, breathing a sigh of relief. The night shift people had left and the room was empty. She made up her mind and quickly crossed the room to Hugh's desk, praying that no one, especially Hugh himself, would come in to start work. There was a folder on the desk, and she slipped the piece of paper in between the pages, then hurried away.

Julia was waiting for her outside. 'Working overtime again?' she teased.

'Lost track of time,' Sylvia replied.

'Let's go and get breakfast. I'm starving.' Julia slipped her arm through her friend's and they made their way to the mess. It was still quite dark, and Sylvia stumbled.

'Careful,' Julia said.

'I don't mind night shift, but I hate going to work in the dark and it still being dark in the morning.'

'At least it's not raining,' Julia said with a laugh.

They reached the mess just as Hugh and Bill were leaving. They both smiled and said 'good morning.'

The girls returned the greeting and hurried inside. Sylvia's heart rate increased and she knew her cheeks were flushed. Just seeing him, even though no words were exchanged beyond the conventional, had made her day. She hoped Julia wouldn't comment on her demeanour or, worse still, tease. It was the cold making her breathless and colouring her cheeks, she told herself.

She hardly said a word through breakfast, a meal of unappetising porridge which she ate mechanically. She pictured Hugh finding her note and tried to imagine his response. Would he be annoyed with her for taking such a risk?

Julia ceased her chatter and said, 'You're quiet this morning.'

'Just tired, as usual. I'm going to try and sleep.'

'Me too.' Julia yawned.

'Really. Things catching up with you?'

'I overdid it yesterday. Could hardly keep awake at work.'

Sylvia wanted to say, 'I told you so,' but she kept quiet.

***

When Sylvia woke a few hours later, Julia was still fast sleep. She got up and dressed quietly so as not to disturb the other sleeping girls. She contemplated waking her friend but decided to leave her.

She needed some fresh air and stepped outside the hut. There was a thin, misty drizzle but it wasn't as cold as yesterday. She walked through the grounds towards the exercise field. The men were doing their PE and she stood watching for a while then, glancing at her watch, she decided to go and get something to eat.

It was noisy in the mess, most tables full and she found a seat with a group of people she didn't know. One of them had just returned from leave and the conversation was all about a visit to London. Sylvia half-listened but she was worrying about the note she left on Hugh's desk. Had he found it? Would he reply?

She pushed the food around her plate. This was ridiculous. How could anyone be expected to have no contact for two years? It was too hard. Better to try and forget him. Hadn't she always been a 'love them and leave them' sort of girl? But that was before she had fallen so hard for the handsome wing commander. Hard as it was to live like this, she would be strong. This time next year, he would be free, and no one could stop them being together.

Of course, that wasn't strictly true. The end of the two year period was just the beginning. It would be several months after that before Hugh would be granted the decree absolute.

'We'll still have to be careful, darling, but at least we'll be able to speak in public,' Hugh had said.

Perhaps they could be married next year in the spring, she thought. At least that was something to look forward to through the long cold winter.

Chapter Seventeen

After a few mild days, the weather turned bitterly cold again. In their off-duty hours, the girls huddled round the stove in the centre of the hut, grumbling a little and often glad to get back to work where the offices were a lot warmer.

As Christmas approached there was little to celebrate. There would be no pantomime this year as everyone was completely engrossed in work and, when not on duty, far too tired.

The long hours took their toll on everyone. Pressure was on to find out what the mysterious objects appearing near the Baltic coast were. Babs confided in Sylvia that she had been told to look out for anything that could not be easily explained.

'You remember the photos taken earlier this year? I've been looking at them again. I'm sure these new objects are connected in some way,' she told Sylvia.

The bad weather over the past few weeks made it even harder to distinguish anything unusual. But Sylvia, anxious to please her superior officer, put everything she had into deciphering the images. The few times she was able to report anything useful lifted her spirits, but only for a while. She tried hard to put Hugh out of her mind, at least until there was any news of his impending divorce.

She eagerly awaited the post each day, hoping that another letter from him would arrive, but since that brief note there had been nothing. Despite her disappointment, she realised he was being sensible. She would just have to be patient.

A couple of days before Christmas she was handed an envelope and her heart leapt, only to come to her senses when she recognised Daisy's handwriting. Still, she ripped it open and eagerly read the contents. It was always good to get news from home.

After saying there had been no news of Chris for some time, Daisy wrote that Mum and Dad were well and sent their love, and Jimmy was enjoying his training as a merchant seaman. She finished with her big news.

'I've got to work through Christmas, but they've given me a day off in January. Lily is coming up to London and I'm going to meet her. She's won tickets for a show and wants to share with me. I'm so excited. I wish you could join us. Could you possibly get time off?'

Could she? Sylvia didn't see why not. How lovely it would be to spend time with her sister and forget the war and her problems for a few hours.

***

Daisy was depressed, despite having a day off with her friend to look forward to. She'd worked extra hard over Christmas, trying to bring some cheer to the young men who came into the NAAFI. But at home it had been difficult, although Mum had done her best to provide a festive meal. It wasn't the same without Jimmy, who'd gone off for his training in November. She'd never dreamed she would miss her annoying little brother. He was still annoying at times with his pranks and teasing, but he had grown up a lot since joining the Home Guard and then left to join the Merchant Navy.

She glanced at the clock on the wall. Nearly time to cash up and go home. She opened the ledger and wrote the date at the top of the page – December 31st, 1943. There would be few New Year's Eve celebrations tonight. She sighed. Everyone seemed to be feeling the strain of four years of war. They had hoped it would be over by now but it seemed as if it would drag on forever, despite rumours that the coming year would see the Allies invading Europe and bringing an end to it.

As far as Daisy knew Chris was still in North Africa. She'd had no letters for ages. She prayed he was all right, having learned from experience that lack of letters didn't necessarily mean bad news. She hadn't heard from Sylvia either and didn't know if she would manage to join her and Lily in London.

She finished her work and said goodnight to Muriel, the manager, before putting on her hat and coat and heading out into the rain and wind. She turned her collar up and trudged along the High Street deep in thought. She was excited about seeing Lily again. It had been so long since her friend had gone to the New Forest to stay with her grandmother. After having her baby, Lily decided to stay on and had worked on a farm while grandma looked after little Mikey. The rest of the Scott family had returned to Sheerness and Mrs. Scott kept Daisy up to date with her friend's progress.

'She couldn't come home with us – not with a baby in tow,' Mrs Scott told Daisy. 'She misses you and the NAAFI girls, but she's made a life for herself down there. They all think she's a war widow.'

Lily had won the tickets for a London show at a village fete and was eager to share them with Daisy. In a way she hoped Sylvia wouldn't be able to get away. Much as she longed to see her sister, it would be nice to have her friend to herself for a while.

***

As the train drew into Victoria station a few days later, Daisy felt a little nervous. She had never been to London by herself and worried that she might not be able to find Lily in the crowds that thronged the concourse. She handed in her ticket and stood for a few moments trying to get her bearings. Lily had said she would be by the W H Smith bookstall.

She spotted the sign and made her way towards it, looking around anxiously. So many people, all rushing here and there. How would she spot her friend? What would she do if she never caught up with her? She glanced at her watch, jumping with fright as arms encircled her from behind. Before she could protest, Lily said, 'Got you,' and turned Daisy round to face her. 'Oh, it's wonderful to see you. You haven't changed at all. I was worried I wouldn't recognise you.'

'Me too,' Daisy said. 'But you haven't changed either.'

'Well, it's only been three years.' Lily patted her tummy. 'Bit slimmer than when we last met.' She laughed.

'And how is little Mikey? I wish I could see him.'

'You will, one day. But I'm not coming back to the island. Perhaps you can visit after the war.'

The girls walked off arm in arm, chattering brightly as they exchanged news of work and family.

'Come on. We need to get a bus,' Lily said.

'Do you know where we're going?'

'It's all written down.' Lily showed Daisy a sheet of paper with the number of the bus, where they had to get off for Lyons Corner House and also how to get to the theatre. 'First, we're going to have lunch, then a look round the shops and afternoon tea, then the Victoria Palace Theatre.' She pointed across the road. 'See, you can't miss it.'

'You've got it all organised. Clever you.'

'Could Sylvia not get time off? You said she might join us.'

'She's going to meet us at the theatre. She's managed to get another ticket. She can't get here any earlier.'

'That's a shame,' Lily said. 'Still, I've got you all to myself and I've so much to tell you.'

They got off the bus outside the restaurant and found a table by the window. Daisy ordered steak and kidney pie, although she was sure it wouldn't be as good as what her mum made. 'What are you having, Lily?'

'Fish and chips,' her friend said. 'It'll remind me of Sheerness. I do miss Jacobs' fish and chips, but I must admit there's not much else I miss.'

Daisy loved her home-town and couldn't imagine living anywhere else but, remembering the cramped wooden cottage with its outside toilet where Lily and her three siblings lived, she could understand her friend's feelings.

'Is it nice, living on a farm?' she asked.

'Bloody hard work – but I love it. The countryside round there is so beautiful.' She smiled. 'It's not just the countryside I love though.'

She paused and Daisy leaned forward smiling too. 'What is it? It must be a man.'

Lily nodded. 'Not just any man. Colin, his name is. Met him at a dance in the village hall. He's so...' She rolled her eyes and grinned.

'A soldier?'

'No. A farmer.'

'I'm pleased for you.' Daisy reached out a hand and touched her friend's arm. 'Does he know about Mikey?'

'I told him the truth – couldn't carry on pretending I was a widow. He was good about it. And he's very good with Mikey, too. He'll be a good step-father.'

Daisy squealed. 'You're going to get married?'

'We haven't set a date yet but yes we are – and you're going to be my bridesmaid.'

***

Sylvia bought her ticket to London and went on to the platform, looking around anxiously in case she saw anyone she knew. Hugh said he would catch the same train but would travel separately, meeting up when they reached Paddington. There was no sign of him on the platform and she had an awful feeling he might have changed his mind. After all, they were taking a tremendous risk.

She half-hoped he wouldn't turn up. She hated the need for secrecy and the furtive way she was behaving. Apart from those cherished moments on the riverbank, she felt she had really done nothing wrong whatever other people might think. And since Hugh's divorce proceedings started, they had avoided each other, only seeing each other briefly in the mess or as they changed shifts. She knew she shouldn't have agreed to spend her day off with him. But it was too good a chance to miss. Anyway, she told herself, there was nothing to be ashamed of in sharing a train journey. If they saw any one they knew they could pass it off as a coincidence and pretend to go their separate ways when they reached London.

She had been in the mess with her friends, telling them about meeting her sister in London. 'It will be wonderful to spend time together. I haven't seen Daisy for ages,' she'd said.

'So exciting,' Julia said. 'Wish I could have a day in London.'

The others joined in the conversation, those who knew London giving advice on where to go and what to see. Hugh had been passing their table and stopped to ask what the excitement was about.

'A day in London, lucky you,' he said, smiling at Sylvia. 'When do you go?'

'On Friday. It's my next day off,' she said.

'Well, have a good time,' he said, walking away.

The next day Sylvia found a note from him in her locker, saying that he too had a day off and was going to London. It would be nice if they could travel together. All perfectly innocent sounding but her heart thumped crazily and, although she knew she shouldn't agree, she quickly wrote a note telling him what train she was catching. She left it on his desk with a report she had typed.

The train pulled in and came to a halt with a hiss of steam. Carriage doors opened and closed with a slam and Sylvia jumped into the first compartment she came to. It was empty except for an old lady knitting.

The woman looked up and smiled. 'Going to London, dear?'

Sylvia nodded. 'Meeting my sister.' It was true, although she had arranged to meet Daisy much later.

'Very smart uniform, dear. I love to see you girls doing your bit for the war effort. Is your sister in the forces too?'

'She's a supervisor in the NAAFI.'

The old lady's questions helped to keep her mind off the coming meeting with Hugh – that's if he turned up. Had he caught the same train? She looked out of the window into the corridor but turned back to answer her fellow passenger who was asking what it was like in the WAAFs. The journey passed quickly, Sylvia glad of the old lady's company. It helped take her mind off her anxiety. Would Hugh be there when she got off the train? Had he changed his mind? She wouldn't blame him. There had been several RAF personnel on the station, some of whom must be known to Hugh. He wouldn't risk jeopardising his divorce by being seen with her.

They pulled into Paddington station and Sylvia got off, standing on the platform and nervously looking around. What would she do if Hugh didn't turn up? She had no idea. A lump rose in her throat and tears threatened. She had dreamed of this day so much, picturing the hours she would spend with him, with no worries about being seen together.

She had arranged to meet Daisy and her friend at the theatre that evening but that was hours away, hours she planned to spend with Hugh. She'd never visited London, only passing through on her way to Norfolk or back home to Sheppey.

Someone jostled her and she came out of her trance and walked towards the barrier. There was no sign of Hugh and her heart sank. He hadn't been able to get the day off then. She handed in her ticket, resigned to spending the day alone until it was time to meet Daisy. She'd find a cafe and have a cup of tea.

She only took two steps, once again lost in thought, when someone grabbed her arm. Before she could protest, she was swung round and pulled into his arms. 'There you are, darling. I thought I'd never find you.'

'Hugh,' she gasped as his lips sought hers and she clung to him in a kiss she wanted to last forever.

When he finally released her, she was so breathless she couldn't speak.

'Forgive me, darling. I was so pleased to see you, I couldn't resist,' Hugh said. 'I was so worried when I didn't see you on the train. I thought you'd missed it or couldn't get away.'

'Me too. I thought you'd changed your mind.'

'How could you think that? It's all I could think of these past couple of days.'

He took her hand and they made their way out into the busy main road, where he raised his hand and hailed a taxi. Sinking into the seat, Sylvia said, 'Where are we going?'

'It's a surprise,' he replied.

Sylvia smiled. 'I love surprises,' she said.

They held hands and Sylvia gazed out of the window, watching as landmarks she had only read about or seen at the cinema flashed by. Was that Marble Arch? And there – Nelson's Column. Uniforms of every service – British, Canadian, American and others she couldn't recognise thronged the streets.

When the taxi pulled up in Park Lane, Sylvia gasped. They were outside the Dorchester Hotel. Her heart sank, remembering another man, another hotel. Was this the surprise? Had he booked a room? She was disappointed in him. Much as she longed to be with him, to make love again, she hadn't thought he would sink to this.

He helped her out of the taxi and turned to pay the driver, then took her arm.

'What are we doing here?' she asked in a small voice.

'Lunch, darling, of course – I've booked a table.'

'Lunch – really?'

He looked closely at her, then burst out laughing. 'You thought...? Oh, my sweet. What sort of a cad do you think I am? Besides, this is definitely not that sort of hotel.'

Sylvia blushed, and stammered. 'I'm sorry.'

'You're forgiven. Now let's go in and find our table. I'm starving.'

The front of the hotel was piled high with sandbags, leaving only a small entrance. The doorman ushered them in to the dining room, the only part of the hotel open to the public. Hugh told her that the main part of the building had been taken over by American officers.

'We were lucky to get a table,' he said. 'I came here with my parents as a young lad for a special treat. I thought it would be nice as a treat for you too.'

She smiled up at him, sorry for misjudging him, but she scarcely touched her first course, and still felt embarrassed at her *faux pas*.

That blissful autumn afternoon on the riverbank had been quite spontaneous and they agreed that, until his divorce was through, it could not happen again. She should have trusted him.

Hugh paused in telling her why he had been late meeting her and said, 'You're not eating. Is the food all right?'

'It's lovely.'

He reached across for her hand. 'You're not upset at me laughing at you?'

'No, of course not. It's just – I feel bad for thinking...'

'I understand, darling. A natural reaction. Just forget it and enjoy your meal.'

She nodded and picked up her fork. 'I've never tasted anything like this before. It's delicious.' She looked around at their sumptuous surroundings. 'This place is out of this world. I love the chandeliers. I could get used to this.'

'This isn't an everyday experience for me either. But, as I said, I wanted to give you a special treat.'

'Thank you. I really am having a wonderful time.'

The main course came, and Sylvia couldn't believe how tender the meat was with its coating of delicious sauce, nothing like the gravy her mother made. After the boring plain food served in the mess it was almost too much for her. And then there was the dessert trolley, a bewildering display of cakes and pastries. How did they manage to produce such fare in wartime, she wondered?

She put down her spoon and fork and sighed. 'I can't eat another thing.'

'Me neither.' Hugh signalled for the bill and, after paying said, 'Now for the next surprise.' He asked the doorman to call a taxi and they set off again.

It wasn't far to Trafalgar Square and the taxi set them down outside the National Gallery.

Sylvia gazed up at Nelson's Column and watched the water playing in the fountains, the crowds of people feeding the pigeons. Hugh hurried her up the steps and into the gallery. She wanted to linger and look at the paintings, the most valuable of which were stored away for the duration of the war for fear of the bombing. Some had been left on display to add atmosphere to the surroundings.

Suddenly she caught the sound of music and Hugh led her into the Octagonal Gallery with its glass dome. The chairs were all full and several people stood around, leaning against the walls or sitting on the floor. Some were even eating sandwiches.

As they came in there was a burst of applause and a few people stood up to leave. Hugh grabbed two empty seats and motioned to Sylvia to sit down. After a few moments, the music began again.

Sylvia craned her neck to look at the platform at the end of the room where a woman played the piano. 'Beethoven,' Hugh whispered. 'We're lucky today. That's Dame Myra Hess.'

The music pulled at Sylvia's heartstrings. She hadn't heard anything like it before. She felt for Hugh's hand and he squeezed it. They both became oblivious to their surroundings, caught up in the music and the joy of being together. It was wonderful to be able to sit so close, holding hands and sharing these magical moments.

The last piece Dame Myra played was *'Jesu, joy of man's desiring'*, a piece Sylvia recognised from childhood church services, and a lump came to her throat.

They came out of the gallery in a daze, still holding hands. Darkness crept over the early winter afternoon, a mist almost obscuring the fountains and the lions on their plinths.

'What next?' Hugh asked. 'It's too early to go and meet your sister.'

'I don't care. I just want to stay here forever.'

'Not possible, I'm afraid. But I know how you feel. Let's walk.'

They strolled along, passing under Admiralty Arch and proceeding along the Mall. It was quiet here with fewer people about and Sylvia found it hard to believe they were at war and that, not far away, streets had been bombed to oblivion.

'Buckingham Palace is up there,' Hugh said, pointing along the Mall. 'They've been bombed several times, but they refuse to move out.'

Sylvia shuddered. 'I'm glad the King and Queen are all right,' she said.

Hugh nodded, then glanced at his watch. 'Better get going. You don't want to be late meeting Daisy.'

They walked back to Whitehall and he summoned a taxi, leaning in to kiss her goodbye. 'I don't want to go. I'd rather stay with you,' she said.

'You can't disappoint her. Besides, you've got her to thank for us being together now with no suspicions from our colleagues. Try to enjoy the show and I'll see you on the platform at Paddington so we can travel back together.'

Sylvia waved as the taxi moved off, and then sat back savouring that last kiss. The memory of their time together would have to suffice for at least a year. Could she bear it? She mustn't cry, she told herself, as tears prickled her eyelids. She still had the journey back to Oxford with him to look forward to.

When the taxi stopped, she fumbled in her purse for the fare and got out, pasting a smile on her face, determined not to let Daisy and her friend see her sadness. Her sister knew she was in love with a married man, but she dared not let her know she had been with him today. It would be different if Daisy were alone - she might be tempted to confide in her. But she didn't really know Lily. Better to keep her secret, she decided.

Chapter Eighteen

Daisy and Lily arrived at the Victoria Palace Theatre ten minutes before the show was due to start. They were both excited about seeing variety artistes they had only read about or heard on the wireless.

It had turned very cold and Lily shivered, hugging herself to keep warm. 'Where's Sylvia then? I hope she won't be late. Don't want to miss the beginning.'

'She'll be here. She promised,' Daisy said.

A taxi drew up alongside them and a young woman in WAAF uniform stepped out.

'Sylvia – is it really you? My goodness – a taxi. How did you afford that?' Without giving her a chance to reply Daisy wrapped her arms around her sister and hugged her tight. 'It's so good to see you.' She turned to Lily. 'You have met Sylvia, haven't you?'

'It seems a long time ago,' Lily replied.

The girls linked arms and hurried into the foyer, handing in their tickets at the box office. They climbed what seemed like a hundred stairs, emerging into a curved gallery overlooking the auditorium.

As they took their seats the music started and they were soon engrossed in the various variety acts – singers, comedians, and conjurors. Daisy stole a glance at her sister wondering if she was really enjoying the show. She seemed lost in another world. Dreaming about her married lover I expect, Daisy thought. Silly girl. She shrugged and turned her attention back to the stage, soon becoming entranced by the colourful show. Such a treat after the drabness of four years of war. By the end, she and Lily had tears of laughter rolling down their faces, while Sylvia just smiled.

'Oh, I did enjoy that,' Daisy said as they joined the laughing, chattering crowds exiting the theatre. 'What did you think, Sylvia? Worth coming?'

Sylvia's face lit up. 'Definitely,' she said. 'Such a shame I have to go so soon. It's been so lovely to see you.'

'Do you have to go just yet?' Daisy said.

'I don't want to miss my train. I need to get a taxi.'

'We haven't had a chance to talk. Walk across to the station with us. You can get a taxi there.'

Victoria station was opposite the theatre, just a short walk away and Sylvia accompanied them. They stood by the taxi rank and Daisy threw her arms round her sister. 'It's been lovely seeing you too, Syl. We must do this again.'

'I'll let you know when I get some leave. Won't be for a long time though. We're so busy these days.' She turned to Lily. 'It's been nice seeing you again. Sorry I have to rush away.'

She got into the taxi and Daisy waved until she was out of sight. She turned to Lily and sighed. 'Pity we didn't have longer to talk. I was hoping she'd come for a cuppa with us before rushing off.'

'She didn't look as if she was really enjoying herself. Don't know why she bothered to come,' Lily said, sounding rather fed up.

'She's probably just tired. She told me she's working twelve-hour shifts.'

'Blimey,' Lily exclaimed. 'I thought I worked hard on the farm, but we do get time off.'

'I'm not sure what she actually does. She was very cagey when I asked her last time she was on leave.'

Lily laughed. 'Perhaps she's a spy.'

Daisy echoed her laughter. 'Don't be daft, Lil,' she said, giving her friend a little push. 'I'm sure she's not just a secretary though.'

At the station they parted, each to a different platform, promising to try and meet more often, war duties permitting.

Daisy managed to find a seat and leaned back, closing her eyes. It had been a grand day out and lovely to see her closest friend after such a long time. They'd had a wonderful time. It had been good to see Sylvia too but she was still worried about her.

She knew the work Sylvia did was important – her sister had told her that much – and the long hours must be taking their toll. But she was sure there was something else on her mind. Maybe if Lily hadn't been there, Sylvia would have confided in her. She hoped it wasn't that married officer making her miserable. She had promised there was nothing in it and Daisy wanted to believe her. She prayed that her sister would not get hurt.

***

The fog had thickened, and the taxi crept slowly through the streets, Sylvia marvelling that the driver could find the way.

'Here we are, miss,' he said, as the bulk of Paddington Station loomed out of the gloom.

She paid him and entered the station, anxiously looking at the platform numbers and praying Hugh would be there. She couldn't bear having to travel back alone.

Even this late in the evening the concourse was crowded and there were so many RAF uniforms she wondered if she would be able to pick him out. But there he was, waving to catch her attention.

She rushed towards him, straight into his arms. It felt as if she hadn't seen him for days, not just a few hours.

He hugged her and kissed her cheek – not the sort of kiss she had been expecting, and she pulled away, embarrassed.

He smiled down at her. 'Sorry, darling. Too many of our chaps around. Let's try to find an empty carriage.'

The train was in, steaming gently. Carriage doors slammed and people shouted farewells. They jumped on board just as the train began to move, pushing their way along the corridor between crowds of servicemen with kitbags. Sylvia was disappointed that they couldn't find the privacy they sought. They wedged themselves in a corner at the end of the corridor, standing close together.

The journey was over far too quickly, and Sylvia dreaded having to say goodbye to him when they got off the train. They hurried through the ticket barrier and out into the cold night.

Sylvia turned to Hugh and said, 'There's a bus due. Better say goodnight now.'

'Oh, no. I've got the car here. If anyone remarks on it, I'll say I bumped into you and offered you a lift.'

Sylvia wasn't happy – more lying and deception, she thought. But the opportunity to spend a little more time in his company won over her misgivings and she nodded.

They sat in the car for a while until the passengers who left the train had dispersed. 'Now I can say goodbye to you properly,' Hugh said, taking her in his arms.

It was the perfect end to a perfect day and Sylvia sighed contentedly, coming back to earth, as Hugh started the car. How long would it be before they could enjoy another perfect day, she wondered?

Later, unable to sleep, she went over every minute of the time spent with Hugh, her emotions in turmoil. It had been wonderful being with him but having to be careful the whole time, even in anonymous London, had taken its toll. How would she cope in the months ahead, catching glimpses of him at work or in the mess and trying to hide her feelings?

She sighed and turned over in bed, telling herself firmly that she had coped so far and she would continue to do so. It would be worth it in the end. As she drifted off to sleep a spasm of guilt woke her. She had been so wrapped up in her own problems that she hadn't spared a thought for Daisy and what she was going through. She hadn't even asked about Chris. How could she have been so selfish? What would her beloved sister think of her? She must write tomorrow and try to make amends.

***

By the time the train pulled into Sheerness station, the excitement of Daisy's day out had somewhat dissipated. She loved being with Lily, amazed that despite their years apart, it had been as if they'd seen each other only yesterday. The worry about Chris was firmly put aside and she had determined to enjoy every minute of this special treat. The London sights, the meal in a nice restaurant and the visit to the theatre all more than met her expectations and she had tried to ignore the sandbagged buildings and other signs of wartime. Now, as she began the walk home from the station, she felt depressed. She had been so looking forward to seeing Sylvia and was disappointed that she could only manage to join them at the theatre. But, besides not having time to really catch up with each other's news, Sylvia had seemed withdrawn. Perhaps she was ill, Daisy thought, remembering the last time her sister had been home. Sick leave she had said, without actually saying what was wrong and begging her not to say anything to their parents. But by the time she'd gone back she had seemed her old self again.

No, not ill, Daisy thought, I'm sure she's pining over that RAF officer. She told me she was going to end it. Just hope she has. It will only mean trouble.

She opened the back gate and walked slowly up the garden path, hoping her parents were in bed. She couldn't face the inevitable questions about her day out. Mum especially would want to hear how Sylvia was. What could she say without worrying her?

She opened the back door quietly, hoping to creep upstairs without disturbing anyone but, as she opened the kitchen door, her mother said, 'You're home, love. I was starting to get worried.'

'Oh, Mum, you shouldn't have waited up. I told you I'd be late.'

'I can't help worrying. It's not every day my girl goes up to London alone.'

'Mum, I'm grown up now. Don't tell me you worry about the others too, Jimmy over in Gloucester, Sylvia...'

'A mother always worries about her children, no matter how old they are,' Dora interrupted. 'Anyway, get your coat off while I make a cup of tea and you can tell me all about it. How was Sylvia?'

The tea made and poured, they sat either side of the range which gave out a good heat and Daisy recounted the whole day in minute detail, interrupted frequently by Dora's questions.

'Lily seems happy then?' Dora asked with a slight frown. Daisy told her some time ago about little Mikey and Lily's decision to keep him.

'Very happy. She's courting.'

Dora was shocked. 'What about the baby?'

'He's not a baby now. Lily showed me a picture. He's growing up into a lovely little boy – blonde curls. Anyway, Lily's going to marry a farmer and he's happy to take on little Mikey.'

'Lucky girl. Not many men would accept another man's child.' Dora took another sip of her tea. 'What about Sylvia? She doesn't say much in her letters. I thought she had a boyfriend?'

'I don't think it came to anything. We didn't really have much time to chat, Mum. She couldn't get away until early evening. We went to the show as I said and then she had to rush off to catch her train. She said they're working twelve-hour shifts.'

'I don't believe it. Isn't she a shorthand typist?'

'I think she's been promoted but she doesn't say much about her work.' Daisy laughed. 'Lily thinks she's a spy!'

Dora laughed too and stood up. 'Silly girl. Well, it's late. You've got work tomorrow - better get to bed.'

***

Sylvia started awake at the hand on her shoulder. 'Come on, sleepyhead,' Julia said. 'Get up and tell us about London. Did you have a nice time with your sister?'

'Couldn't you wait till I was awake?' Sylvia asked with a yawn. 'I got back late and couldn't get to sleep for ages.'

'Well, I've just come off duty and longing for my bed, but I thought we could go over to breakfast together and you can give me all the details.'

'Well, I'm awake now so just wait while I get dressed.'

Breakfast was lumpy porridge and cold toast which Sylvia couldn't help contrasting with the meal she'd had at the Dorchester Hotel. She couldn't tell Julia about that though. Her friend wanted to hear every detail of her day and Sylvia managed to give a good account without raising any suspicions. She wished she didn't have to lie. It would be wonderful to tell her friend what she'd really done.

'We were very extravagant – taxis everywhere,' she said. 'And we went to a concert in the National Gallery.' That was true at least. 'Then in the evening we went to a show at the Victoria Palace Theatre.' She was on safer ground now and she went into some detail about the various acts and what fun it had been.

'Lucky you,' Julia said. 'Next time we have a day off together, we must go. I've heard about the concerts. Did you see Dame Myra Hess?'

'Yes. She was amazing.'

Julia finished her breakfast and stood up. 'I'm off for some shuteye before another long, boring shift.'

As she left, a group of girls came in and joined Sylvia, all wanting to hear about London. She managed to get away and went back to the hut, claiming tiredness. She too must get some sleep before starting yet another night shift later on. And she must write that letter to Daisy.

Chapter Nineteen

Her first shift after returning from London plunged her straight back into work that needed intense concentration and within a couple of hours it was as if she had never been away from her desk.

Her team had already seen photographs taken the previous December of a prison in North East France just outside Amiens. Now there was information from a French resistance group that many of the prisoners held important information which must not get into the hands of the enemy. Word came down to Sylvia and her colleagues that these photographs must be analysed more carefully.

'They need to know the thickness and height of the walls, as much information as we can give them,' Babs told Sylvia.

'Whatever for? It can't be that important surely.'

'We don't need to know why. Just give the powers that be the information they ask for,' Babs replied rather sharply.

Sylvia nodded and went back to her desk. It was the usual story. So often they had no idea what they were looking for or why. It was sometimes very frustrating.

A little later Babs approached her. 'Sorry about that,' she said. 'I do have an idea what's up but, please, don't breathe a word. They're going to attempt the rescue of some important prisoners held there and calling it Operation Jericho.'

'I see. Don't worry, I'll keep mum.' Sylvia was pleased that Babs trusted her. She went back to studying the photos, noting details of machine gun posts, the guards' quarters, and anything else that might be useful.

A few weeks later, Babs called Sylvia over. 'They did it. Appalling weather, which might have actually helped. We've just had film of the damage assessment.'

'Did our work help?' Sylvia asked.

'I'm sure it did.' Babs smiled. 'I don't know much more, but I did hear that prisoners were seen running across the snow away from the bombed building.'

'I hope they got away,' Sylvia said. She carried on to the end of her shift feeling quite elated, despite her exhaustion. It was good to know that what she was doing had helped the war effort in some small way.

With Operation Jericho successfully concluded it was back to scrutinising photos of what they thought might be launching ramps for the pilotless aircraft they had discovered. Bombing raids had been carried out in the early months of the year but the structures were soon replaced and more carefully hidden among trees. Sylvia needed all her skills to find these in the often-blurred photos.

The long hours of intense concentration were taking their toll, not just on Sylvia but on all her friends. Back at the hut on a dark early morning, she noticed that they were all looking tired. Even Marion, who claimed she only needed two hours of sleep, had bags under her eyes. And Iris was so pale and thin, she looked as if she was fading away. How long can we keep this up, Sylvia asked herself. As long as the war lasts, was her answer and she resolved to carry on and try not to complain.

At least the long shifts and exhaustion helped to stop her dwelling too much on the situation with Hugh. It also seemed to make the time pass more quickly and she counted off the weeks and months until his divorce case was heard in court. Hugh hadn't been able to contact her at all, just brief greetings as the

214

shifts changed over. She had no idea of the date of the court hearing, although it was probably still several months away.

***

Hugh opened the letter from his solicitor with shaking hands. What was it this time? Had Margaret changed her mind? He unfolded the single sheet of paper, hardly daring to look.

As he perused the letter, trying to make sense of the legal jargon, his heart started to race. Did it mean what he thought it meant? Margaret had informed her own solicitor that their separation had started in 1941 when she first went to Scotland.

Hugh had to affirm that they had not lived as man and wife since that date. Their only meetings had been to discuss the children's welfare. He sighed and leaned back in his chair. What about that visit last year when she had begged him to rent a cottage for them? She hadn't wanted them to split up then? What had changed?

He read the letter again, mulling over the details. He was being sued for desertion which was fine with him if it meant less chance of a scandal. He was thinking of Sylvia, anxious to protect her from being involved.

Now, he worried about Margaret's stay at the Horse and Hounds last year. Everyone knew who she was and her behaviour with the servicemen had been seen. But on the other hand, there were witnesses that Hugh had not stayed with her, going back to his quarters at Medmenham after each meeting.

He answered the solicitor's letter straight away, saying he would sign an affidavit that he had been apart from Margaret since 1941. He didn't say that she had left him and was quite happy to accept the blame for their separation.

He answered the questions posed by the solicitor as honestly as he could and signed the letter. As he sealed it into its envelope he sighed with relief. It was almost over. If the dates they'd given were accepted in law, the divorce hearing would take place very soon, then there would be the three months wait for the decree absolute and he would be free.

Free, he thought. He'd be able to court Sylvia openly, buy her a ring, set a date for their wedding. He jumped up, almost pushing his chair over, grabbed his cap and rushed out of the door. He would drive into town and post the letter instead of using the post box near the gate. It would get there sooner, he hoped.

As he drove, he started to sing one of the popular songs that he'd heard on the wireless – *'You'll never know – just how much I love you.'*

He hoped he could catch Sylvia as she came off duty the next day. He couldn't wait to share the good news with her. Of course, there were practical things to consider, mainly the future of his two sons. He ought to try and get some leave, visit them and explain. Who knows what Margaret may have told them, he thought.

When he got back from posting the letter, he decided to write to Margaret. He would have to set the right tone though. He knew that if he sounded too relieved and happy about the situation, she would be likely to change her mind, just for spite.

***

Sylvia found the note on her desk when she arrived for her next shift. She had seen Hugh in the mess earlier. She'd been with two other girls and he sat at a table with Bill James. As she passed with her tray he had looked up and smiled.

'Good evening, sir,' she said and went to walk past, determined to maintain a facade of formality in front of other people. She longed to stop and ask if there was any news, but she dare not in the presence of her colleagues. Her hands were shaking, and a spoon fell from her tray.

Hugh bent to pick it up and, as he handed it to her, he squeezed her hand and smiled. She hoped no one noticed as she hurried to her table and joined her friends for supper.

She ate quickly, anxious to get to work and immerse herself in the piles of photographs she knew awaited her. She wouldn't think about that smile and the pressure of his hand on hers.

As she unfolded the note and started to read, she drew in a deep breath. She read it twice to be sure she'd understood. The divorce hearing was in two weeks. 'I will explain when I see you,' the note said and went on to suggest that they meet the next time their days off coincided.

For the first time, Sylvia found it hard to give her attention to her work, her mind going off at a tangent every few minutes. After staring at one photograph for some time without really seeing it, she shook her head and put it down, reaching for another. This would not do. She would find out what Hugh meant when they met. Until then she must concentrate. She glanced across to Babs's workstation. The older woman looked in her direction, frowning.

'Anything wrong?' she called.

Sylvia shook her head.

'Shall I have a look?' Babs asked.

'It's all right. I thought I saw something but it's just a shadow. I've made a note.'

After that exchange Sylvia knuckled down, determinedly pushing thoughts of Hugh aside. It was hard, but once she became immersed in the work, the fascination of trying to interpret the images took precedence over everything else.

However, by the end of her shift she had the beginnings of a headache and, as she walked out into a bright spring morning, she decided to walk around the grounds for a while to try to shift it.

Since she came to Medmenham, much of the grounds had been built on and now the once pristine lawns were covered with Nissen huts. Sylvia walked down the drive towards the road. She would go as far as the gate and then return to her hut for some much-needed sleep.

Some of the topiary which lined the drive remained and the grass verges were studded with primrose and violets. The birds were singing their hearts out. It was all so different from her home-town. Sometimes it was hard to recall that other life, before the war. Medmenham was her home now. But where would she go when the war ended, as it surely must before much longer?

She tried to imagine being married to Hugh. Would he expect her to give up her career and be a 'service wife'? Would she be willing to do that – even for love? She wasn't sure. They had never discussed it. And then there were his sons. They hadn't discussed them either.

She was roused from her thoughts when a car approached along the drive. She turned round and recognised Hugh's Alvis. Where was he off to so early in the morning?

He stopped the car and leaned across to open the door. 'Going anywhere special?' he asked.

Sylvia shook her head.

'Good. I spotted you walking this way. A good opportunity for that talk. Jump in.'

She settled herself in the passenger seat and said. 'I got your note. What's happened?'

'Good news. Look, let's go and park by the river. It will be quiet this early. There's a lot to discuss.' Without waiting for a reply, he started the car and drove towards Henley.

Sylvia managed to contain her impatience for the few minutes it took to reach a quiet stretch of the river with a parking space nearby.

They walked hand in hand along the river path then sat on a bench under a tree.

Hugh put his arms around her and pulled her towards him. The kiss was long and passionate, and Sylvia was breathless when he released her. 'God, I've been wanting to do that for so long,' he murmured.

He reached for her again, but Sylvia gently pushed him away. 'You said there's lots to talk about. Please – I need to know what's happening.'

'All right, darling, here's the good news. The hearing's in two weeks. We don't have to wait till December. After that we have to wait three months until it's final – the decree absolute. So, instead of having to wait another year, we can be married sooner.'

'That's wonderful – but how?'

'Here – read the solicitor's letter.' He took it out of his pocket and handed it to her but, without giving her a chance to read it, he went on to explain that Margaret had cited him for desertion from early 1941. 'So, we've been apart for much longer than two years.'

'But, I don't understand,' Sylvia said, looking down at the letter. 'What about when she visited you last year? The two years isn't up for another eight months.'

'Margaret wants it over quickly. She is prepared to swear that her visit was solely to discuss the boys' future.'

Sylvia frowned. 'But that's not really true, is it?'

'No. Although I did think that's why she'd come. We did talk about it very briefly, but we argued. I could see there was no future for us. It was over long before I met you, Sylvia my love. I did try to make a go of it.' He sighed. 'I'm just relieved that she's come

219

to realise that too. Now, I think she just wants it to be over as soon as possible. In her last letter she talked about making a new life for herself.'

'Will she stay in Scotland do you think? And what about your sons?'

'I don't know her plans but I'd like to have custody of the boys. I think they'd be better off with me. Margaret's drinking worries me. She'll fight me, of course.'

'I hate to say it, Hugh, but I think you're right. I saw what she was like when she stayed at the Hare and Hounds that time.'

'I know. Nobody said anything to my face, but I know there was gossip about her.'

'Hugh, darling, I'm so sorry you've had to go through all this. But I'm happy that we can be together soon.' She reached for him now and for some time they were lost in the bliss of being so close after such a long time apart.

When they drew apart, Hugh kept hold of her hands and said, 'There's one thing we haven't discussed – the boys.'

'Yes, poor lads. I hope they won't be too upset by all this. I suppose being away at school will make it easier. They're used to not seeing you much. But if you get custody, how will you manage?'

'That's not what I meant, darling. You haven't met them yet, but when we're married you will become their step-mother. How will you cope with that? It's a bit unfair to land you with a ready-made family.'

Sylvia was silent for a few moments. Then she said, 'I hadn't really thought about it but I'm sure we'll manage. As you say, they're away during term time and I expect Margaret will want to see them in the holidays. We'll work something out.' In truth, Sylvia had often day-dreamed about being married to Hugh and caring for his two sons – a proper family. But when she faced reality, she imagined his wife would have custody and she would continue with her WAAF career. Now, she wondered, did she really want that, and would she be able to be a mother to two little boys?

Hugh kissed her again and said, 'You'll be a wonderful mother to them. I hope you can get to know them soon.'

'Me too,' she said, dismissing her concerns and snuggling up to him on the bench, happy just to be with him.

They sat for a long while, each engrossed in their thoughts, content in each others' company, watching the flowing river and the ducks and swans paddling in the weeds.

Sylvia was feeling sleepy now and she yawned. Hugh immediately sat up straight.

'Forgive me, darling. I should take you back. You must be exhausted after your night shift.' He stood up and reached for her hand. 'Come on.'

'Let's stay a little longer,' she pleaded.

'I'd love to, but you need your sleep.'

She gave in and stood up, smoothing down her skirt and tucking stray strands of hair into her cap. They walked back to the car, Sylvia doing a little skip and hop every few minutes, unable to contain her elation.

Hugh laughed and said, 'Behave yourself.' And then, more seriously, 'We'll still have to be careful, my love. I'll drop you off just before we get to the gate.'

'I'm so happy. I want to tell everybody.' Sylvia laughed. 'Don't worry, I'll be discreet. We've managed to keep it secret all this time, haven't we?'

A few yards from the main gate and out of sight of the guard, Hugh pulled over and Sylvia got out. She watched him turn in through the gates and when he was out of sight began the walk up the drive, nodding a good morning to the guard.

Entering the hut, she was relieved that it was empty except for two of her colleagues asleep in the far corner. Julia must have gone out, she thought.

She started to undress, her head still whirling with excitement. It was really happening. She and Hugh could be married much sooner than she'd hoped and, most importantly, she would not have to keep their relationship secret for much longer.

As she went to climb into bed, she turned sharply as a voice accosted her. 'Where have you been this bright early morning? Up to something, no doubt.'

It was Marion, leaning up on one elbow and staring at Sylvia with a cynical smile.

'Not at all, I went for a walk to clear my head. Had an awful headache but it's gone now.'

'Sez you. I know you're up to something. You never come out with the rest of us so where do you go on your days off?'

Sylvia sat on the edge of her bed. 'We're all doing different shifts now and you're in a different section to me so it's a bit difficult for us all to get together, isn't it?'

'I know you were seeing that soldier – Harry isn't it – but he's been posted overseas. So, who are you seeing now?'

'No one. I write to Harry but there's no one else.' Sylvia could feel her face flushing and she climbed into bed, hoping Marion hadn't noticed. 'Now, please, let me sleep. I'm exhausted.'

But Marion wouldn't leave her alone. 'Vera and me reckon you've got a secret lover. We've been trying to guess who it is.'

'What nonsense.' Sylvia managed a laugh. 'Who do you suggest then? Boring academics, officers old enough to be my father? Give it rest Marion and let me sleep.'

'We thought it might be Bill James – you spent a lot of time with him doing the pantomime last year. But he and Iris are going steady now so it's not him.'

Sylvia didn't reply and burrowed under the covers, Marion's voice echoing in her head. Was she just teasing and, if she really suspected something, how long before she latched on to Hugh's name? I'm not going to think about it, she told herself. We've been discreet and we won't have to hide for much longer.

But she couldn't sleep for worry. Marion loved to gossip and if she found out, it would be all over the station. She couldn't bear it if, so near to the court hearing, something happened to stop it. Hugh would not be able to claim the divorce was due to desertion if it became known that he had been seeing another woman. Worse still, if Margaret found out, she would change her plea to adultery and name Sylvia.

But how could Margaret find out? She was far away on the west coast of Scotland.

Chapter Twenty

Only one more week till the court hearing, Hugh thought. What could go wrong in a week? But still, his stomach churned, and he found it hard to concentrate on the prints on his desk.

They now knew that the strange objects that had been appearing over the past months were definitely launch sites for rockets and the race was on to find and identify them before they could be launched. They were also trying to find the rocket factories which were very well camouflaged.

Babs discovered that what looked like farm buildings were being used as cover and Hugh found time to congratulate her. 'It wasn't easy to identify them,' she said. 'SO Bishop was a great help. She has a keen eye.'

Hugh tried to hide his pleasure at her praise for Sylvia and said. 'I know, she's very good.'

He was working hard in a race against time but a few days later he received word from above that the hunt for the rocket sites and factories would be suspended as preparations were made for the invasion of Normandy.

He was going through some reports when a message was handed to him. 'A lady at the main gate wishes to see you. I can't let her in without a pass and she asks you to meet her at the village pub when you come off duty.'

A lady? he thought, knowing straight away who it must be. What was she doing here? He had been dreading seeing her in court, but to turn up here a week early. What did she want? Had she changed her mind?

He should finish his shift, but he knew he wouldn't be able to work efficiently until he found out what Margaret was up to. He threw down his pen and shuffled the pages of the report together, slipped them into a folder, placed it in a drawer and locked it.

He knocked on his superior officer's door and went in. 'Sorry to interrupt, sir, but a family problem has cropped up. Permission to take a few hours off to sort it out?'

'Can't it wait, Smythe?'

'Not really, sir. My wife's come down from Scotland, says it's urgent. I'd be grateful if you'd allow me to see her. I'm sure it won't take long.'

'Something to do with the children, is it?'

Hugh nodded, not wanting to lie. Besides, for all he knew, it might be a problem with the boys.

'Very well. Don't take too long.'

'Thank you, sir.' Hugh saluted and left, heaving a sigh of relief. He had expected his request to be turned down. Not that he wanted to see his wife. But he could just imagine her, the worse for drink, turning up at the gate and forcing herself past the guard.

It was only a short walk to the village, but he got the car out. Not wanting to risk a scene in the pub, he decided to drive somewhere where they could talk privately.

She was in the public bar chatting to the barman but when he came in she swooped towards him, throwing her arms around him. 'So lovely to see you, darling,' she cried. 'I knew you'd manage to get away from your, oh so important, work.'

'I don't have long,' Hugh said, gently disentangling himself from her embrace. 'Why are you here? What do you want?'

She ignored the question and said, 'Aren't you going to buy me a drink?'

'No. We haven't got time. I must get back soon. So come on, let's go for a drive. We can talk on the way.'

'Why not here?'

Hugh glanced round the bar which was almost empty. Still, he didn't want everyone hearing what she had to say and someone from the base could come in at any moment. 'More private,' he said, walking towards the door.

She followed slowly and reluctantly got into the car.

He drove out of the village and parked on the edge of a wood. They sat in silence for a few moments while Margaret fiddled in her handbag for a cigarette. 'Well?' she said, taking a long drag.

'Well what? You came to see me so tell me why so that I can get back to work.' He tried to remain calm but the urge to shake her was hard to resist.

'Oh, your precious job. Much more important than me and the boys.'

Hugh didn't answer and she went on. 'The divorce, darling. Thank God, it'll soon be over. But we need to talk about the future.'

'If it's about the boys, I won't fight you for custody if that's what you're worried about,' he lied.

She took another long drag at the cigarette. 'Well, yes, it is about the boys. But I don't want custody.'

'You don't?' Hugh was astonished. He'd been so sure he'd have a battle on his hands. What was she up to?'

'Well, I can't take them to America, can I?'

'America? What are you talking about?'

'I've met someone. An American naval officer. He's based in Oban, but he wants to take me back to the States after the war.'

'It's serious then? Not one of your casual conquests?' Hugh didn't really believe her. She had always been a flirt and enjoyed the company of other men. But he had never thought she was actually unfaithful.

'Deadly serious, darling. I'm in love.' She finished her cigarette and threw the stub out of the window, then turning to him she pleaded, 'You won't spoil it for me will you, Hugh? You'll take care of the boys, won't you?'

'I don't know. Are you sure about this? They need their mother.' Although he wanted custody of his sons, he wasn't going to give in so easily. If she knew how he felt she would fight him just for spite.

She fumbled in her bag again and drew out a letter, thrusting it in front of him. 'Perhaps your little floozy can be a mother to them. You can marry her when the divorce is final.'

Hugh tried to grab the letter. 'Floozy – there is no floozy! Where did you get that idea?' His stomach churned and his brain whirled.

'I don't know her name but someone's seen you together and put two and two together. It's all in here,' she said, waving the letter under his nose.

He snatched it from her. 'It's a lie. Who wrote that?'

She laughed. 'No signature. A jealous rival perhaps?'

'Don't talk rot,' he snapped.

'Oh, Hugh. Did you really think you'd get away with it?' She laughed again. 'Divorce on the grounds of desertion! I must have been mad to agree to it. Well, we'll see what they say in court next week when I tell them what you've been up to.'

'Hang on a minute, Margaret. You can't do that.'

'And why not? It seems you've been carrying on with one of your WAAF officers for months.'

Hugh didn't like the phrase 'carrying on', it sounded so sordid. His feelings for Sylvia were nothing like the casual affair Margaret was accusing him of.

He had the perfect comeback. 'Well, for a start, you've just admitted to me that you've been 'carrying on' as you put it. And besides, you need proof of infidelity.'

'You're worried now, aren't you? Thought you'd get away with it.'

'You're talking nonsense. Besides, you can't change things now. You want a divorce as much as I do. Your Yank is welcome to you.'

She pouted and bit her lip then turned to him with a bitter smile. 'Don't worry. I'm not going to make waves. I just wanted to make you sweat. We'll let the court hearing go through. And then, in three months, we'll be free of each other.'

'But what about the boys?'

'That's your problem. It's about time you started taking some responsibility instead of focusing on your career.'

'Margaret, you know it hasn't been my fault, not seeing them for so long. There is a war on, you know. And I'm doing important work.'

'Try explaining that to them then.' Margaret shoved the letter in her bag, lit another cigarette and leaned back in the seat.

Hugh sighed. What could he say? She was right in a way – no use trying to explain the guilt he felt. He put the car in gear and started to drive off.

'That's it then? You've nothing more to say?' Margaret took a puff of her cigarette.

'I'll drive you to the station. Did you book a sleeper?'

'I'm not going back to Scotland. I'm off to London. I'll stay there till the hearing.'

As he saw her off on the London train, he said, 'See you in court next week. We'll sort out the children then.'

He drove back to Medmenham his mind full of questions. Who had written to Margaret? Who knew about his feelings for Sylvia? Bill James suspected there was more than friendship between them, and he thought Sylvia's friend Julia had probably guessed. But they were friends. Who among their acquaintance would stoop to such a malicious act?

***

On the day of the court hearing, Sylvia woke with a sick feeling in her stomach. She had only slept for a couple of hours since coming off duty and, although she needed the rest, she couldn't get back to sleep again.

She kept thinking about the anonymous letter Hugh told her about. He assured her there was nothing to worry about. Remembering Marion's jibes a few days ago, she was sure she must be responsible. She wondered why the other girl disliked her so much. It must have been her. If Margaret produced the letter during the hearing, how would that affect the court's decision? One thing was sure, Hugh would be in deep trouble for lying about the grounds for a divorce. He could be charged with perjury. But surely Margaret wouldn't do anything to prolong the proceedings. Hugh said she wanted the divorce as much as he did.

It was no use lying here going over everything, she told herself, as she started to dress. At least she didn't have to worry about the case being reported in the newspapers. That had been a real worry, especially as a high-profile case had recently been splashed all over the tabloids. 'Scandal sheets' her dad called them, but he still avidly read the 'News of the World', commenting loudly on the goings on. She couldn't bear the thought of her name being used in that way. Hugh assured her that nothing of the kind would happen to them as the divorce would not be contested. She just had to believe him.

Once dressed, she wandered over to the mess, hoping to find someone she could talk to take her mind off the court case. She wondered if Hugh had confided in any of his friends, and if anyone knew the reason he had gone to London today.

She spotted Bill and Iris at a table in the corner, but they were engrossed in each other and she didn't want to disturb them. She walked over to the counter and ordered tea and toast, turning as Iris called her name.

'Come over. I've got something to show you,' she said, a huge smile on her face.

Bill was grinning too, and Sylvia hurried over with her tray, wondering what was afoot.

Iris held out her left hand, showing off the diamond ring on her finger. 'Aren't you going to congratulate us? We're engaged.'

'That's wonderful Iris. Congratulations – and you too, Bill. When did this happen?'

'Yesterday. We both had the day off and went into town to buy the ring.' She held out her hand again, admiring it. 'Oh, Sylvia, I'm so happy.'

'Are you going to let everyone know? I thought you might have to keep quiet about it. You know - the rule about WAAFs and officers?'

'I had to ask my superior officer for permission,' Bill said. 'Anyway, it's casual affairs they're down on. It was obvious to everyone we were serious about each other.'

'I'm pleased for you both,' Sylvia said sincerely. It was good to have something nice to think about amidst the gloom of the war and her own problems.

Iris touched Sylvia's arm. 'You next,' she said quietly.

They both turned to Bill as he started to cough, his face turning bright red. Iris handed him a glass of water and Sylvia took a bite of her toast, hoping she wasn't as flushed as Bill.

'Something went down the wrong way,' he said.

'So, when's the wedding?' Sylvia asked, pretending she hadn't noticed anything amiss.

'We haven't decided. I've got to tell my parents. And we need to put in for some leave.'

'Not that we're likely to get any at the moment,' Bill said. 'All the signs are that there's likely to be an invasion some time soon. Something big's building up.'

Sylvia nodded. 'We're not supposed to know exactly what's going on but it's fairly obvious.'

The talk turned back to the couple's engagement and plans for the future and Sylvia joined in, pleased to share in the couple's happiness and for the moment, distracted from what was happening in London. She would hear soon enough. And then, although they couldn't actually get engaged until the divorce was final in three months, she and Hugh could also begin to make plans for their future.

It wasn't until she was back in her billet that she began to contemplate the implications of that future. If Hugh gained custody of his sons, as he wanted, she would become their step-mother. She had never had a lot to do with young children, except for sometimes looking after her little brother. She had often thought about having her own children, but that was something in the distant future when the war ended, and she left the WAAFs. She loved the thought of having Hugh's child. But a ready-made family? She wasn't sure.

**

Hugh sighed as the train pulled out of Paddington station – a sigh of relief. It was over. He was a free man – well, almost, he amended. He had the decree nisi, signed by the judge, in his inside pocket. The document finalising his divorce, the decree absolute, would be sent to him in three months' time. He did the calculation in his head. In theory, he and Sylvia could be married at the end of the summer, but a lot could happen in three months. With the progress of the war

231

at a critical point, his work would become more important and he, along with everyone else, would not be allowed leave. They could of course rush off to a registry office between shifts. But he didn't want that for Sylvia. She would want a proper wedding with her family there – almost impossible in wartime. Could he bear to wait?

The court hearing had gone more smoothly than he had anticipated. Right up to the last minute he dreaded that Margaret would accuse him of infidelity and get the case thrown out. He imagined her brandishing the anonymous letter and screaming insults at him.

Thank God it hadn't happened. Now, though, he had a new worry. His sons. He supposed they knew nothing of their parents' separation and divorce. He hadn't been able to bring himself to tell them in a letter and he didn't think Margaret had either. The boys were tucked away at their boarding school, safe from bombs and the war, shielded from their mother's drinking and his and Margaret's rows.

How would they cope with their mother going off to America with a strange man? And, more importantly, how would they take to a new woman in their father's life?

As the train steamed through the late spring countryside Hugh forced himself to face up to his main worry. How would Sylvia feel about taking on two small boys? They had never really discussed it. But it would have to be faced and he dreaded it.

Chapter Twenty One

Sylvia waited impatiently all afternoon, hoping that Hugh would find some way to let her know the outcome of his visit to London. Surely, if everything had gone well, he would get a message to her somehow. She hung around in the mess for ages, the only place where they could talk freely without causing comment.

She had to start her shift soon. How could she get through the long hours without knowing? She went to her billet to tidy up before reporting for duty, telling herself sternly that the job came first. She would lose herself in the work and the time would pass quickly as it always did once she got her head down over the stereoscope and became immersed in the mysteries of photo interpretation.

After several hours she straightened her shoulders and picked up the cup which had been left on the desk beside her. Cold tea was quite refreshing she had discovered. She looked at her watch and realised her shift was ending in minutes. Where had the time gone?

She tidied her desk, stood up and stretched. Only then did she allow herself to think of Hugh, to wonder if he had returned from London with good news.

She went outside with the other girls from her shift, but she hardly listened to their chatter. She was wondering how she would fill the time until she could discreetly find out where Hugh was and wangle a meeting as if by chance.

She walked down the path towards her billet so deep in thought she didn't notice when someone stepped out from behind one of the topiary bushes and grabbed her arm.

Before she could scream, Hugh pulled her into the shade of the bush. Then his arms came around her and he covered her mouth with his. The kiss ended at last and Hugh, panting, said with a grin, 'It's over. I'm free.' He took a document out of his pocket and showed it to her. 'There, you see. Signed by a judge.'

Sylvia, still breathless from that kiss, snatched the document from him and read quickly, hardly able to believe it. But there it was, in black and white.

Tears welled up and she couldn't speak for a few moments. Then, 'Oh, Hugh. It's really happened. Can we tell everyone?'

'Not yet, darling. We still need to be discreet, at least until the final decree. Then we won't have to hide away anymore.'

'Wonderful. I can't wait.' She gave a little laugh. 'I'm so happy. But you're right.' She paused. 'I won't say anything to the girls, but I must write and tell Daisy. We've never had secrets from each other - always shared everything and it's been hard, not telling her about you.' She mentally crossed her fingers, remembering the confidences shared when she'd been home on leave as well as the hints dropped in letters.

***

Daisy walked in through the Garrison gate on a bright May morning feeling on top of the world. She greeted the guards with a smile and hurried into her office. Three letters from Chris had arrived that morning. No time to read them before leaving for work. And no time to read them now.

234

The manager, Muriel Green, had a day off so Daisy went through to the kitchen and made sure everything was ready for opening, then went into the canteen. Ruby was already there, wiping down the tables and Daisy greeted her with a cheerful smile.

'You're chirpy this morning,' Ruby said.

'Letters from Chris.'

'Wonderful. You must be so relieved after so long without hearing.'

'Haven't had time to read them yet. So I'm going to leave you in charge of the till and do it now before we get busy. When the others arrive, tell them I don't want to be disturbed.'

'OK. Hope it's good news.' Ruby went back to her task and Daisy hurried into her office.

She tore open the first letter which had been written several weeks before. She'd known Chris had been in Italy since January but there had been no news of the allies' progress for some time. His letter was brief as usual not giving anything away about where he was.

'Been dug in here at a place called (the word had been blacked out by the censor) *for weeks, nothing seems to be happening. Lads are fed up with no progress. I'm Ok though so no need to worry. I love you so much and can't wait to get out of this hellhole and back to you my darling.'*

The rest of the single sheet of paper was covered with crosses for kisses and pictures of a heart with an arrow through it with their initials. She would treasure this one, along with the others and the card with its loving poem.

Daisy wondered where he was. Dad had marked the progress of the war on Jimmy's school atlas so when she got home from work, she'd ask him to show her on the map where Chris was most likely to be.

The rest of his letters were in much the same vein although he did say they might be moving on soon. She skimmed through them and kissed the place where he signed his name, putting them in her bag to read properly later on.

It was so good to hear from him, but her happiness was tempered by the knowledge that the letters were written weeks ago. Anything could have happened to him since then. She would just have to keep hoping and praying. With a sigh, she drew a pile of invoices towards her and started work.

She had just become engrossed when there was a tap on the door and Ruby came in. 'Post,' she said, handing a batch of letters to Daisy.

'Thanks.' She took the batch and was about to put them on her desk to read later when the handwriting on the top one made her gasp.

Why was Sylvia sending letters here instead of home? Had something happened to her?

Remembering her sister's last visit home and her confidences about the married officer she was in love with, Daisy reluctantly opened the envelope. It must be something she didn't want their parents to know about. It was impossible to keep secrets in the Bishop household.

'Divorce'. The word leapt out at her before she had time to take in the whole content of the letter. To Daisy it meant scandal and she recalled reading in the 'News of the World' about a famous film star's divorce. What had Sylvia got herself into?

She read through the letter quickly, sighing with relief. No scandal, thank God. Sylvia explained about the two-year separation and reassured her sister that Hugh had not involved her in any way. *'No one knows about us,'* she wrote, *'and in three months' time when it is finalised, we'll be able to get engaged. Until then please don't tell Mum and Dad.'*

Daisy read the letter again, a smile creeping across her face. Sylvia was getting engaged. Three months, she mused. A long time to keep her sister's secret. But she was so thrilled she must tell somebody. I'll write to Lily, she thought.

***

Somehow or other, due to the mysterious grapevine which circulated gossip around the station, word of Hugh's divorce leaked out. No one mentioned it to him directly of course, but he was conscious of knowing looks and barely concealed whispers whenever he entered the mess.

He wished he could confront the gossipmongers with the truth, but he was still afraid that Sylvia would be hurt and wanted to keep her name out of it. Once their relationship became public, he knew that wouldn't be possible and she too would be the subject of innuendo and sly looks.

Personal problems had to be put aside however as it became clear that the invasion of France was close. Operation Overlord, as it was labelled, was due to happen in the first week of June. Far from the work slowing down at Medmenham, the PIs were busier than ever with very little time off. Despite this, Hugh and Sylvia managed to steal a few moments together, sitting close together in the pub, hoping no one they knew would come in.

'It's so good to be with you, darling,' Hugh said, squeezing her hand under the table. 'I wish we could be together more often but...'

'I know. There's so much going on. Hard as it is, we must put our own feelings aside and concentrate on work.' Sylvia sighed. 'Perhaps the war will be over soon, the way things are going.'

Hugh glanced round the bar to make sure they were not overheard. 'I think we've a long way to go yet. The invasion is just the beginning. And we've got those rockets to deal with yet.'

'Let's not talk about the war, Hugh.' Sylvia leaned against him, wishing they could be closer, longing for a kiss and an embrace. Sometimes she wished he wasn't so sensible.

'You're right. We need to talk about us, our future.'

'I've been dreaming about it. Being with you. It won't be long now.'

Hugh kissed her cheek, not the sort of kiss she longed for but better than nothing. 'Can't come soon enough for me, my love. But we must be practical. There are things to discuss.'

As Sylvia went to interrupt, he put his finger to her lips. 'Not now, darling. Let's just enjoy these few moments together. We'll have to go back soon.'

***

When Sylvia got back to her hut, she could hear laughter from within. She paused on the threshold, wanting to savour her time with Hugh before joining her colleagues. But she had to get ready to go on duty and she took a deep breath before opening the door.

Silence greeted her and she looked around at their embarrassed faces. 'So, what's so funny?' she demanded.

When there was no reply, she said, 'Come on, share the joke.'

'It's nothing, Syl,' Julia said. 'Just Marion being silly.'

'I just heard that Wing Commander Smythe has got divorced. I thought it was quite amusing – he's so strait-laced, such a stickler for rules and regulations. I didn't think he was the sort to get involved in a scandal.'

Sylvia was furious at Marion's snide tone but before she could reply, Julia stepped in and said, 'Told you she was being silly.' She turned to Marion. 'There's no scandal. He and his wife separated by mutual consent. All perfectly legal and besides, none of our business.'

'Julia's right,' Iris said. 'Bill told me about it. He said Hugh didn't want it talked about until the final decree.' She appealed to Sylvia. 'I haven't said a word, I promise. Please believe me.'

'It's all right, Iris. Actually, Hugh told me himself. And I agree. It's none of our business.'

She turned her back and concentrated on getting ready for her shift, tensed for another of Marion's barbed comments. But other girl remained silent. Sylvia was now certain that it was she who had sent Margaret that poisonous letter. What have I done to her to make her so vindictive? Sylvia asked herself.

She walked across to the main house still seething. What a bitch Marion was. She'd always had a down on Sylvia, never losing an opportunity to play on her own superior education, her wealthy background, mentioning her cook or chauffeur at every opportunity. What difference did it make when they were all doing the same important work?

Julia caught up with her at the side door. 'Don't take any notice of her. She's just jealous.'

'Jealous of me? Don't talk rot. She's got nothing to be jealous about.'

Julia smiled. 'You think so? She was furious when she suspected you and the Wingco were sweet on each other.'

Sylvia gasped. 'How does she know?'

'Guessed probably.' Julia laughed. 'I knew how you felt about him from the start. You couldn't hide it whenever we saw him, especially if he spoke to you. Your blushes spoke volumes. When the other girls twigged, I persuaded them it was just a girly crush. It wasn't though, was it?'

Sylvia shook her head. 'I love him,' she whispered.

Julia nodded. 'I thought so. And how does he feel?'

'The same.' Sylvia clutched Julia's arm. 'You won't tell, please. We have to keep quiet for a bit longer.'

'You can trust me. And I'll try and keep Marion off your back.'

'Thanks.' Sylvia shook her head. 'I still don't know why she hates me.'

'Don't you? She wanted him herself, made a play for him when we were in Norfolk, always smiling at him, hanging on his every word. But he wasn't interested.'

'She knew he was married though.'

'That didn't bother her. She just wanted another conquest.' Julia looked at her watch. 'Better go in. Don't want to be late. We'll talk more later.'

Sylvia was grateful for Julia's support and relieved that her friend knew her secret. She knew Julia wouldn't gossip and it was good to have someone to confide in.

Chapter Twenty Two

There was a bit of a party atmosphere on June 7th when Sylvia and her hut mates gathered in the mess with Babs, Hugh, Bill and several more of their colleagues. Word had come through that the invasion of northern France the previous day had been successful.

'A bit soon to celebrate though,' Bill said. 'There's a long way to go yet.'

'Oh, Bill, don't be such a pessimist. Surely we're on our way to victory,' Julia said.

'And the Allies are in Rome now. We're coming at them from both ends,' Hugh said.

'Still, it's going to be a long hard slog,' Bill insisted.

They all nodded agreement, but Julia wasn't about to let him dampen the party atmosphere. 'Let's drink to eventual victory then,' she said, raising her glass.

They all raised their glasses and the talk became general. Hugh leaned close to Sylvia and said, 'You're very quiet. Anything wrong?'

'It was the mention of Rome. My sister's boyfriend is in Italy. From what she said in her last letter, I think he was at Anzio and there was some hard fighting there. She doesn't even know if he's all right.'

Hugh nodded. 'I hope he is. But Bill's right. It's not over yet. At least with the landings in Normandy there's cause for hope.' He squeezed her hand and she smiled up at him.

It would be a couple more months before they could display their feelings openly but among friends she felt confident that no one would betray them. She was still a bit wary of Marion, but the other girl left her alone lately. She had met an American officer and was so taken up with her new romance had stopped picking on Sylvia. She was standing across the room now, her arm hooked through the American's, staring triumphantly at her friends. Hugh could not compare with a high-ranking Yank who could give her everything she desired.

'Come on, boys and girls. Back to work. The war's not over yet and there's plenty still for us to do.' Babs's voice interrupted Sylvia's thoughts and she drained her glass, following the general move towards the exit.

Hugh was on a different shift to Sylvia and, as they crossed the grass towards the house, he arranged to meet her when she finished work.

She.was smiling happily as she seated herself at her desk, but the smile vanished when Babs called her over, a worried frown on her face.

'I've been looking back at some of the earlier prints. I think we missed something. Look at this.' Babs handed her two prints and asked her to compare them. 'I think that's a flying bomb. In fact, I'm sure of it.'

Sylvia felt a fluttering in her stomach. She was excited that they appeared to have solved the mystery but apprehensive too. Could these new weapons reach their shores? It was quite a blow after the euphoria of D Day. She frowned as the implications of the new weapons dawned on her. Kent would be in the firing line once more.

Now, for Sylvia, the hunt for the launching sites became even more imperative.

***

A few days later she sat in the mess with Hugh, Bill and Iris when Julia came in, her face white.

'Have you heard? London's been bombed again – badly this time.'

'Bombed? No.' Sylvia couldn't believe it.

'It's not the usual bombing raid. I heard one of the officers saying it's these rockets we've been hearing about.'

'But we've been bombing the sites. How could this happen?' Sylvia turned to Hugh.

'We're doing our best but...'

'We should be going after the factories but they're too well camouflaged,' Bill said.

A sombre mood settled over the group and shortly afterwards they broke up, Hugh to start his shift and Sylvia back to the hut to write to Daisy. She had been feeling so happy recently but now a new threat had appeared and her happiness was tempered by the new danger to her family.

***

'Doodlebugs, Mum. That's what they're calling them now. Better get to the shelter,' Daisy said as the siren wailed its warning.

'Nasty things. Poor old London getting it again. We'll be all right, Daisy.'

'You can't be sure. Yes, they're aimed at London but lots of them have fallen short.'

'I can't be running to the shelter every five minutes. I've got your dad's tea to get. He'll be back from the allotment soon.' Dora carried on peeling potatoes.

Daisy shrugged. After the first few weeks of what they were now calling the second blitz, most people carried on as normal. So far none of the doodlebugs had landed on Sheppey but there was never much warning.

They had got used to the guns up on the seafront blazing away at all hours trying to bring the doodlebugs down in the sea before they reached London.

The siren's wail died away as Dora put the potatoes on to boil. She stirred the mince and onions in the pan ready for the shepherd's pie while Daisy shelled peas and chopped carrots.

When the pie was in the oven, Dora made a cup of tea while Daisy cleared up and laid the table ready for their meal. They sat down together enjoying a quiet moment before Stan came in and switched on the wireless. He still followed the news avidly and, since the Home Guard had been stood down, spent hours poring over the maps in Jimmy's old atlas, marking the progress of the Allies in red colouring pencil.

Daisy refused to listen to the news, although it seemed to be a bit more optimistic these days. She couldn't join in the general euphoria over D Day, her thoughts constantly on what was happening in Italy. All the place names in his letters were heavily blacked out so she could only guess where he was.

She worried constantly that he was all right. The fighting had been hard, and the troops made little progress until a month ago. She had been quite excited when her father told her that the Allies had reached Rome after months of being dug in at Anzio. But it wasn't over yet and there was still fighting as they made their way north to Florence. And she still didn't really know where Chris was.

The back door opening interrupted Daisy's gloomy thoughts.

'Something smells good,' Stan said, taking off his boots in the scullery before coming into the kitchen.

Daisy switched on a smile for her father. 'Your favourite, Dad.'

'Lovely. Any word from Jimmy?' he asked, glancing up at the mantelpiece.

'No – and nothing from Chris either before you ask,' Daisy said.

'Don't worry, love. You'll probably get a whole bundle of letters now they're in Rome, like you did before.'

Dora poured her husband a cup of tea and told him the meal would soon be ready.

He sat down at the kitchen table and said. 'Just had a word with Mrs Gardner. She's worried about Bob. She's heard nothing either.' He looked at the clock and leaned over to switch the wireless on. Daisy sighed. No escaping the news tonight.

***

Chris was not with his platoon pressing on towards Florence. He was lying in a field hospital just outside Rome. He mumbled deliriously as the nurses came to change his dressings, calling for Daisy.

'Lie still, Sergeant, 'the nurse said. 'We'll soon have you feeling better.'

'I want Daisy,' he muttered.

'When you're well enough to move, we'll send you home. You'll see your Daisy then,' the nurse said.

She turned away and spoke to the doctor. Chris could only make out a few words but heard the word 'amputation' and struggled to sit up.

'Not my leg. You can't take my leg off.'

'Now then, laddie. We'll not do that. I was saying to nurse that the infection is healing. There'll be no need for amputation.' He turned to the nurse. 'I think he can be moved on now. Next ship home. He's a lucky chap.'

Home, Chris thought, a smile stealing across his face, only to be replaced by a grimace of pain. When the spasm passed, he thought of Daisy and their reunion. Would she still want him with a gammy leg? He might not be able to work. All the plans for 'after the war' which had sustained him during the long days of fighting at Anzio and beyond seemed

245

impossible now. He'd been dreaming of opening a garage specialising in motorcycles, but would he ever be fit enough?

He only had a hazy recollection of what happened to him. He had been speeding up the mountainside carrying an urgent message when the grenade went off, sending him flying, the motorcycle falling on top of him.

His head hurt and there was a searing pain down his right leg. He had passed out, only coming to when he realised he was being carried. Bob was at is side telling him over and over that he was going to be all right.

When they reached the field hospital Bob was shooed out but not before Chris grabbed his arm. 'Letter, in my pocket. Send it for me. I wrote it before... Don't tell her – don't want her to worry.'

'Ok, mate. I'll do that. You can tell yourself when you're well again.'

Apart from his shattered leg, Chris had broken his wrist and was covered in cuts and abrasions. The leg became infected and his other injuries took a long time to heal. Weeks later, he was still unable to hold a pen. He just hoped Bob had posted the letter he'd written to Daisy before his injury. He would wait till he was completely well before writing to her again.

As he gradually healed and the delirium passed, one of the nurses asked if she could write a letter for him. 'I know you have a girl back home,' she said. 'You've been talking about her non-stop while you were ill.'

He knew his parents back in Bromley would have been informed of his injury and when he felt a bit better, he would write to reassure them that he was on the mend. But he felt it would be unfair to let Daisy know how close he had come to losing his leg.

The nurse waited for his reply and he said, 'I don't want her to know. She'll worry and there's nothing she can do.'

'I think she'd like to be told. She's probably worrying anyway if she hasn't heard from you.'

'I suppose so.'

'Let me write a little note for you. She doesn't have to know how badly you were wounded. Just say you hurt your hand and can't hold a pen – it's the truth after all.'

Chris gave in and dictated a few stilted words.

'I'll get this off right away. Once she knows where you are, you'll get letters back. That will be nice, won't it?'

'Thank you, nurse.'

Chris lay back on his pillow and sighed. He tried to picture Daisy's face when she got the letter. How he wished he could be with her, feel her arms around him, telling him she loved him.

***

Sylvia had always been dedicated to her work as a PI. She loved the challenge of trying to interpret the often-murky photos and the sense of satisfaction when she managed to work out what she was seeing. Now the task took on a new dimension and she was determined to find the launching sites for the V1 rockets, which were constantly being moved.

A hundred of the deadly weapons reached London every day and, as well as this, many fell short of the target, landing on Kent and Sussex. So far, none had fallen on Sheppey but Sylvia knew it could happen any day. Her fears for her family filled her waking hours.

The hunt was on for the factories too. It seemed the enemy had an inexhaustible supply of fuel and materials. As the summer progressed Sylvia could think of nothing else. She was even able to put her relationship with Hugh to the back of her mind - at least while she was at work.

She found it easier now – only a few weeks until his divorce was final, and they need not meet secretly anymore. Their friends seemed to have accepted them as a couple, just as Bill and Iris were. In their rare leisure moments, they went out together as a foursome, walking along the riverbank in the summer sunshine or going to the cinema.

'You're looking happy,' Julia remarked when Sylvia returned from one of their outings.

'I am. It's so good not having to be secretive. I hated all that slinking around.'

'I'm pleased for you. It's nice to see someone happy amidst all this doom and gloom.'

Sylvia sighed. 'I feel guilty though.'

'What for? You have nothing to feel guilty about.'

'Oh, not about Hugh. It's just – I feel I shouldn't be so happy with so much going on – these awful doodlebugs. And we're not stopping them. As fast as we find one site, they pop up somewhere else. It's so frustrating.'

Julia nodded. 'Still, there's not so many now. Let's hope there'll soon be an end to it.'

'I hope so. I worry about my family down in Kent. They're right in the path of the bloody things.'

Chapter Twenty Three

Sylvia had been marking the days off on her calendar and, on a warm September morning she did a little dance as she realised it was only a week until Hugh received his decree absolute. Then he would be really free. She couldn't wait to write to her parents and tell them that she was getting engaged.

She hummed happily as she made her way over to the mess, the frustrations of her recently finished shift forgotten.

Her smile faded as she went inside and immediately sensed the atmosphere. Something awful must have happened. She joined her friends who were talking quietly at their table.

'What is it?' she asked, putting her tray down.

'A dreadful explosion in Chiswick. They're giving out that it was a gas main, but we know it wasn't,' Bill said.

'It couldn't have been a doodlebug. It caused far more damage than those things,' Hugh said.

'So what was it?'

'We've known for some time that the Germans were working on another type of weapon. The doodlebugs are nothing in comparison.' Bill shrugged his shoulders helplessly. 'We must find the factories but they're so well camouflaged.'

'Can't our chaps shoot them down as they come over like they've been doing?' Julia asked.

'They're trying of course but...'

A gloomy silence descended on the group.

'I feel like going back to work right now and not stopping till we've found the factories,' Sylvia said.

'We all feel the same, but you've just come off a night shift. You need your rest – you all do,' Hugh said, looking round at them all. 'We're doing all we can.'

The group broke up and Hugh walked across to the hut with Sylvia. 'Try to rest, darling,' he said. 'I'll see you later.'

Sylvia nodded. 'I was so happy this morning thinking we only had another week to wait. But that doesn't seem so important now.'

'Not important?' Hugh teased, smiling down at her.

'Oh, you know what I mean. It's just...'

'I understand. How can we think of our own happiness when so many are suffering? But we have to carry on. The war will end one day. Hold on to that thought and we'll get through.'

He bent and kissed her cheek and said goodbye.

***

Sylvia woke with a pleasant feeling of anticipation. She and Hugh both had an afternoon off – a very rare event. They were going into Oxford to buy her an engagement ring.

'I wanted it to be a surprise,' he'd said. 'But I thought you'd like to choose.'

'Thank you. I don't really want a conventional diamond, although I'm not sure exactly what I do want.' She smiled up at him. 'It will be fun choosing and I'll know it when I see it.'

The morning was filled with boring chores, washing her smalls, ironing her blouse and then, the inevitable physical jerks with her hut mates –as they called them. She had to admit she felt better for the exercise. After so many hours hunched over a desk, it toned up her mind as well as her body.

PT finished, she strolled over to the mess with her friends, intending to have a quick lunch before meeting Hugh.

As she reached the entrance Hugh caught up with them. 'Got away early,' he said. 'How about we lunch out and then do our shopping?'

'Sounds good,' she said, turning to her friends. 'See you later then.'

'Have fun,' Julia said with a laugh.

'Do they know where we're going?' Hugh asked.

'I haven't said a word.'

'Wait here while I get the car,' he said when they reached the gate.

While she waited, she chatted to the guard on duty, remarking on the mild autumn weather. It was a pleasure to be able to do this, she thought, instead of pretending she was going to catch the bus. No more sneaking around, she thought happily as she spotted the Alvis coming down the drive.

She climbed into the car and waved cheekily to the guard as they set off, giggling a little at his shocked look.

'I don't care,' she said. 'I can't believe it's almost over. Only a few more days.' She looked at Hugh, who was concentrating on the road. 'Nothing can go wrong now – can it?' she asked, an anxious frown creasing her forehead.

Hugh reached across and took her hand. 'Stop worrying, darling. If Margaret was going to cause trouble, she'd have done it by now. Besides, she's got her Yank. She'll be glad to be rid of me.'

Sylvia smiled. 'I suppose you're right.' She leaned back in her seat and told herself nothing could interfere with her happiness now.

Instead of taking the main road into Oxford, Hugh turned off along a quiet lane which ran alongside the river. Sylvia looked out of the car window at the trees now turning red and gold, remembering that day nearly two years ago when she first realised that

Hugh loved her as much as she loved him. It had been worth the wait, not to mention the furtive meetings, deceiving her friends and family. She hoped her parents would understand when she was finally able to tell them.

After parking the car, they found a little cafe which did simple home-cooked meals.

Sylvia enjoyed it far more than the posh London hotel where she had felt a little out of place. Being an officer had introduced her to another way of life and she knew how to conduct herself, but sometimes she longed for the ordinary life she'd grown up with.

When they were in London, she worried that Hugh would expect her to get used to 'posh' hotels and dinners. She glanced up at him now to see that he was eating his sausage and mash with enjoyment. He seemed quite at ease.

He looked up and smiled. 'Just like mother used to make,' he said. He sighed. 'She's not well enough to cook now. A nurse comes in to look after her. She was never the same after my father was killed in the last war.'

'Does she know about us?'

Hugh shook his head. 'She doesn't know about the divorce either. I can't tell her. She's very frail. The shock...' He shook his head.

Sylvia reached out and took his hand. 'I wish you'd told me before.'

'I envy you your close family,' he said.

'Well, maybe you'll meet them one day.' It was the first time she dared to think of taking him home to meet her family.

'I can't wait. I'd love to meet your parents and your brother and sister. I've heard so much about them.'

They finished their meal and set off in search of a jeweller, ending up at a tiny little shop tucked away down a side street.

The shop keeper brought out a couple of trays of rings, pointing out the typical diamond engagement rings.

'I really want something different,' Sylvia said. 'Nothing too flashy though.'

'What about this one?' Hugh asked, pointing to a huge sapphire surrounded by tiny diamonds.

Sylvia shook her head. 'I said not too flashy,' she said with a smile. She bent over the tray, then pounced. 'This one,' she said, holding it up so that the light caught the changing blues and greens, shot with a streak of purple.

'The jeweller shook his head. 'Not for an engagement, miss. Opals are said to bring bad luck.'

'What rot. I don't believe all that nonsense.' She turned to Hugh. 'What do you think, darling?'

'It's beautiful. If you want it...' He took the ring from her and slipped it onto her finger. 'There – a perfect fit.' He turned to the jeweller. 'We'll take it.' He took his wallet out and paid, while Sylvia stood, holding her hand up to watch the play of light on the stone.

They walked back to the car hand in hand, Sylvia with a dreamy smile on her face. On the journey back she kept twisting the ring around and stretching her hand out to admire it. She could hardly believe they were really engaged at last. She couldn't wait to get back and tell her friends. And then she must write and tell Daisy her exciting news.

***

'Letter for you,' Julia said the minute Sylvia entered the hut.

'I'll read it later. Look.' She held out her hand for inspection and Julia squealed with delight.

'You're engaged? Really? Did he go down on one knee and pop the question?' The questions came tumbling out and before Sylvia could answer, Julia called to the other girls in the hut. 'Come and see Sylvia's ring.'

They crowded round exclaiming over the beautiful stone. They all seemed pleased for her except Marion, of course. She frowned and said, 'Very pretty but it's not a proper engagement ring, is it? Anyway, don't you know that opals are unlucky?'

'Rubbish,' Julia retorted. 'Don't take any notice, Syl.' She turned to the others. 'Party time, I think. Hare and Hounds later? Iris, get Bill to round up some of his mates – and Hugh, of course.'

Marion and Jane couldn't join them as they were on duty but some of the girls from Hut Five joined them, as well as Bill James and a crowd of his friends. It was a merry party that gathered in the pub that evening.

Holding on to Hugh's arm and sipping a gin and tonic, Sylvia surveyed the crowd, wondering how many of them, apart from her closest friends, had known about her liaison with him.

Everyone seemed very pleased for them anyway she thought, smiling.

Hugh put his drink down and turned to her. 'They all seem to be having a good time. Do you think we can slip away without being noticed? I want to be alone with you.'

'Me too,' Sylvia said, quickly finishing her drink.

They pushed through the crowd fending off good wishes and ribald comments, out into the blessedly fresh air of an autumn evening.

Hugh drove out of the village and parked. 'Let's walk a little.' He held the door open and then, hand in hand, they wandered along a path beside a field, now harvested, the corn standing in stooks.

'You're very quiet,' Hugh said. 'Not about to change your mind, I hope.'

'Of course not, silly.' She sighed, a happy sigh. 'It's just – I'm feeling a bit overwhelmed. All those people back there in the pub, being so nice. I was dreading everyone knowing about us and...'

'I think most of our friends knew or guessed. They were very discreet.' He stopped walking and drew her to him, leaning against a farm gate. 'We are so lucky – *I'm* so lucky. Finding someone like you, someone willing to wait so long, not knowing how it would turn out.'

His lips sought hers, tenderness turning to passion and Sylvia gave herself to him willingly. It was what she had dreamed of through all the months of secrecy and deception. It had all been worth it.

At last, they drew apart and Hugh said, huskily, 'Let's get married right away. I can't wait.'

'I'd love to Hugh. But...'

'Why not? Please, darling.'

'I want my family there and you haven't even met them yet. I can't rush off to a registry office with only a couple of witnesses. My mother would never forgive me.'

Hugh sighed. 'You're right, of course. I don't have any family – only my mother and she can't come, much too frail.'

'It won't hurt to wait a little longer. Perhaps we can get a forty-eight hour pass together and go down and see my parents.'

'All right. I'll be patient.' He kissed her again, releasing her with a sigh. 'You do realise you're torturing me, don't you?'

She laughed. 'Don't exaggerate. Anyway, I've been tortured too – for more than two years.'

She stepped back and walked away, her heart beating fast. She wanted to stay, of course she did, but they had promised to wait until they were finally married, however hard it was.

***

As she got ready for bed later that evening, still dreamily reliving those magic hours with Hugh, she suddenly remembered that she hadn't read her letter. In the excitement of showing her friends her engagement ring she had quite forgotten about it. She sat up and rummaged in her locker for the envelope and a torch.

'Dear Sylvia', she read. *'I have just had the most dreadful news. Chris has been badly wounded and is in hospital somewhere in Italy. I've had a short note from him, written by a nurse, as he can't write himself. He is on the mend and makes light of his injuries. But Mrs Gardner next door has heard from Bob and she said Chris is in a bad way. Bob was with him when he was hurt and last saw him as he was being stretchered to a field hospital. I can't bear it, not knowing how badly he's hurt and if he will survive to come back to me. I want to rush over there and look after him. I've tried to be brave and not upset Mum and Dad by weeping and wailing. You know Dad and his stiff upper lip and Mum only starts crying too, the big softie. Sorry to be so dismal. I'll try to write a more cheerful letter when I have some news. I have to keep hoping and praying that it will be good news. Your loving sister Daisy.*

PS The Home Guard was stood down in June and Dad doesn't know what to do with himself.'

Sylvia leaned back against the pillows, the letter crumpled in her hand. She smiled at the PS. Dad had enjoyed his stint in the Home Guard and was probably driving Mum mad stuck at home. Then she frowned. Poor Daisy. How awful, just when she herself was feeling so happy. She felt a spasm of guilt. How could she write and tell her sister about her engagement? It would be too cruel. But she had to let her family know about Hugh. She didn't think she'd get away with concealing the fact of his divorce. Mum, especially, would be planning a big white wedding at

Holy Trinity Church. She would never understand why Sylvia would choose a registry office.

She didn't care for herself. All she wanted was to marry Hugh. She turned over and thumped the pillow. Why was life so complicated? As she drifted off to sleep another worry surfaced. Hugh's two little sons. Would they accept her, or had they heard too many fairy stories about wicked step-mothers?

***

Once the novelty of being engaged wore off, Sylvia was forced to put her worries to one side and knuckle down to work once more. The V2 rockets were causing so much devastation and accurately pinpointing where the factories were became paramount. Everyone was exhausted but there was cause for hope. The Allies were making progress – Paris had been liberated in August amid great rejoicing.

Sylvia had hoped to be married by now but there was little time to spend with Hugh to discuss their wedding. But at last on one rainy day in October they both had a little time off and drove into town.

Hugh parked in the market square and they hurried through the downpour into the little cafe where they first had tea all those months ago. The miserable weather kept people away and they had the place to themselves.

The waitress brought tea and sandwiches and then they were alone, the first time for several weeks

Ignoring the refreshments, Hugh reached for Sylvia's hand. 'I hoped we'd have set a date by now, but it seems the fates are against us. With all this extra work it's impossible to get time off to go and visit your parents. We could go into Oxford and get a special licence...'

Before he could continue, Sylvia began to protest. He squeezed her hand. 'I know, darling. I was just about to say – I know you don't want that and I'm willing to wait, however hard that is.'

'I'm sorry, Hugh. It's just, I always dreamed of having Daisy as my bridesmaid. I know we can't have a church wedding, but I still want my family there, do things properly.'

'I understand, really I do. When things calm down, we'll get some leave together and travel down to Kent to see your family.'

'There's something else we must talk about,' Sylvia said.

'I know, but we haven't had much time to plan anything – where we'll live for instance when the war's over.'

'I was thinking more about your sons. I haven't even met them. Do they even know about me?'

'Don't worry about it, darling. Of course, I must tell them about us. But it's difficult in a letter and there's no way I can go up to Scotland to see them. I don't even know if Margaret's told them she'd going to America – and leaving them behind.'

'The poor little mites. Such an upheaval for them.' Sylvia swallowed a lump in her throat. She couldn't imagine what it must be like for them, sent away to school so young and not seeing either of their parents for such a long time. She remembered how unhappy Jimmy had been, evacuated to the other side of the country. So unhappy that he'd run away and made his way home from Wales to Sheppey. She prayed that Hugh's boys were not suffering as Jimmy had.

Hugh interrupted her thoughts. 'They're still at boarding school and Margaret tells me they're happy there. Things won't change for them for a while and once we're settled, they can come for a visit.'

Sylvia didn't think it would be as simple as that, but she nodded. The prospect of taking on two little boys was a bit daunting, but she would do her best although she knew she could never take their mother's place.

'I'm longing to meet them,' she said, 'but I'm a bit nervous.'

'No need to be. I'm sure they'll love you – as I do.' He leaned across the table and kissed her cheek.

'But I'm sure they'll miss their mother and hate me for taking her place.'

'Of course they won't hate you, darling.'

Sylvia wasn't so sure. The very thought of meeting them and trying to get to know them terrified her. Suppose they didn't get on. A little spurt of anger made her bite her lip before she could say anything. How could Margaret plan to go off to America and leave them? Perhaps she would change her mind at the last minute and take them with her. In a way Sylvia hoped so. She could cope with having the boys to stay in the holidays – she just wasn't sure about being a full-time mother to them, which is what Hugh seemed to want.

Hugh sensed her distress and took her hand again. 'Stop worrying, my love. There's plenty of time to work out what arrangements we need to make. Let's think about the wedding first.'

'I sometimes think there won't be a wedding. This bloody war drags on and on and we're so busy we can't get any leave.' She choked back a little sob. 'Oh, Hugh, what shall we do?'

'I'm just as frustrated as you are. I want us to be married as soon as possible.' He paused. 'Look, do you really want to wait until your family can be there? If we got a special licence you could be Mrs Smythe in a couple of hours.'

Sylvia smiled. 'I love the idea, but...'

'I just want you to be happy. I know, why don't you ask Daisy to come up here and be a witness? I'm sure she could get away just for a day.'

***

Daisy tore open the envelope and gasped as she took in the contents. 'Married! Mum, Sylvia's getting married.'

Dora paused in her pastry rolling and looked up. 'What are you talking about?'

'I didn't tell you she was courting because she's been waiting for Hugh's divorce to be finalised.'

'What? Divorce. Oh, goodness me.' Dora put a hand over her chest and sank into a chair. 'What has my girl been up to?'

Daisy shook her head impatiently. 'She hasn't been up to anything, Mum. It's all been done properly, no funny business.'

'You knew about this, didn't you?' Dora's lips tightened. 'How could you both deceive me like this?'

'We didn't. Sylvia kept it quiet because she knew how upset you'd be. She wanted to wait till everything was settled.'

'Divorce,' Dora repeated. 'There's never been anything like that in this family. I expect it'll be in the Sunday papers. What will the WVS ladies think? I won't be able to hold my head up...'

Daisy held out the letter. 'Read it for yourself, Mum. There was no scandal so nothing in the papers. It was all done very quietly and with no blame on Sylvia or Hugh. He hadn't seen his wife for years. She left him and took the children to Scotland at the beginning of the war.'

'Children? Oh dear, it gets worse.' Dora took a deep breath. 'Whatever is your dad going to say?'

Daisy was worried. Her mother looked pale and seemed on the verge of tears. It should have been good news – and, as far as Daisy was concerned, it was. But how to convince her parents of that? She wished now that she'd given some hint of Sylvia's involvement with her officer. It would have been less of a shock.

She had just succeeded in calming her mother down when Stan came in from the allotment. He

260

looked from one to the other and frowned. 'What's up? Is it our Jimmy?'

'No, Dad. Jimmy's OK,' Daisy reassured him. 'Mum's had a bit of a shock, that's all. Sylvia's getting married.'

'Why the long faces? That's good news surely. When's she coming home? Have they set a date?' Before either of them could answer, he went on, 'Who's she marrying anyway? We haven't even met the bloke. What's he like?'

'He's a wing commander – name's Hugh Smythe. He was her boss when she was in Norfolk,' Daisy told them. 'They met up again when she was posted to Buckinghamshire and they got to know each other.'

'An officer,' Stan said. 'Hope he's not like that snooty bloke she brought home a few years back – acting like he was too good for us.'

'He's nothing like that,' Daisy protested, remembering what a rat Roland had turned out to be. Sylvia assured her that Hugh was a perfect gentleman and she believed her.

'I hope so. Anyway, why are they in such a hurry to get married?' Stan clapped a hand over his forehead. 'She's not pregnant is she?'

'No, Dad. Of course not. Stop worrying.'

'It's worse than that,' Dora snapped. 'He's divorced.'

'Oh, well, nothing wrong with that, I suppose' Stan said. 'Unless she's the guilty party.'

'Of course she isn't. How can you think that of your own daughter?' Dora slapped his arm.

'Sorry, love. Look, when she comes home, we can meet the bloke and judge for ourselves. Then we can plan the wedding.'

'She's not coming home, Dad. Here, read her letter.'

'Not coming home? But I was looking forward to walking her down the aisle at Holy Trinity.'

261

'Stan, she can't get married in church, can she? They don't allow divorcees to marry in church.'

His face fell. 'I didn't think of that. So, it's the registry office then.'

'In Oxford,' Daisy said. 'She and Hugh can't get leave at this stage of the war. They're far too busy. But they want me to be a witness. I'm sure I can get time off to go up there – just for a day. Sylvia's going to let me know when they've set a date.'

'Why can't they at least come here for the wedding?' Dora seemed to have recovered from the shock. 'We could have a small reception in the church hall. I'm sure that would be allowed even if they don't marry in church. I'll talk to the Vicar. Surely she'll want her family there.'

'Don't get excited, Mum. They won't be able to get leave to come all this way.'

Dora shook her head. 'This wasn't what I dreamed of for my eldest daughter.'

'Me neither. But we must make the best of it, I suppose.' Stan turned to Daisy. 'At least I've got one daughter I can still walk down the aisle. We'll have a big do for your wedding, love.'

Daisy burst into tears. 'Oh, Dad, I don't even know if Chris is all right. I haven't heard anything since that note the nurse wrote. And Mrs Gardner told me Bob was with him when he was wounded, and he was in a bad way.'

'Sorry, love. I didn't think.' Stan awkwardly patted her shoulder. 'Don't get upset, love. I'm sure he'll be OK.'

Daisy shrugged him off and went through to the scullery to fill the kettle. She had been trying not to think about Chris, trying not to feel envious that her sister was about to marry the man she loved. She was pleased for Sylvia – of course she was – but it seemed so unfair.

As she lit the gas under the kettle and got out the cups and saucers, she could hear her parents' voices from the other room. She was surprised that Dad seemed to have accepted Sylvia's decision to marry a divorced man. Mum was more upset. She had always worried about what the neighbours thought.

The kettle boiled and she filled the teapot and put it on the tray. She was about to take it in when she heard her father say, 'At least she's getting married, not having an affair. It seems from her letter they're doing the right thing.'

'Daisy told me she's known him for some time, but they've not done anything wrong – if you can believe that,' Dora said.

'Don't say that. We brought our girls up right. It must have been hard waiting for him to be free.'

They stopped talking when Daisy came through with the tea tray. She could tell her mother was still annoyed with her for keeping her sister's relationship secret.

By mutual consent nothing more was said about Sylvia and the talk turned to Jimmy and his training. He was doing very well and would soon be joining his first ship.

Chapter Twenty Four

'Have you set a date yet?' Julia asked as they hurried across to the mess one wet and windy November morning.

Sylvia shook her head. 'Hugh's getting impatient. He wants us to take a couple of hours off and rush off to the registry office and then back to work.'

'Why not? At least you'll be married then. You told me Hugh's already paid the rent on a flat in Henley. You could move in straight away and at least be able to spend some time together.'

'I must admit it's tempting but I want to wait until we can get some leave together. And I'm determined to have my sister as a bridesmaid.'

'Do you have bridesmaids at a registry office wedding?' Julia asked.

'I'm not sure, but I want her there anyway. We always promised each other we would be bridesmaids or maids of honour at our weddings.'

'I understand. You're very close, aren't you? I sometimes wish I had a sister.'

'We always did everything together as children. I just want her here. I'll send for her as soon as we have a date.'

'Still, it might be a long wait, given how things are with our work now. Nobody's allowed leave at the moment.'

Sylvia sighed. 'I know. It was so exciting after the Normandy landings - we thought it would all be over in weeks. But now...'

'Instead, we're busier than ever. What with the bloody rockets and the Germans fighting back in Belgium. They don't want to give up.'

'No wedding yet then,' Sylvia said. 'My mum thinks we ought to wait till after the war.'

'I can't imagine Hugh will agree to that.'

'I can't either. I want to be married soon. We've waited long enough.'

Julia agreed. 'It hasn't been easy for you. I'm glad it all worked out in the end.'

'I still think something could go wrong. I won't really believe it until we're finally married,' Sylvia said.

'Well, no use brooding about it. Anyway, duty calls. Better finish our breakfast and get on.'

***

Leaning back in her chair Sylvia took her glasses off and rubbed her eyes at the end of what had been a particularly gruelling shift.

Far from resting on their laurels and thinking the war would soon be over, the photo interpreters were being kept just as busy as before. They were doing their best to monitor the advance of the enemy and pass that crucial information on to the defending allies.

There had been some good news. Brussels had been liberated by the Americans in September and Antwerp was captured undamaged by the Allies. But the Allies' first rapid advance had slowed to a crawl and there was fierce fighting. The Germans were resisting determinedly and were advancing through dense forest towards Bastogne.

The thick cover made it hard for the PIs to decipher the photos that came in hourly. Sylvia sighed. It was frustrating not to have anything worthwhile to pass on to the higher ups. She would like to have stayed on until she finished the batch of prints she had been studying but she was so tired she knew she would not be able to do them justice. Better to hand over to her replacement and get some rest.

Hugh was now working the same shift and Sylvia looked forward to spending the evening with him. She didn't fancy going to the pub but that was the only chance they had to be alone.

She hurried over to her hut to get ready, having agreed to meet him in the mess. There was a letter from Daisy waiting for her and she knew what it would say. Her sister had been badgering her in every letter wanting to know when she should book time off to come up for the wedding. The letter was longer than usual and on the first page there was no mention of the wedding. Daisy was excited that Chris was being brought home from Italy.

'He is still very poorly and not able to walk yet but he sounds quite cheerful. They are sending him to a military hospital in Portsmouth. A long way to go to visit but i can't wait to see him.' Sylvia turned the page. *'Don't worry I'll be there for your wedding. Mum has put a new collar and cuffs on my jacket to make it look more dressy. I know I can't wear a proper bridesmaid's dress especially as you told me you'd be in uniform. I hope you're not too upset at not having a proper wedding.'*

Of course I'm not upset, Sylvia thought. I just want to be married. That's the most important thing. She pictured herself with Hugh in the flat he had rented. It wasn't the home of her dreams - just the top floor of a terraced house in Henley. The furniture wasn't to her taste, but she knew she could make it cosy and homelike.

She put Daisy's letter in her bag, intending to answer it later that evening. She glanced at her watch and hastily tidied her hair and added a dash of lipstick. She didn't want to be late – every moment spent with Hugh was precious.

A misty rain still fell as she ran across the grass to the mess.

Hugh was waiting for her by the entrance.

'I'm not late, am I?' she asked breathlessly and, without waiting for an answer reached up for a kiss.

He linked his arm in hers and they set off across the grounds to where he parked the Alvis.

'I don't fancy the pub this evening,' Sylvia said as she settled herself in the passenger seat.

'Where to then?'

She smiled shyly. 'I thought we could go to the flat.'

Hugh grinned. 'I was hoping you'd suggest that but I'm not sure we should.'

'Why not?'

'You know why, you little minx. Are you trying to tempt me? You know we promised to wait...'

'I'm fed up with waiting. Besides, if it wasn't for the bloody war and our work, we'd be married by now.'

'You're right, darling. All right, let's go.' He put the car in gear and drove off, much faster than he should.

Sylvia gripped the sides of the seat, biting her lip, wondering if she'd been too forward. But it was true. They should have been married by now. As they drove into Henley and drew up in front of a row of terraced houses, she forced herself to relax. Too late to change her mind now.

Hugh opened the passenger door and took her hand. He led her up the steps to the front door, which opened on to a dimly lit passage. A steep staircase loomed in front of them.

Sylvia followed him upstairs, her heart beating faster in anticipation.

'Your new home,' Hugh declared, opening a door on the left. He did not switch the light on, although the blackout restrictions had been eased a little over the past couple of months. A little light came from the bulb on the landing and Sylvia stepped into the room which was barely furnished. A table and chairs and two armchairs took up most of the cramped space. 'The kitchen is through there,' he said pointing.

Sylvia laughed nervously. 'I didn't come here to look at the kitchen,' she said.

Hugh laughed too. 'All right - follow me.'

They went along a short passage to a room at the front of the house. He threw open the door, gesturing apologetically. 'It's not quite the Ritz, darling,' he said.

'I don't care.' Sylvia put her arms around him. 'It doesn't matter where we are so long as I'm with you.'

'Sylvia, my love.' He pulled her towards him and sought her lips. The kiss grew ever more passionate and, almost without realising it, Sylvia found herself lying across the bed. At last, after all those months of being 'sensible', she was able to show him how much she loved him.

Later, as they lay entwined in each other's arms, Sylvia smiled contentedly.

'So much more comfortable than a damp riverbank,' Hugh murmured.

She giggled, remembering the first and only time they made love. 'We were very naughty, weren't we?' she said.

'Yes, but now it's time to be sensible. I would love to stay here all night, but we should get back.'

'I suppose you're right.' Sylvia sighed and reached for her clothes.

'It won't be long now. Then we can spend every night here in our own little love nest.' He switched on the light and for the first time Sylvia took in their surroundings.

Not much of a love nest, she thought. The faded wallpaper and threadbare carpet were only partially brightened by the pink satin eiderdown and green curtains. But she didn't care. She would soon turn it into a cosy home, and she looked forward to the day when they could move in permanently.

Chapter Twenty Five

Sylvia opened her eyes and looked around the hut which had been her home for the last three years. It was the last time she would sleep in this bed, she thought with a little thrill of anticipation. Her best dress uniform, freshly cleaned and brushed, hung on a hook behind the door. It should have been a long white dress with a veil. But Sylvia didn't care. Today she would become Mrs Hugh Smythe.

She leapt out of bed and gave Julia and shake.

'What – what's the rush?' muttered her friend.

'I'm getting married. Come on, sleepyhead. You're supposed to be helping me get ready.' Sylvia could not contain her excitement.

Julia fumbled for her watch on the bedside locker. 'Plenty of time yet.'

Sylvia shook her again. 'I need you to fix my hair. And you were going into the village to fetch my flowers. Oh, goodness, there's so much to do.'

'Stop panicking. It's all in hand. I'm borrowing Jane's bike to get the flowers.' Julia got out of bed and began to dress. 'Bill's going to fetch your sister from the station, but she won't be here for ages. I'll fetch the flowers and you'd better be washed and dressed by the time I get back. Then I'll do your hair.'

Their chatter woke the other girls who started to get washed and dressed. while offering encouragement and advice to Sylvia. All except Marion, of course.

'I don't know what all the fuss is about. You've both been behaving like a married couple for ages,' she sneered.

'What do you mean by that?' Iris asked, leaping to Sylvia's defence.

'She knows what I mean - sneaking around while he was still married.'

Sylvia felt her face grow hot and was about to retort when Julia said, 'Don't talk such rot, Marion. You're just jealous 'cause you haven't got a handsome officer to walk you down the aisle.'

'Now who's talking rot?' Marion snapped.

'Well, your Yank's not here, is he, and he didn't give you a ring before he left.'

'Girls, please,' Iris interrupted. 'Don't spoil Sylvia's big day.' She turned to Marion. 'Aren't you supposed to be on duty this morning? You don't want to be late.'

Marion snatched up her cap and walked out, slamming the door behind her.

'I'm off too,' Jane announced. 'Julia, make sure you put my bike away this time.' She turned to Sylvia. 'Good luck, Syl.'

Julia pulled on her great coat. 'Good job it's not raining. It won't take long to cycle into the village and I'll be back in two ticks.'

It was quiet in the hut when they'd gone and Sylvia sighed and sat down on her bed, still in her satin slip. 'I don't know why she has to be so horrible,' she said.

Iris turned from brushing her hair. 'It's like Julia said – she's jealous.'

'I shouldn't let her get to me. Oh, well, at least I have some good friends and I'm so pleased you were able to get time off to come to my wedding.'

Iris laughed. 'Not exactly time off. I start a night shift this evening.'

Julia came back with the flowers. 'Lucky to get these, they told me.' She put them down on her locker. 'They did their best.'

Sylvia rushed over and picked up the little posy. 'It's lovely, just what I ordered. Roses in November and these lily things. So pretty.'

'Perfect,' Iris said. 'A traditional bouquet wouldn't look right with your uniform.'

'That's what I thought.'

'Now then, time to get your hair done,' Julia advanced on her, brush in hand.

'I don't know what you have in mind. It'll only get squashed by my cap anyway,' Sylvia said.

'Leave it to me. You won't be wearing your cap in the registry office and you want to look your best. Bill has a camera and is going to take photos.'

Sylvia gave a mock groan. 'Don't mention photos today. I don't want to think about work.'

The others laughed and Julia got busy with her brush. Sylvia usually wore her hair up, covered by her cap but Julia brushed it out and smoothed it into a shining pageboy style. She teased a few strands out and twisted them to fall each side of Sylvia's face.

'There, what do you think?' She held up a hand mirror for Sylvia's inspection.

'Oh, Julia, it doesn't look like me.'

'Don't you like it?'

'Of course I do. It's lovely.' Sylvia reached up and fingered a curl.

'Don't fiddle with it; you'll spoil it. Now – makeup.'

'Not too much, please.'

'You don't need much with that lovely complexion,' Julia said enviously.

The makeup done, Sylvia put on her stockings, making sure the seams were straight. Then she donned her uniform, only half wishing she could wear a proper wedding dress. She would wear rags if it meant getting married to Hugh.

She looked at her watch. 'Hugh should be here soon.'

'It doesn't feel right, going to your wedding in your future husband's car. It should be your father giving you away,' Julia said.

'Well, Dad's not here and I'm certainly not going into Oxford on the bus,' Sylvia replied with a laugh, rushing to the door as she heard a toot on the horn from outside. 'He's here. Come on you two.'

Laughing, they piled into the Alvis, Sylvia in the front seat, grasping Hugh's hand, unable to control the butterflies in her stomach. It was really happening at last. She was on her way to her wedding.

When Hugh pulled up outside the registry office, she looked round for Daisy. She should be here by now.

Disappointed, she whispered to Julia, 'Daisy's not here.'

'Neither is Bill,' Julia said. 'Perhaps the train was late.'

'Don't worry, she'll be here. We won't start till she arrives,' Hugh said, taking her hand and leading her into the building.

The foyer was crowded and, before she could take in who was there she was surrounded. With cries of 'surprise', her mother and father hugged her, Daisy too.

Sylvia turned to Hugh, tears in her eyes to see that he was grinning, as were Bill and her two friends. 'You knew?'

'You don't know how hard it was to keep it secret,' Julia said. 'Hugh arranged it.'

'Hugh, darling. Thank you. You've made my day.' She turned to her family. 'Oh, it's so lovely to see you all. So much to talk about.'

'And plenty of time to talk later,' Hugh said. 'Now, let's get married.'

Sylvia passed the short ceremony in a daze, gripping Hugh's hand tightly throughout.

'You may kiss the bride,' the registrar announced with a smile and Hugh lost no time in taking her in his arms.

She thought he would never let her go but at last they turned round, and she smiled to see her father grinning and her mother sniffing into a lace handkerchief. Daisy hugged her and kissed her. 'Congratulations, sis. He's gorgeous,' she whispered.

Outside, Bill gathered them into a group and focused his camera. 'Smile please,' he said, not that they needed telling.

He took a photo of the two of them, then a group with Sylvia's family and another of Sylvia with her two best friends.

The hotel where Bill and Iris had arranged a meal for them all was only a short walk away. The party was greeted with glasses of sparkling wine.

'Sorry we couldn't get real champagne,' Bill said.

As they sipped their drinks, Hugh said, 'Before we go in to eat, I think Sylvia would like a few moments with her family.' He indicated a seating area by the window.

Sylvia smiled gratefully at him. He was so thoughtful. She sat on a sofa between her parents, Daisy seated opposite. For a moment she couldn't speak for the lump in her throat.

She took a sip of her wine. 'I can't believe you're really here. I was only expecting Daisy and I wasn't even sure she'd make it.' She turned to her sister. 'Have you heard from Chris? I thought you might be visiting him rather than coming all this way.'

'I'm going down next week. He wasn't allowed visitors before. I can't wait to see him.' Her face clouded. 'I'm not sure what to expect. He's very optimistic that he'll be all right, but I think he might just be trying to cheer me up.'

'Oh, Daisy. I don't know what to say.'

'I wasn't going to tell you – didn't want to spoil your big day.'

Sylvia hugged her. 'I'm glad you did tell me.' She turned to her parents. 'It's so wonderful to have you all here.'

Stan grinned. 'You didn't think we'd let our eldest daughter get married without us?' he said. 'Anyway, it was your young man's idea.'

'Really?' Sylvia smiled up at Hugh who stood watching the family reunion with a smile.

'He wrote us a lovely letter,' Dora said. 'Said he was sorry we couldn't meet before the wedding and hoped we would accept him as a son-in-law.'

'Which we do,' Stan said heartily.

'Mum, Dad, I'm so sorry we had to keep it secret. I really wanted to tell you about Hugh.' She took her mother's hand. 'I know how you feel about divorce,' she whispered. 'But I promise we did nothing wrong.'

'I know, dear. Anyway, you're married now. And he does seem a very nice young man, very thoughtful. He's arranged for us to stay here overnight. So we'll have time to talk before we go home.'

Bill came over and told them the food was served and they all trooped into the dining room where a splendid buffet had been laid out.

'You wouldn't think there was rationing,' Julia said, helping herself to salmon.

'They've done us proud,' Bill said.

Very soon the room grew noisy with laughter and chatter until Bill banged on the table for quiet.

'Please – no speeches,' Hugh said with a laugh.

'Can't have a wedding without a toast and speeches,' Bill replied. 'Anyway, I just want to say how pleased we all are that Hugh and Sylvia have finally got together and we wish them all the happiness in the world.' He raised his glass. 'Sylvia and Hugh.'

They all echoed the toast and drank. Then the friends announced that they must get back to work. 'The war won't stop just for a wedding,' Bill said.

'I suppose it is very important, what you're doing?' Stan said.

Sylvia nodded, unsure what to say. She knew her family didn't think being a shorthand typist was very important. Hugh saved her from having to reply.

'I always say that everyone's work is important in a war situation – from the lowliest kitchen orderly to the highest-ranking officer.' He put his arm around Sylvia and smiled down at her. 'Luckily, the powers that be have granted us two a couple of day's respite. Time to settle into our new home.'

'You're not leaving now, are you?' Daisy asked. 'We haven't had time to talk properly. I thought you'd be staying here too. We have so much to talk about.'

'We want to spend our first night together in our flat,' Sylvia said with a shy smile.

'I understand,' Daisy said with a grin.

'We'll come over in the morning, see you all off on the train,' Hugh said. He shook hands with Stan and kissed Dora and Daisy's cheeks.

Sylvia hugged her parents and turned to Daisy, who kissed her and whispered, 'All the best, sis – and no more secrets, eh?'

Sylvia nodded and smiled.

She and Hugh went outside to the Alvis and the family waved them off. As they drove away, Sylvia thought, Yes, no more secrets, thank goodness – but, of course, there was one secret she could never divulge. Even when the war ended, she would still be bound by the Official Secrets Act and no one would ever know just how important her work had been.

She reached for Hugh's hand and with a feeling of warm contentment, mixed with a flutter of excitement, she looked forward to their life in their new home.

The End

If you enjoyed this book, please leave the author a review.

After 22 years of handling other people's books while working as a library assistant Roberta Grieve decided it was time to fulfil a long-held ambition and start writing her own. Her novels are mainly historical romances and she enjoys researching and writing stories set during the Second World War.

Roberta lives in a small village near Chichester, Sussex, and when not writing enjoys walking her son's dog.

Website: www.robertagrieve.co.uk

Printed in Poland
by Amazon Fulfillment
Poland Sp. z o.o., Wrocław

64360297R00164